The Pool in Bethesda

Adventures of the Quiet Stranger in the Black Hat

Paul John Hausleben

The cover artwork and computer retouch, cover design, and cover concept by Paul John Hausleben
The photographs of the author and the Quiet Stranger are by Paul John Hausleben
Scripture reference is from the King James Version, Holy Bible, public domain

Published by God Bless the Keg Publishing
Somewhere, U.S.A.

ISBN: 978-0-9986300-5-2

The Pool in Bethesda

Dedication

To everyone who stands on the precipice of wonder and asks the simple question of, "What if?"

The Pool in Bethesda

Adventures of the Quiet Stranger in the Black Hat

Paul John Hausleben

Contents

Acknowledgements

Thank you to my friends and my family. Thank you to Paul Edmund Hausleben for his expert advice on video games and the world of gamers. Thank you to Mr. Mark Knopfler OBE, for the inspiration and for some amazing words.

"Can you imagine how wonderful this world could be if we could just stop and think before we react? If only, for a pause, this world would be so much better of a place."

Paul John Hausleben

05 March 2019

680 Kilohertz

A novella of crime and fantasy

The Fig and the Thistle

A novelette of fantasy mixed with the power of love and of faith

Echo of a Requiem

A short story about perseverance

If Only for a Pause

A novella of crime and fantasy
Introducing the character of "Winterkill."

Preface from the Author

Late in the year 2017, I diligently worked to lay out a game plan and an outline for my future work and material. After some slicing, some dicing, and some prioritizing of the plan, one of the books that remained at the top of the list was to bring back the ever mysterious, but always interesting, character of the quiet stranger in the black hat. Our goal was to have a collection composed of mostly novellas and novelettes, with a short story sandwiched somewhere in between.

When it came down to actually beginning work on the collection, I found that I had three very strong themes and three solid outlines for the stories for the book. Yet, I felt as if I was missing a central story for the book and the all-important "anchor" story for the collection. I also searched for a character that could be a reoccurring character to pair with the quiet stranger in further adventures, much as I created in the characters of Charles "Chuck" McCracken and Mr. and Mrs. Jimmy Reeves. There was little doubt that my future visions included a composition including all of these characters in a "no-holds-barred" effort to assist the dark stranger in his quest to defeat evil, and to assist persons in need, in what he often portrays to be a "weary world."

Regardless, the final story and the perfect character required for it proved a bit evasive.

Then as it often does come to PJH, inspiration unexpectedly arrived.

It seemed as if it was going to be a very quiet evening for PJH. I sat on an open-air patio of a restaurant in Florida while traveling on business. For the end of June, in Florida, it was not a gruesome, hot and humid Florida evening; it actually was rather pleasant, with a gentle breeze and fading sunlight. Those people close to me know how I despise the heat and humidity; therefore, for PJH to sit outside in an open-air restaurant patio in Florida, it must have been an exceptionally pleasant evening.

The evening proved to be quite memorable in many ways.

I ordered a chicken dish and a beer and when I took my first sips, I spotted a very pretty, rather petite restaurant server flirting with a patron who was sitting a few tables away from where I sat. The patron was a tall, lanky sort of young man, with floppy, long hair, and he wore black canvas sneakers similar to my own and a tee shirt printed with the logo and name of a well-known video game. He also sported and fiddled with multiple cellphones. No doubt, modern technology captivated him. However, when he did not have his nose in those cellphones, he was smiling and happily interacting with the server. By his body language, the flicker in his eyes, and his smile, it appeared as if the young man was quite cocky in his demeanor, as well as extremely confident. While I studied the interaction, his personality traits became more obvious as the two of them flirted and shared some laughter together. I thought that they made such a cute couple, and I hoped that if they were not a couple now that their future would be bright and they would spend it together.

Another sip or two of beer might have induced some type of hazy influence because I felt inspiration overtake my mind and soul. The cute couple suddenly became characters, slowly evolving within my mind. I did my best to take as many mental notes as I could while sitting there and to carry the inspiration with me.

That evening, while back in my hotel room, the quiet stranger in the black hat, made an appearance, and he tipped his famous hat in my direction once again and walked briskly into the pages of a draft outline for the anchor story for the potential manuscript. It seems as if he is a rather persistent chap and follows me around quite a bit.

On the airplane flight back home, I pondered the potential storylines for the anchor story. It all evolved rather slowly in my mind's eye and after making some random outline notes, a song by the great, singer and songwriter and former front man for the legendary rock band Dire Straits, Mr. Mark Knopfler OBE, sounded in the ear buds stuck in my ears. Mr. Knopfler used a word within his lyrics and it fixed in my mind as a perfect name for my own floppy-haired, geeky, but cocky and confident, video gaming character. I wrote a character's name on the hotel notepad that I stuffed in my pocket. "Winterkill," was the name I scrawled on the pad, and when I arrived home, a few title names for stories appeared and I set to work on the draft of the first story. Shortly after the initial words flowed, I bogged down a bit with wavering and at times, unconfident writing.

A change in my moods caused a shift in the title names for the stories. I ran new title names around within my mind and after some internal debate; I narrowed the titles down to those used herein.

The revised titles proved to be the final pieces of inspiration and I wrote hard and dove into the words with the titles, outlines, and themes for all the stories all now under my belt. Just as I often write a story into an ending, I also write a story into titles, especially if the words invoke a certain mood.

The entire book became a draft reality in about four weeks of intense writing. I felt it was a solid draft and when I finished the work, once more, the quiet stranger tipped his hat at me and in his strange sort of way, considerably improved my own world.

I think that is part of the magic of the stranger and a

large portion of his appeal with many of our readers. Through the stranger's adventures and his empowerment of his chosen allies, his character somehow provides hope and love to everyone he touches. Furthermore, whatever a reader's faith or religious beliefs are, or might not be, the stranger endorses a sort of ecumenical type of faith. Even I, as his eccentric creator, feel his presence and admittedly, I enjoy his adventures and feel as if somewhere in the deepest and darkest shadows of the world, he actually does watch and wait and tries to make sure that we do not make such a terrible mess of things. I think that I will use some of my privileges as the creator and steal some of Winterkill's thunder by quoting his words, "When the games are all won and the bad guys are all defeated, love is all that remains and all that really counts in this weary world."

Indeed.

It is my hope that you enjoy reading this collection of stories as much as I enjoyed the experience of writing them.

Thank you for reading them.

Paul John Hausleben

05 March 2019

Prologue

Mr. Davis Taylor had been fishing the same spot here at the watershed on the outskirts of the city for many years. In the spring, the summer, and even the fall, he fished. Ever since he retired after working for nearly forty-five years in the dye factory on Laidlaw Street in the old mill section of Paterson, New Jersey, fishing became his passion. Mr. Taylor would still be working, if he had his way about it. His mind was still sharp, his body was still strong and solid, and his eyes still keen, but when management closed the factory and the parent company that bought them a few years earlier, moved the entire operation overseas to China, then Davis Taylor knew he reached the end of the road.

He retired before they retired him. Davis always wanted to go out on his own terms and not theirs.

It was a good run. He never made a ton of money, but he fed his family, had a modest house in the Hillcrest section of the city and he drove an older car, but he always had decent tires and he kept up on the oil changes. In fact, the same car was parked just down the road a piece from where he sat on an upturned bucket, while enjoying the cool breeze of springtime. He was watching the end of his fishing line for a bite, while it gently waved in the breeze. The car had some rust now and a few more creaks and squeals from the springs and the belts, but the engine burned little oil and it always started, even on the coldest days. Davis always parked in the same spot and the local police knew his car, so they looked the other way at the "No Parking" sign posted above where Davis parked his car. He was alone now. His wife passed on about five years ago, and his two sons long since moved out of New Jersey. They constantly told their father to sell the house and join one of them and enjoy his family in his retirement. However, Paterson, despite the flaws and wounds, was his home. Now, he fished three or four times a week during the pleasant weather, hung around a local bar with some old buddies, watched sports on television, he cut his grass, and fixed things around his home. It was a simple life, but after all those years of punching a time clock and getting out of bed at five in the morning, Davis felt pretty good about sitting on an old bucket watching his fishing line.

He deserved it.

This was a good spot and the watershed, while not huge, did cover quite a few acres of land and it was quiet and beautiful. This was one of the main sources of water for the city, and while the fish and wildlife department did not stock the waters with fish, there was a generous population of fish inhabiting the clear and clean waters of the reservoir.

Davis always managed to catch a few fish and enjoy the day. Sunnies, catfish, calico bass, yellow and white perch, large mouthed bass and a rare pickerel or two. There were the occasional rumors of a few of the local anglers pulling a good-sized rainbow or brown trout or two out of the watershed, but Davis was never so lucky and he doubted that the trout even existed in the reservoir. It was just hearsay and "fishing talk." He never kept any of the fish, he just enjoyed the lure, and the hunt, and the fight, and then tossed them back into the water to catch another day.

His old, but still sharp, gray eyes studied the water, and a few pieces of his white hair floated away from his scalp in the gentle breeze. Davis reached up and pushed the strands of hair back down on his head and then, frustrated with the breeze, he reached next to his tackle box and grabbed his baseball cap and plopped it on his head to hold his hair down. A small transistor radio played some broadcasted music while it sat at his feet and a thermos of coffee sat next to the radio. It had been an extra-long winter, and it felt good to be out on the bank of the water once again and suck in some springtime air. He had a flask of whiskey in his tackle box in case that the early spring breeze was nippy, but right now . . . the coffee was fine.

He had not had a nibble yet, but it was early and the water was still cold from the winter months.

Old Davis looked up to the asphalt path that surrounded the body of water because he heard a noise. He could not quite place it, but it was a rhythmic "clicking noise" as if someone or something was moving on the path or walking. The old man listened for a few moments until his curiosity got the best of him. He stood up and he poked his head just enough to see over the bank and to where the asphalt path twisted in his direction. He saw a man walking in his direction. While the man walked, his boots made the clicking noise as they struck hard upon the asphalt surface of the path. Davis surmised that his boots had metal tips on them in order for them to make such an unusual, but strangely captivating sound. This was not a fellow fisherman, or a game warden, or a police officer checking in to make sure that Davis was okay down here. No, not at all. This man might have been the largest man that Davis had ever seen. Davis stood up, and at first, he wondered if he should grab his gear, his car keys and dash off to safety or if he should grab his cellphone and dial, 9-1-1, but the hint of a smile on the man's face gave Davis some sort of comfort. Honestly, the man's strange and unusual appearance captivated Davis too much for the old man to do more than only stare at him.

The man was dressed all in black, he wore a black vest covering a perfectly pressed, black buttoned-up shirt, and his sharply creased, black trousers had not a single ripple or a wrinkle in them. There was nothing out of place on this man—nothing at all. He was impeccable, immaculate. His features were dark; he wore on his face, a finely trimmed beard, closely framing a perfectly chiseled face, and he walked silently while watching with dark, piercing black eyes. Dark eyes that were staring straight ahead, emotionless, expressionless. On his head, he wore a black hat, pulled down to where his facial features were not easily seen, but still slightly visible. No doubt, he was a striking and handsome man.

He was the quiet stranger in the black hat.

The stranger stopped walking on the path when he reached the spot where Davis stood, and he smiled once again at Davis as he turned off the path. Despite his fancy black boots, he easily and deftly made his way down the side of the bank, while walking on the dirt and in a few short seconds; he stood next to Davis on the edge of the water, with his dark eyes carefully studying the water. Davis carefully watched the silent stranger and the old man admired the deep sparkle in the dark eyes of the stranger. After a careful study of the stranger, Davis slowly stood up, he leaned over and turned the volume down on the radio.

"Well, good morning there, stranger! How are you today? I have to say that ya sure are dressed fancy for a trip to the edge of the watershed. Ya gave me a bit of a start until ya smiled a little." Davis pointed at the boots on the stranger's feet and commented, "Gonna need to brush off the dirt and mud off those fancy-ass boots. Be a shame to get them all dirty."

Davis rubbed his eyes as he stared at the boots. Because despite the hike down the bank and the walk along the asphalt path, the boots did not have a speck of dust or any mud or dirt upon them. The stranger still did not say a word and Davis slowly sat down on the top of his upturned bucket. Occasionally, local photographers wandered by to snap some scenic landscape shots, but this man held no photographic gear. Therefore, Davis surmised that the stranger was just a sightseer. While it seemed as if he just stepped out of a time machine from another era, and he was the size of a mountain, Davis felt that he meant him no harm.

"Nothing biting yet. Too cold. Can I offer you a sip of coffee or a nip of some whiskey? You have a hat on, and a mighty fine hat it is too, but that vest might not hold back the cool spring breeze."

The stranger still did not answer. He only stood there and allowed his dark eyes to study the old man and capture the sparkle of the sunlight. The old man shrugged at his silence and picked up his fishing pole out of the fork that stuck in the sandy bank of the watershed and he tweaked the reel a little to bring his line up tighter.

"Suit yaself. Guess it is a beautiful spot to enjoy the world from and admire all of it. People hardly can imagine the perfect picture that God painted here . . . just a few miles away from the grit of the city. They don't understand how beautiful New Jersey can be."

The stranger now smiled widely, and finally, spoke in a deep, melodious voice, "Indeed. God's handiwork is beyond any understanding. I agree with you, Mr. Taylor. Thank you for the offer, but I just stopped here for a moment or two."

Davis was surprised that the quiet stranger not only finally spoke, but he was shocked that he knew who he was.

"Hey, nice, I get it. Admire the view and check it out for some fishing or perhaps, some picture taking. You know my name, huh? Do I know you? Might be that we crossed paths or worked together years ago? I think that I would recall a man such as you are, but I am getting a little older and things escape me, especially people's names and faces. C'mon and sit down next to me for a bit and we can shoot the breeze. I would enjoy the company. Gets a little lonely at times."

The stranger did not immediately answer Mr. Davis Taylor. Instead, he walked down to the water's edge, and he gently placed his right hand in the water. Davis thought it was strange behavior. The old man watched as the stranger moved his hand rapidly about in the water, and his old eyes widened as the stranger's actions seemed to cause ripples across the entire surface of the watershed. Davis tested the breeze with his hands and quickly determined that the breeze stirred the water, and it was simply a coincidence that the large and powerful ripples arrived when the stranger touched the water.

The stranger spoke while he continued slowly stirring the water around as Davis carefully listened, "Oh, perhaps, somehow there is a chance that you might know me. Somehow. I would like to stay a bit but have to be on my way. There are a few things that need my attention, but I wish you the best of luck today. Maybe, a trout or two will come along and you will finally put an end to the wonder of their existence. There are many unknown wonders in the world, Mr. Taylor. So many. God's gifts of wonder and of beauty are some of our greatest gifts."

The stranger tipped his hat and smiled again and after he finished stirring the water, he stood back up, made his way up the path and once more began walking briskly down the asphalt pathway.

Davis recovered from the strange encounter and called out, "Ah, now, I get it. Ya, a fisherman like me. Just wanted to see how cold the water is, huh? Well, it was a long winter, and it is still very cold. Well, thanks for stopping by and the well-wishes, but as far as trout go, I might be out of luck. It is just an old fishing tale 'bout those trout swimming 'round in here. Have a good day, stranger!"

The dark stranger did not turn around, nor did he acknowledge the words of Davis, and the old man stood and watched and listened to the metal tips of the stranger's boots, until both the stranger and the sound of his boots faded from view. Davis shook his head once more, took his seat upon the upturned bucket and he stared at the flask of whiskey in his tackle box.

While turning the volume back up on his radio, Davis mumbled, "Geez, maybe I have lost my mind or dipped into the hooch and just don't remember it. He had to stir the water in order to test how cold it is, huh? He could've just asked and I would have told him. Okay, he seems to be a bit of a loony tune there. That sure was one weird experience. Nice guy, but he sure was a strange one."

Davis was going to reach for the flask, when his line suddenly shot straight out into the water. The fishing pole lurched forward in the fork, and the force of the strike on the line almost pulled the pole into the water.

"Holy Mollie!" Davis screamed, and he picked up his pole just before the fish pulled the entire fishing pole into the water. The old man stood up, clicked the bail open on the reel to feed the fish extra line and then clicked it shut again. Davis eased back on the pole as the fish ran hard. When he felt the weight and power of the fish on the end of his line and on the tip of the pole, then old Davis knew this was the fish of a lifetime. When the fish swam hard and then jumped out of the water, Davis felt his heart jump in his chest. The colors of the fish in the fantastic sunlight were as if they arrived straight from Heaven and the fish leaped in the air, turned and twisted and fought and then crashed back into the water.

"Geez, I might be a crazy old geezer, seeing dark strangers dressed in black, but dang, if that doesn't look like a rainbow trout on the end of my line!" The old man proclaimed as he let the fish run some more and the fight was on. Davis tugged a little; he only had a ten-pound test line loaded on this reel, because sunfish usually do not weigh too much! The fish ran again and Davis let the fish run, easing the line here and there and being gentle as the fight elevated to an intense battle. Davis never fought a fish so long and so hard, but as the fish eventually tired and Davis had some more courage to reel the fish into the shore. He felt his heart race even more when he caught sight of the fish in front of him in the clear, bright water.

It was a rainbow trout! At least thirty inches long and the fish was stocky, powerful and thick in girth. What a fish! A glorious and amazing fish! Davis carefully set his pole down and waded to the water's edge and with the greatest of care; he gently captured the fish and held it in his hands. Never was there such a glorious fish. It was gorgeous beyond description. All the amazing colors of the rainbow glistened in the old man's eyes. As the fish gasped for air with its mouth open, and its gills working, Davis knew that he had to release the amazing creature that God created back to its kingdom. Not before, Davis snapped off many pictures to show his drinking buddies, though! He grabbed his cellphone and carefully maneuvered the camera of the phone, as well as the fish, to take a few solid snapshots. When the photographic evidence was gathered, Davis measured the length of the fish with his tape measure and proved that it was just a tad over thirty inches long. Now, it came time to release the fish.

Davis carefully freed the hook from the mouth of the trout and then he gently held the fish under the water, watching the fish recover as it worked its gills and gently flapped its fins. When the powerful fish recovered and it began to squirm in an effort to find its freedom, Davis released his grip on the fish and it quickly darted off and disappeared into the cold water.

"Thank you, for a glorious day and a remarkable experience. Live a long life, dear trout. A long and glorious life."

The old man stood on the bank and he pursed his lips and blinked his eyes. He took his hat off, smoothed his hair down upon his head once again, and realized that he had some tears of joy in his eyes.

The sunlight glistened upon the waves of the water, the patterns set into the waves with colors of flickering light, and the wind danced the timing of the waves as if it was a beat of a melody from Heaven.

While admiring and taking in all the beauty of the glorious scene in front of his eyes, the old man mumbled, "Yes, indeed, I have lived a long and glorious life, too. There are many unknown wonders in the world. So many. I ain't ever been much of a churchgoing man, but I know that God exists. I agree with you, dark stranger that God's gifts of wonder and of beauty are some of our greatest gifts."

680 Kilohertz

It was a Monday morning, late in March, and it was unusually cold for this time of the year. Almost like a winter cold. Northern New Jersey had its share of harsh winters, snowfall, and cold, but this day was unusually cold. After all, it was almost April and the last snow was only a day or so before Saint Patrick's Day or thereabouts.

It was well past the time to usher in springtime.

Mr. Arthur Doogan turned the key in the door lock and gave it a good twist. Actually, he gave it a hard twist to the left with a tiny jiggle of the door handle right at the end of the twist. The lock had been sticky and troublesome for quite a bit of time, and Arthur kept reminding himself that he needed to put a squeeze of some graphite lubricant in the lock cylinder or take it apart and repair it.

'One of these days, I will lubricate and fix that stupid lock,' Arthur thought, as the lock finally spun free and the door swung open. The little silver bell, mounted on a bracket on the top of the front door, jingled while it gently swung, tinkling the telltale signal that the door was active. Arthur slowly guided the door back to a closed position, and he pushed his shoulder into the door until he heard the lock snap closed.

The door closed better than it unlocked.

Arthur Doogan could walk the interior of his shop blindfolded and the fact that the morning remained dark and the day overcast almost forced him to feel for the light switch and grope along the wall for the telltale cover plate covering the bank of light switches. After all, Mr. Doogan had been flipping these same light switches on in the interior of "Doogie's Television and Radio Repair Shop," nearly every day for the last forty-three years or thereabouts. Ever since, he returned home after his discharge from the United States Navy after the big war. In the Navy, Arthur Doogan earned his nickname of "Doogie" and he learned his trade of electronics repair, as well as a few other skills and lessons while serving as a radioman, onboard various aircraft carriers and while being crisscrossed across the Pacific Ocean combat theatres. Arthur Doogan returned home physically unscathed, and he was always thankful for that fact.

Very thankful.

When Doogie returned home, he married his high school sweetheart, and after a short stint working for a large telecommunications corporation as an electronics repairman, with his loyal wife's unending love and support, Mr. Doogan opened his own electronics repair shop. It was a dream that came true for him.

Now, here he was, all of these years later, still unlocking the door to his shop. Arthur's back caused him some pain now, because of some arthritis in his lower spine. Doogie surmised that it was because of his age, as well as the wear and tears of lifting unreasonably heavy television sets over the years. Yet, despite his age, his blue eyes remained keen and sharp and his thick chock of white hair layered over easily across his head. His features were soft and smooth and, in his day, he certainly could make the young ladies swoon. Despite that fact, Arthur "Doogie" Doogan only had eyes for one gal. He married her and his life was grand. He made a very good living over the years in his business. He worked very hard, he worked long hours and Saturdays and put his two children through college on the money earned here and paid off two mortgages, too. Arthur Doogan treated his customers fairly and honestly, and he was lucky enough to have worked as his own boss for all of these years.

During the heyday of the electronics business, Arthur

employed two bench technicians, two road technicians, a full-time salesman on the sales floor, selling radios, televisions, stereo systems and small electronics and his business grew until he could purchase the building where the shop and store were located. The corner of Fifth Street and Main Street, just off the outskirts of downtown in good old Paterson, New Jersey. As his business grew, Arthur took over the space next door, which had been at one time, until the tailor passed away, a tailor and garment shop. He knocked a wall down in the shop's rear and expanded the building to add a small loading dock to allow for easier unloading and loading of the televisions and larger goods. The loading dock area also gave the road technicians a place to park the service vans off the busy city streets. Investing in the building turned out to be a wise move because the two apartments above the shop and stores proved to provide some additional income that came in handy and helped to pay off the mortgage on the entire building. Then the world and advanced technology caught up with the business. As American corporations looked to maximize profits at any cost, the business slowly dried up as consumer electronics moved overseas with manufacturing. The service business dried up as the goods became cheaper, shinier, and repairs became prohibitive except for the high-end electronics. Fewer and fewer persons repaired their televisions, radios, and other electronics, and instead, when they malfunctioned and wore out, they tossed them away and bought new ones. The "new" economy labeled them "consumers" and that is exactly what they did.

As the years flew by, the business went the opposite way and as quickly as the expansion occurred, now, the shrinking occurred just as quickly. Presently, the shop occupied a small nook at the far end of the building that Arthur Doogan owned. A liquor store rented the space next door, and Arthur moved the walls of the store and shop and adjusted the footprint of the shop to create space next door to rent out to a dry-cleaning operation.

Arthur Doogan adapted his skills too, realizing that the number of televisions and radios to repair was rapidly shrinking, and modern electronics proved more reliable as the technology evolved, Doogie repaired much more than electronics in his shop. He rewired expensive heirloom light fixtures and chandeliers. He learned to repair computers and video games and established a reputation for being able to repair just about anything, with a "plug and a cord." Whereas the large majority of the old television and radio repair shops in the area closed as the business dried up, Doogie's shop stayed open, because of the flexibility and ingenuity of the owner. The shop eked out a small profit. Arthur did not really need the money from repairs any longer, because the rental of the other stores and the apartments provided most of his income.

Mr. and Mrs. Arthur Doogan invested wisely and lived within their means, and now Arthur just wanted to cruise one more year until he was seventy years old, collect his retirement payments, sell the building, and join his children in Florida. Arthur Doogan was now a widower, having lost his beloved wife after forty-five years of marriage, about one year previous to this very day. Now, flipping the lights on his small shop and counting the days until retirement kept him from losing his mind and, mostly, each day seemed just the same as the previous day was.

Mostly.

A flip of the switches with his fingers caused a snap, a pop, a brief whiff of ozone in the air of the repair shop as the ballasts fired, and the old fluorescent light tubes of the light fixtures sprung to life. Doogie sighed. His eyes scanned the shop, and he took a few shuffles and then a few longer steps as he made his way through the front of the shop. The distinctive, musty smell of old electronics filled the air. The odor of old electrolytic capacitors and ceramic capacitors, resistors, wire, the smell of coils and transformers, and over forty years of melted solder smoke lingered in the air. A lifetime of telltale signs of the trade, countless repairs and thousands upon thousands of memories. Too many to count.

Arthur Doogan slowly made his way through a few random displays of used televisions for sale, a few old radios, a display of used video game consoles, and some assorted electronic parts for sale. All of this was sure a far cry from the rows upon rows of polished televisions, radios and high-tech stereo systems that the store used to sell back in the heyday. Now, if he sold a battery or two, it was a big sale for the day. It was fine with Arthur "Doogie" Doogan. He was in the homestretch now, a year or so more, and then it was off to the Sunshine State and a well-deserved retirement.

For today, he had a mission or two. First, he promised Mrs. Gunter that he would replace the cord and the plug on her vacuum cleaner and have the vacuum cleaner ready for her to clean the carpets before her company arrived for the weekend. Wilhelm, that new and frisky puppy of hers, loves to chew on that cord. It will be the third time that Arthur has had to replace it.

It was a good thing that it was unplugged. . ..

Second, he had to see if he could get the stuck video game disc out of the Millhouse's video game. The Millhouse's young son was driving his old man crazy, bugging his father every day because the game was in the repair shop. Yes indeed, a few missions, but mostly, each day felt about the same as all the other days did.

Mostly.

Detective Barclay Millhouse had no choice but to become a police officer on the police force in Paterson, New Jersey. It was in his genes from birth. Barclay's father, Captain Percy Millhouse, just retired a few months ago, after a nearly forty-year career on the Paterson police force. Barclay's grandfather, Theodore Millhouse, was also a captain on the force, and he served for forty-two years as a police officer. Yes, indeed, from the very first diaper that Barclay wore, his dear mother joked that he should wear a police badge hung on the corner of his diaper. Now, with the Millhouse's son nearly eleven years old, and their daughter around eight, it appeared as if the legacy of honorable service of the Millhouse family in the line of law enforcement in Paterson might have a good chance to continue. Becoming a police officer was all that their son, Joseph, spoke of these days and their daughter, Pearl, while still very young, followed the chatter on the heels of her older brother. Pearl might just become the first female police officer in the family's history. While he tied his shoes in front of his locker in the precinct headquarters, Barclay chuckled at his own thoughts, because Pearl certainly was tough enough. She gave her older brother hell on a daily basis, and it was a good thing that Joseph was a gifted athlete and could run fast.

Very fast.

Barclay was a handsome man. Both his mother and his wife felt as if he was the spitting image of his father. Barclay was tall, around six feet two or thereabouts, and he was muscular, with broad shoulders and powerful biceps. As his father did, Barclay had riveting hazel eyes, and his face had chiseled features and his head sported blonde hair, buzzed close to his head. One glance at him and it said "Policeman" in a bright, loud, and clear broadcast. His look was no nonsense. None whatsoever, yet, Barclay enjoyed life, and he loved his wife and kids with all of his heart and soul, and he loved what he did for a living.

Detective Millhouse slipped his suit jacket on, grabbed the police badge out of the pocket of the jacket, and clipped it on his belt. He felt for his service revolver tucked neatly in a shoulder holster and double-checked his body for all the parts and pieces to be in the correct locations. He no longer wore a police officer's issued daily uniform, but he still had the tools hidden away that a street cop carries. Handcuffs, a can of mace, a small knife tucked in his belt, a multi-tool and flashlight tucked into two small sheaths hanging on his belt under his suit jacket.

Old and young habits die-hard. Habits are habits.

His daily, double-check was a habit that Barclay developed upon solid advice offered by his grandfather, "Once you are dressed and holster your weapon, give your body and equipment the good old, double-check or two. Make sure you are ready for whatever comes your way in a day's work. Not only to enforce the law and to do your duty, but to protect your own ass too."

It was only one month ago that Barclay received the promotion to a detective. The glances and vague nods from his fellow police officers told him that the jealousy and animosity still ran high as Barclay received the rank over what some of his fellow officers, and in some cases, old friends, felt were more experienced and deserving officers. The word in the locker room was that Barclay only received the detective position because of his family's legacy, and nothing that Barclay had done in his short service career of about three years or thereabouts warranted such a quick and high promotion.

The banter was, "He walked a beat for only two years and then sat in a patrol car for a little over a year. He got lucky and made one big bust. Big deal. The detective rank is all because of his old man and his grandfather."

Barclay walked out of the locker room, and only received some weak nods and a mumble or two of, "Good morning," from some of his fellow officers, while others, purposely held their heads down and did not even look his way. They used to drink beer together and talk about the hockey games after work in "Smitty's Tavern" and now, these same guys could not even say, "Hello."

He was an outsider now. No longer one of the "Boys."

Barclay thought how it was time to clean out his locker and move into the detective's office with his new daily co-workers. So far, the detective force warmly welcomed him. He was a fresh face, a fresh and young mind and despite the complaints about his track record, Barclay did have a short, but distinguished service record. After graduation from a local university with a criminal justice degree and a two-year stint in the military reserves, Barclay hit the streets hard, and he quickly developed a reputation as a city kid who grew up here and had the toughness, honesty and street senses to be an exceptional police officer. His initial response to a murder crime scene and keen observations written into his report led to the breakup of a large crime ring. Barclay's role in the subsequent arrest of the crime ring's notorious kingpin, working out of Paterson's rough and tough North Ward section and his eye for detail, caught the eye of one of the head detectives. That report, the arrests, the investigation and the recommendation of the head detective triggered his promotion to a detective.

Now Barclay gradually adjusted to his new position. Admittedly, it was still very early in the game of his new career, but it required some adjustment on his part. Sitting at a desk, for the long, boring, hours upon hours, was a large adjustment from the life of a street cop in the city of Paterson, New Jersey. This was a difficult, old city and as many old cities are in America these days, urban life brings its dark side, and crime while not rampant as it was in the

1970s, sure had its moments. Barclay tagged along on a few investigations, but for the most part, his chain of command gave him routine reports to write, and paperwork of current and past investigations to review, along with internet investigations and telephone calls to make in order to follow up on leads. A large part of his day seemed to be surfing the social media sites of known street thugs and criminals, trying to determine their latest intentions and potential criminal activities from their postings. He often chuckled at how dumb some of these bums were as they posted enough material to open the door to their own arrests and investigations as they tried to impress the world and demonstrate how "bad" they were.

His latest target was a typical street punk who was now peddling drugs and stolen goods here and there in Barclay's old beat neighborhood of the lower numbered streets of Third, Fourth, Fifth and Sixth Street and Main Street, just off the outskirts of the downtown area of the city. The street punk was from some country that Barclay never really heard of, with a name that he could not pronounce. Somehow, the young man entered this country on some type of work authorization, and Barclay sensed an evil connection there. A payoff to someone in order to be here in the United States of America. This guy had no real job, other than committing petty crimes and dealing some weed and pills, or on the other hand was there more to this guy than just that? Barclay sipped a fresh cup of coffee and waited for his computer to flicker to life. Today's first assignment was to check the social postings of this punk and see what he decided to brag about to his street buddies, using his stupid code words . . . code words that the entire detective bureau understood the meaning of and code words that told telltale clues of the latest activities. Certainly, they would eventually round up this punk, but the goal was to round up a few levels above him, too. Time would tell, and Barclay was street savvy enough to understand where and how to look in order to make it happen.

Thinking of his old beat neighborhood, Barclay pulled out a notepad and wrote a reminder to stop by Doogie's Television and Radio Repair Shop and see if his old buddy, Arthur Doogan had any luck extracting the video game disc that was stuck in Joseph's game console. Barclay knew that the second he arrived home from work today that Joseph would ask him once more for about the millionth time if Doogie had repaired the unit and pulled the stuck disc out. Over the last weekend, their son had bugged his parents so much about the video game that Mrs. Millhouse asked if he really was too young for Barclay to take him downtown to the military recruiters and sign their son up for a quick stint. It made Barclay long for the days of his own youth, when stickball in the streets and endless games of street hockey, kept kids occupied forever, rather than killing aliens, saving the world as a superhero and tracking down computer generated criminals while playing video games in their bedrooms.

Oh well, Barclay thought as he clicked his button on the mouse and began to surf the social media sites for clues. The video world might actually serve some useful purpose. It might be good training for tracking down real-life bad guys someday in the future.

Someday, and there sure were enough bad guys out there to hunt down too.

As well as a world to save.

Later that same morning, inside Doogie's Television and Radio Repair Shop, Mr. Arthur Doogan fished around in his toolbox for a specific tool. He knew it was in there somewhere; he opened each drawer and compartment to the toolbox, and as he did so, his eyes scanned the contents and after not finding the tool, he then moved on to searching the next drawer. He knew what the tool looked like. It had a cushion-grip black handle with a red stripe on the end. Arthur had begun the process of extracting the video disc from the inside of Joseph Millhouse's video game, and already Arthur had hit an obstacle. These newfangled video games could not use the standard Phillips-head screws that the entire world used forever. No, that would be too easy. Instead, the game console had some new star-head screws that required a special driver to remove. As he searched for the wayward tool, Doogie thought about how this modern world had to always go and change the standards and add confusion and nonsense to the mix. For no reason other than to sell more tools or screws. There was nothing wrong with the old Phillips-head screws. . ..

His old repair bench also served as a front counter to his shop and store and on the bench was a set of various meters and other assorted electronic test instruments as well as the most used hand tools, some repair tickets, pens, a small brew-type coffee maker and a cash register on the far end of the bench. The tool chests, various shelves, and an assortment of storage drawers full of various parts and supplies lined the rear wall behind the bench. Since Arthur had gradually condensed the repairs and sales operations and the footprint of his shop and store grew considerably smaller over the years, things became a little tight.

The old loading dock area behind the building now served the liquor store next door to allow easy deliveries and the loading and unloading of goods. The "new" rear area of his shop now only had a small bathroom, an area of a "graveyard" of sorts, where he kept various parts, old televisions, and various electronics, as well as categorized boxes of old repair manuals and schematic diagrams. On one entire wall of the rear area, there was a custom array of a floor-to-ceiling wooden wall of shelves built by Doogie many years ago. The wall housed a vast collection of old vacuum tubes. Hundreds and hundreds of dusty, old cardboard boxes with old manufacturers' famous logos and the tube numbers stamped on the ends of the cardboard tube holders faced proudly outward. They were all in numerical and alphabetical order, and Doogie knew the functions and numbers of the vacuum tubes all by heart. 12AX7, 6GH8, 6B6, 6BQ5, 6SN7, and 5U4s and many other tubes. . ..

On and on they went, all the way to the higher numbers and the letter, Z. The display was worthy of a corner of a museum somewhere. A proud display of a bygone but a glorious era in the world of electronics. Standing next to the tube display was a medium-sized safe that Doogie now used very infrequently. It was not as it was in the old days, when he did enough business to need a safe to lock up cash, checks, or other valuables, until he could run to the bank.

It was so busy in those days, however, now. . ..

Next to the safe, sat a small refrigerator stocked with a few six-packs of cold beer, some water bottles, half-and-half cream for his coffee, some soda bottles, and his daily lunch, neatly tucked into a corner of the rear area. That was about it.

However, these days, it was all that Arthur needed or wanted as he headed into the twilight of his long working career.

"Here it is!" Arthur exclaimed aloud to no one except the small table radio that he always kept playing in the shop. Arthur enjoyed listening to some background music, news broadcasts, weather reports, and when it was hockey season, and he was in the shop late or on a Saturday, he listened to the hockey games. Arthur eagerly picked up the tool and, with his weapon-in-hand, the old repairman turned back to the bench and prepared to lay bare the video game and expose the precious contents contained therein. Just as Arthur turned, the little silver bell mounted on the front door of the store jingled while it gently swung, tinkling the telltale signal that a customer had arrived. Arthur looked up and peered down the short row of displays, half-expecting the visitor to be Mrs. Gunter, with Wilhelm the mad-chewer in tow. First thing this morning, Arthur had replaced the cord and the plug on her vacuum, and left her a message that it was ready and she could come by to pick the cleaner up.

It was not Mrs. Gunter, with or without Wilhelm.

Instead, it was a man . . . an immense man. Tall, lean, but powerfully built. While Arthur watched, the man took a few steps inside the front door; he stopped and allowed the door to close behind him. Arthur could tell by the way the latch sounded that it did not catch all the way, and he was once more reminded that he had to repair that door lock and latch. The man stood there for a few seconds, his eyes scanning the inside of the shop and his head turning here and there, as if he was determining exactly where he was. After his eyes settled on the front of the store and the shop area, the man turned and he began to walk through the rows of displays. The old repairman thought how this man might be the largest person that he had ever seen in his long life. While his size and physical appearance were impressive enough, as he began to walk to the front repair area, Arthur picked up a strange but slightly captivating noise and another fascinating nuance of the large man. The boots on his feet were highly polished black boots, buffed to a mirror shine, and Arthur bet that if he bent down and looked at them that he could see his reflection in them. They reminded Arthur of his own dress shoes from his old Navy days, and of when he handsomely paraded around downtown Paterson, while wearing his best dress white Navy uniform with spit-shined, low-quarters on his feet, and his lovely wife on his arm. Yet the polish and shine of the man's boots were only one fascinating aspect of the footwear, because the boots had metal tips on them and while he walked, they made a loud and distinct clicking noise as they struck the floor of the store in rhythm to his walking.

With what appeared to be a very old radio tucked neatly under his very large and muscular arm, the man walked with a purpose, his dark eyes piercing the air as they focused upon Arthur and the front of the shop. As he walked closer, Arthur set the coveted tool upon the surface of the workbench. He slowly sank down and sat on his trusty old wooden bench stool and studied the immense man approaching the bench area. The man was dressed all in black; he wore a black vest covering a perfectly pressed, black buttoned-up shirt, and his sharply creased, black trousers had not a single ripple or a wrinkle in them. There was nothing out of place on this man—nothing at all. He was impeccable, immaculate. His features were dark; he wore on his face, a finely trimmed beard, closely framing a perfectly chiseled face, and he walked silently while watching with dark, piercing black eyes. Dark eyes that were staring straight ahead, emotionless, expressionless. On his head, he wore a black hat, pulled down to where his facial features were not easily seen, but still slightly visible. No doubt, he was a striking and handsome man.

He was the quiet stranger in the black hat.

Finally, after what seemed as it was hundreds of yards but actually was only a journey of a few short feet, the man arrived at the front counter and Arthur smiled and slowly stood up as his eyes now fell upon the radio that the man carried. The customer's clothes and his general appearance seemed to give the impression that it was as if he emerged from a bygone era, and the vintage radio tucked under his arm only helped to enhance that appearance. Arthur immediately recognized the make and model of the radio and it was a table radio that collectors of electronics and hobbyists now considered a coveted antique collector's item amongst radio collections. Arthur knew his radios. He had not seen one of these radios in a very long time, and his eyes widened at the prospect of studying this vintage radio and obtaining a closer look at it. Even tucked under the man's arm, the wooden cabinet glowed as the lights mounted above the radio bench reflected the immaculate, golden finish of the solid oak cabinet of the radio.

"Well now, good morning and my goodness, what have you got there? An old radio, but an exceptional one at that. Worked on quite a few of them over my many years, but I have to say, I have not seen one of these puppies in a few years. Go on there and set it up there on the edge of the bench, on that pad, right there. The pad will protect the finish. That looks as if it is a radio in mint condition. Almost brand new. What a beauty!" Arthur found it difficult to contain his enthusiasm at the grand appearance and condition of the old radio. He pointed at a clear section on the repair bench and added, "I know they weigh a few pounds too, solid copper transformers in those radios from the old days. When quality was foremost and we actually made things here in this country. Yes, that is one heavy radio. However, for a man of your size and your muscles, I bet ya can carry one under each arm and not even breathe heavy."

So far, the stranger had not yet said a single word . . . he only nodded, and then he rather effortlessly lifted the table radio and carefully set it upon the pad on the repair bench in the location that Arthur had requested. Arthur immediately leaned in and studied the radio, and his eyes glowed at the quality and the condition of the radio. The old repairman gently ran his hands over the wood of the radio, and then the control knobs, and he took the tuning knob in his hands and slowly and carefully tuned the dial pointer across the band markers.

"Remarkable radio, amazing. It looks as if it is brand new. Right out of the box," Arthur spouted in a low voice, full of praise as he admired the remarkable radio. To a radioman such as Doogie Doogan, this was a glorious moment in time. Equivalent to splitting a glorious diamond for a diamond cutter, or a longtime car mechanic finally having the opportunity to work on the classic car of his dreams.

While still focused on the radio, Doogie explained, "I have a reputation for resurrecting the old ones and I keep a collection of vintage parts here in stock. I might have the widest and best collection of vacuum tubes, remaining in any active repair shop around these parts, but parts for these radios . . . well, understandably, they are getting kinda difficult to find. Luckily, I can still wind my own coils and even a transformer or two, and we can work a little magic here and there on these. I often have radios shipped into the shop for repair from all over the state and even the country, but none of those radios, are ever close to this one in condition. So, my friend, welcome to Doogie's Television and Radio Repair Shop. What is wrong with this glorious radio? How can I help you?"

The stranger finally spoke, in a low, deep, and melodious voice, a voice, which sounded as if he could have been the perfect radio or television broadcaster or a professional reader of poetry. No hard New Jersey accent, such as Doogie possessed, just a gloriously clear voice.

"Yes, it is a grand radio. It has been around for quite a long time. I enjoy listening to the station broadcasting out of Wayne, New Jersey. Six-eighty on the A.M. band. As of late, it is difficult to tune in that station and the other stations too. It seems as if the radio picks up strange broadcasts and various stations at random. Not all the time. Intermittently. I think you have to listen for and find the ghost."

Doogie nodded and took the eyeglasses hanging on a chain around his neck and placed them over his eyes.

He carefully examined and turned the tuning dial once again and said, "Intermittent, huh? Find the ghost. I understand that it seems haunted. Working one minute and not working the next. Six-eighty on the A.M. band, huh? Not sure that I have ever heard of that station. Wow! The tuning dial is razor sharp. Like it is still brand-new. Sometimes, the old dial cords, get old, lose their grip on the variable tuning capacitor shafts, and you have to re-string 'em. It is a bit of a pain in the old, you-know-what, but old Doogie can do it." Doogie laughed as he recalled that he still kept a roll of the special waxed dial cord in a drawer in the storage cabinet behind him. "I have the dial cord in stock. Anyway, okay, well, these guys did drift until they warmed up a bit. Could be the alignment or a front-end tube getting noisy when it heats up a bit. I will tell you what, I will plug it in here and give it a listen while I work on other repairs and see how it goes. If it is intermittent, then we will give it a good play and see what I find with it. If it drifts off, then I can jump right on it. Nothing more than I would like then to get this baby back in tip-top shape for ya." Doogie turned and pointed at his old faithful radio playing on the shelf next to the bench and said, "I always keep a radio playing in order to keep me company and catch the hockey games. Gets kinda lonely in the shop these days. In fact, it is kinda lonely all around these days. Anyway, I will shut down my old radio and use yours for a few days. Does that sound like a plan, my friend?"

The stranger only nodded and said no words.

'My goodness, this guy hardly speaks,' Arthur thought, while he reached over and grabbed a repair ticket off the stack that he kept on the end of the repair bench.

It was a stack of slightly yellowed paper tickets. Doogie did not use as many of the tickets as he had in previous years. Still, he kept a good stack of them, right next to the old cash register. You never know when he might have a busy time with demand repairs.

Arthur took his pen out of his shirt pocket, clicked the top, and poised the pen over the top of the repair ticket.

"Your name, my friend?" Doogie Doogan asked.

The melodious voice resonated once again, "Black. Just write down, black."

Doogie nodded, and his eyes scanned the stranger's attire.

'Fitting name,' Doogie thought.

"Here . . . I am going to be away on . . . business for a month or so. That is why I thought it was the perfect time to drop off the radio to you for repair. Since it is so intermittent. Here is a deposit for the repairs and your time. Will this be enough until my return?"

Doogie looked up, and the stranger was holding out three crisp, one-hundred-dollar bills.

"Oh yes, more than enough, Mr. Black." Doogie took the bills and explained as he wrote on the repair ticket, "Okay, I will record this deposit in cash, right here on the repair ticket and I will sign it. I will give you a copy of the ticket. A three-hundred-dollar deposit towards the repairs. Can I have an address or a telephone number, Mr. Black?"

The stranger did not respond right away unless a shake of his head counted towards a response of some sort.

After a few seconds passed away, once more, the melodious voice resonated throughout the old repair shop, "My business causes me to move around a lot and contact numbers really don't exist, nor do they work. I am . . . difficult to reach. I will stop back in when I return."

"Ah okay, I understand. Yes, please stop back in when you return to Paterson. Here is the ticket number." Mr. Doogan tore off the ticket stub on the end of the repair ticket and handed it to the quiet stranger. "Thank you, Mr. Black, and I assure you," Doogie gently patted the top of the old radio and smiled, as the old repairman explained, "Doogie will take good care of this beauty for you." Doogie reached down, tore off the top copy of the repair ticket, and went to hand it off to the quiet stranger in the black hat.

"Here, ya go, Mr. Black. Here is a copy of the receipt for the deposit and for your radio. I have a copy here, but please make sure to hang on to it."

With a smile on his handsome face, the stranger said, "Please keep the ticket. I trust you. The word is that you are the man, as they tend to say these days. I am counting on you. In many ways."

He tipped the edge of his black hat to Arthur, turned, and walked briskly away. Arthur "Doogie" Doogan leaned in over his repair bench and carefully studied the quiet stranger as he exited the store. The metal tips of his boots made that same glorious and distinctive sound as they struck the hard tiles of the floor of the old store. Arthur watched until the stranger reached the front door. He gently pushed it open and walked out into the madness of the city streets.

Curiosity over the unique stranger in the black hat's appearance and the entire experience of meeting the stranger overwhelmed Arthur Doogan. The old radioman hustled as best he could, from behind the repair bench, through the maze of old store displays and to the front door. Arthur pushed open the front door to his establishment and watched as his eyes followed the quiet stranger in the black hat and his ears listened to the distinctive click of his boots on the sidewalk. Arthur watched and listened while standing silently in the threshold of the front door as the noise from the tips of his boots sounded loudly and echoed along the city street. He watched until the stranger faded from view and the noise of his boots was lost in the madness and noise of the city.

Suddenly, this day did not feel the same as all the other days did.

No, this day was decidedly different.

Very different.

It was almost two o'clock in the afternoon when Doogie finally successfully extracted the stubborn disc from the blessed video game console. It appeared as if the paper label on the disc somehow peeled off on one corner and caused all the trouble. Doogie gave the disc a little kiss as he pulled it from its hidden lair. The disc was a worthy opponent in battle, but old Arthur Doogan was a bit too stubborn and too skilled to lose. After he reassembled the game console and tested the game out by hooking it up to a special test television monitor and wiping out a few bad guys on his own, (old Doogie was not too bad at playing these modern games) it was then that Arthur's eyes scanned the old table radio. He had become so lost in the video game battle that he had forgotten to plug in the antique radio, to silence his own radio and to give the old radio a test drive or two.

Doogie picked up the telephone and left a message for Detective Millhouse that he could pick up the video game, and he sat on his stool and wrapped up the repair job. While he wrote out the service ticket for the video game and added the price and the sales tax, Doogie thought about how this had been a productive day. Mrs. Gunter came in around noon and picked up the rewired vacuum cleaner. She scolded poor Wilhelm the entire way out the door. Thinking of vacuums, Mr. Bernstein dropped by and while Mr. Bernstein waited for the repair, Doogie rewired the wires on the cords to the speakers for his stereo system. Mrs. Bernstein sucked the cords up in her vacuum and tore the living hell out of them. He had known the Bernstein family forever and a little more. They lived in a large house, around the corner, over on Fourth Street, and they had been customers since when Doogie first opened the doors to his establishment. In fact, Doogie swore that he sold them the stereo system, which, despite the best efforts of errant vacuuming, was still going strong. Quality products. American-made quality from a different era. Of course, the highlight of the day was the classic radio, meeting the strange, but honestly, fascinating Mr. Black, and now, with the majority of the repairs out of the way, it was time to plug in the golden radio and give it a test whirl.

Arthur unplugged his old, faithful radio, and he plugged in Mr. Black's radio. He turned the on/off knob to the "on" position and with a loud and solid "click," the dial lights flickered to life and soft, captivating orange glows overtook the tuning dial.

'Quality. Even the switches are solid and made to last a lifetime,' Arthur thought as he waited for the tubes to warm up.

A bygone era . . . an era of waiting for radio and television sets to warm up.

Leaning over and peering into the ventilation holes in the rear of the cabinet, told the keen eyes of the old radioman that indeed, the tubes were flowing electrons and soon, the magic of radio would come to life. The orange and yellow glows of the filaments in the vacuum tubes told the story of the progression of the electrons, and Arthur gently sniffed the holes for any telltale signs of smoke or a malfunction. His years of training forced him to keep his hand on the plug while he scanned and sniffed, keeping on guard to unplug the radio very quickly at the first signs of trouble. Old electrolytic filter capacitors in the power supplies can dry up and pop as if they are firecrackers on these old sets. The radio was in mint condition, but it was very old and you cannot take any chances with a classic and priceless radio such as this one was.

Arthur Doogan had fixed more radio and television sets than he could ever dream of counting, but he had seen a few go up in smoke too.

A gentle smile broke across Arthur's face as the speaker crackled to life, and at first, a rush of static filled the air, then with a quick fiddle of the tuning knob, a local news station came in loud and clear. Doogie was in awe of the amazing sound quality of the radio as the deep tones of the speaker thumped inside the solid oak wood cabinet, producing tones comparable to some of the finest audio reproductions. Even in the monaural mode on the usually noisy A.M. radio band, it sounded as if the broadcaster was sitting right next to the old radioman.

Arthur slowly tuned across the band and as he did so, he settled on each station and made a note of the crisp response of the radio. Recalling the words and testimony of the stranger in black, Doogie tuned down the band to the six-eighty kilohertz setting on the dial and sure enough, a radio station boomed in loud and clear. While sitting back on his stool, Doogie took his glasses off and allowed them to hang on his neck chain; he folded his arms across his chest and carefully listened while thinking how he never knew there was a local station at 680 on the dial.

"Must be a new radio station or I just never tuned this far down the band in a long time," Doogie mumbled aloud as the broadcaster read a listing of sports scores and news. Arthur was an avid ice hockey fan and a dedicated follower of the New York Rovers hockey club. His ears perked up when the radio announcer relayed the score from the latest Rovers hockey game.

On the other hand, it was what seemed as it had been the latest game . . . or was Doogie not fully paying attention here?

"Last night, it was the Rovers over their archrivals, the Boston Bears, by a score of two goals to zero. In the first of a home-at-home series, the Rovers goalie, Watson Shambley outplayed the Bears superstar goaltender, Vance Howard and Shambley turned in an outstanding performance in front of an enthusiastic home crowd at their home ice rink. Shambley was remarkable in the net for the Rovers, turning away all thirty-six shots on goal and recording his second shutout of the season. Davis and Potter were the goal scorers for the Rovers. . ..”

Doogie Doogan leaned forward on the stool behind his repair bench, as if he wanted to lend a closer ear to the radio broadcast. He was puzzled because he swore that this was Monday and that the Rovers did not play last evening. He followed the schedule closely and he would not have intentionally missed a chance to catch a hockey game on a Sunday evening while relaxing at home. Doogie certainly did not have too much else on his schedule for lonely Sunday nights in his home. A hockey game, with his favorite hockey club playing their archrivals, would have been entertaining company to while away the lonesome evening.

“Hmm, I must have missed that game. I swore that the Bears did not come into the big city until tonight for the first game of the home-at-home with them goin’ up to Boston on Tuesday night. Oh well. It is a shame that I missed that game. Would’ve been fun to watch that one. A big shutout for the goalie. That is very nice. Especially against the Bears,” Arthur mumbled aloud and for a brief moment, he glanced over at today’s newspaper sitting on the repair bench. Doogie debated grabbing the paper and checking the article about the game. The tattletale jingle of the bell on the front door interrupted his thoughts.

A wide smile broke over the old repairman’s face as he spotted his old friend, as well as a good customer, Detective Barclay Millhouse, walking through the front door. It would be impossible to miss the big man as he made his way through the door and while he made his way through the maze of store displays. Arthur glanced at his watch, amazed at how much time had passed since he first warmed up the old radio. The time seemed to have passed by in the blink of an eye. It was about two minutes to six o'clock in the afternoon, and it was just about time to lock up the shop for the day and call it quits.

"Wow! Just made it, Doogie. Traffic was a little crazy, and I got stuck a little longer than I wanted to at headquarters. I was hoping and praying that you would still be open. If I did not bring that video game console and disc home tonight, the wife would send Joseph packing. It is all he has been talkin' 'bout and askin' us 'bout." the detective's hard New Jersey accent kicked in while he waved his arms in the air as if to capture Doogie's attention. The detective loudly explained his situation and conveyed his enthusiasm for the fact that Arthur had the video game console repaired and ready to go.

Doogie waved his hand in the air and reassured his friend, "Oh no, Barclay, no way would I lock up without waiting for you. I know how anxious the young man has been to get his game back. I would've waited. Besides, I want to hear all 'bout the new job. Honestly, I lost track of the time. It seems as if it was just two in the afternoon."

Detective Millhouse reached the front counter and bench area and leaned in, warmly smiled, and reached out to shake his old friend's hand. The two men exchanged a handshake, and Doogie had a thought.

Doogie said, "Say, I know ya had a long day and all, but ya want to share a beer? I want to hear all 'bout the new job and catch up a bit. I miss when you used to stop in on your old beat days."

Doogie laughed and for just a few seconds he became pensive in his thoughts.

He said in a lower-in-volume-voice while remaining pensive, "Actually, I miss when your grandfather and your old man used to stop by and chat. Back in the day. I guess . . . old Doogie has been around for a very long time. When ya are young, ya never think 'bout lookin' back on the good old days. I guess that I am at that point in my life now.

Everything ya see, observe, and think 'bout brings ya back to the good old days. It is all around me. On every street, in every room and hidden within most sounds that I hear."

The good detective knew that he should pick up the video game console and hustle home for dinner and family time, but he sensed the old man's loneliness and his need for camaraderie. Barclay's hesitation at accepting the invitation proved to be fleeting.

"Sure, sure, a beer will taste good, Doogie. I can stay for a few minutes. Sure. I would enjoy that. Thank you."

Arthur's face lit up at the acceptance of his invitation and the prospect of the company and he fished around in the front pocket of his pants, pulled out the keys to the front door and tossed them in the air to Detective Millhouse.

Barclay deftly caught the keys out of the air and listened while Doogie said, "Great! Please do me a favor and lock the front door. Ya gotta fiddle with the lock a little bit. It is stubborn. I have to fix it and lube it up. While you lock up, I will scoot in the back and get us a few beers. I just stocked up with a few six-packs of Big Boulder beer. They oughta be ice cold by now."

While Barclay locked the front door, Doogie happily walked into the rear storage area of the shop and pulled two ice-cold beers out of the small refrigerator. The prospect of good company with a friend and sharing a beer or two was an unexpectedly happy conclusion to what had turned out to be a very good day. Doogie returned to the repair bench and the front of the shop to find that Barclay Millhouse had already locked the front door, returned to the front, found the extra stool from behind the bench and he now sat on the stool while admiring the classic radio brought in by the quiet stranger dressed all in black. One at a time, Doogie spun the top off the beer bottles and tossed the caps in the trash bucket.

While handing Barclay his beer, Doogie kidded, "I guess

my ass is old and dragging now. You locked the door, walked twenty feet further than I did and you still beat me. Here. Cheers. Ice-cold. Nuthin' like it."

The two men touched glasses in a toast, and they each took the first blessed sip of the ice-cold beer.

Indeed, there are few simple pleasures in this world that match that first ice-cold sip of beer.

With a smack of his lips and a wipe of his mouth with the edges of his fingers, Doogie slowly sank into his stool behind the bench and placed his beer bottle on the bench.

"It's amazing . . . huh?" Doogie asked Barclay while pointing at the old radio.

"Yeah, geez, it is. Remarkable. Like it is in showroom condition, Doogie. Looks like a museum piece. Must be worth a good buck or two. It looks as if ya just unpacked it out of the original box." Barclay gently ran his hand over the wooden cabinet and after taking another sip of his beer and setting the bottle down upon the bench, the detective asked, "Where did ya get it? Sounds like nuthin' but static coming out of the speaker. Is that what's wrong with it? It doesn't receive any stations?" Barclay asked, and then he turned to look at his friend for an explanation.

It was then that Doogie realized that the station that he had been listening to now had gone off into radio oblivion. Yes, indeed, there was nothing but a rush of static flowing out of the radio's speaker. Six-eighty kilohertz was a rush of static now and that glorious amplitude modulation and the enjoyable sound of the radio station had now disappeared into the maze of noise.

Arthur Doogan jumped up, and he gently slid past his friend and with his expert hand gliding over the tuning knob, Arthur adjusted the tuning knob. Up the band and then down again. Nothing. The band was dead as a doornail.

"Ah yeah, well, to answer your question, Barclay . . . yes and no. It does receive stations, but the customer's complaint was that they intermittently fade away. Seems as if he is correct. I will have to check out the front-end tubes tomorrow. They must heat up and go noisy or it has a poor solder joint on the point-to-point wiring. Just before you came in, I was listening to this station here at six-eighty on the A.M. dial. The signals were booming in here rather strongly, and the reception was crystal clear. I guess it faded away when we were talkin'."

Barclay nodded at the testimony, reached for his beer, and took another sip.

With the beer bottle still in his hand, Barclay used the top of the bottle as a pointer and while pointing at the radio, Barclay commented, "Well, you are the best that there is. Ya will fix it back up. It is gorgeous. Did it come in for repair today? Lemme guess. Some very old guy brought it in. He had it in storage for years."

"He was not old. No, in fact, not at all. On the other hand, then again, I am not sure. The customer was very strange."

Detective Barclay kicked into police mode and his brow furrowed as he took another sip of his beer and asked, "Strange? How?"

Now resigned to the fact that the radio band was void of any stations and that he would need to work on the radio tomorrow, Doogie flipped the radio to the "off" position. Sensing his friend's concern over his pronouncement of Mr. Black as strange, Doogie waved his hand in the air in an effort to calm the testimony and his friend's concern.

He walked over to his beer, sat down on the stool, picked it up, took another sip and then explained, "Ah no, trouble. He was a very polite man. Extremely so. Good thing too, cuz, lemme tell ya, he was the biggest man that I have ever seen. You are a big guy, Barclay, and your old man too, but this guy, he makes ya both look small. Must be six feet eight at least. Maybe more. Looks strong as a bull too. Not fat, but lean, and he was very muscular.

Bigger than even those huge football players are. He was unusual. Maybe, strange was the wrong word for me to use to describe him. It was just his appearance. Immaculate. Nothing out of place or a bare thread in any of his expensive clothes. He dressed all in black. Black pants, black shirt, an expensive black vest and a wide brim black hat. He had these amazing black boots. They looked as if they were expensive as hell, with metal clips on them that made this clicking noise on the floor when he walked. Top-notch clothes . . . the best. Must have cost a fortune."

Barclay nodded but did not say a word, while Doogie continued to explain, "Handsome as a movie star too."

"No kiddin'? Movie star, huh? Ya think he is one?"

"Nah, too quiet. The guy hardly said a word. Just e'nuff to tell me what was wrong with the radio and give me basic information. He was as if he popped up out of the same era that the radio did. Or someplace else. I dunno, maybe I am wrong, cuz, he was not old-fashioned as much as a fish out of water type of thing. He did not have a New Jersey accent. Perfect speech. And get this . . . he gave me a deposit of three hundred bucks . . . cash-a-roo-ski to repair the rig."

Doogie leaned back on his stool, reached into the front pocket of his pants, and pulled out the three crisp bills to show Barclay his good fortune.

Barclay whistled a low and admiring whistle at the sight of the cash; he then nodded and smiled while mumbling, "Nice. Guess he can afford it. From what ya tell me. A high roller type of dude. Why did he give you so much dough upfront?"

"Said that he was going out of town for a few weeks, or so. I guess he left the dough as a deposit so that I did not think he was gonna stiff me for the cost of the repairs. But with a radio like that, my goodness it is worth a good buck."

Barclay looked over at the radio and it seemed as if his

police sense tingled for a few seconds over the testimony of the unusual man, but he recovered and mumbled, "Yeah, right. Enough collateral for sure." His voice grew louder and as if to make a mental note and in a return to his police mode, Barclay asked, "Say, what was this guy's name?"

Doogie huffed out a chuckle and then he followed with a grin and, while tilting the beer bottle back for a last drop, said, "Get this. Mr. Black."

"Ha! Appropriate! Well, I guess that explains some of his dress. It must be some kind of image bullshit," Barclay said, while smiling and downing the last of his beer.

"A'nudder?"

"Sure. One more, then I gotta run. The wife is gonna be lookin' for me soon. Not to mention Joseph lookin' for the video game."

Doogie grabbed the empty bottles, tossed them in the trash, and walked into the back to retrieve two more beers. He was back in a flash and once more, the two friends sat and enjoyed the cold beers together.

"So, how is the new job goin'?"

"Well, Doogie, it is still early in the hockey game, but it is good. I guess. Different. Ya know, lots of desk work and paperwork, and workin' the internet for clues and preludes to investigations. I guess that I gotta warm up to it all. I am a street guy. Even though accordin' to some, I am still a rook. They forget that I grew up here and in a family of policemen. It is in my blood. I am young in age and long in experience. Even though, I was only out there a relatively short amount of time, I am used to pounding the pavement and rolling the streets. The kinda cop that reads body language. I stare into eyes, feel the pulse of what is happenin' and gauge the inflections in a voice. That is difficult to do from sittin' behind a desk and staring at a screen."

Doogie nodded and said, "I understand. You go with your gut feelings and that is hard to do right now, because you are not out in the thick of the battle. I get it. However, as you said, it is early in the hockey game. Very early. First period. Right after the opening face-off. You need to find your way. You are a very smart man and a very honest man. It will come to you. It is just time. Patience, my young friend. Remember that hard work always prevails."

Barclay nodded, took a long sip of beer and pondered the very wise words of his friend. No doubt that Doogie was the man.

He had been around the block a few times.

And a few times more.

Barclay continued for a few minutes while explaining various details of his early days in his new career as a detective. He told Doogie about how right now he was working behind a desk, surfing around the internet, while stalking the social media sites of known criminals and petty street thugs while looking for connections and insight that could nail not only the petty activities, but the big dogs too. He told Arthur how large criminal organizations feed these street punks and that is where Barclay's chain of command wanted him to focus and for him to gather more information. Between sips of his beer, Arthur nodded as he listened.

Finally, after Barclay had outlined some of his early discomfort with some aspects of his new position, the old radio repairman commented, "Well, use your street smarts that you inherited and your police genes that your heritage passed off to you. When you are working the angles on the internet, maybe, look past the street thug's persona and feel your soul for something deeper. Do just as you did when walking the beat or ridin' in a patrol car and listenin' to stories and lessons from your grandfather and your father. Recall when you would eye a suspicious character walking your neighborhood. It is different, because you are in a computer la-la-land, but still use your street sense. It will not fail ya."

Detective Barclay Millhouse sat for a brief second while pensively capturing the advice of his old friend, and he smiled when it occurred to him that it was very good advice.

Timely advice too.

Before he was able to comment, Doogie added, "Hey, as we said, it is early in the hockey game, my friend. Very early. Speaking of which, I heard the Rovers shutout the Bears last night. Watson Shambley shut them down two goals to nuthin'. I heard that Shambley played one helluva game. Apparently, he stood on his head makin' saves. Shambley is finally playing better now. 'Bout damn time, if they are gonna make a last run at the playoffs. Season is almost over now."

Barclay looked puzzled and as he drained the last sip from his beer bottle, slowly stood up and tossed the dead soldier of a brew into the trash can.

Barclay said, "You heard? Guess ya did not watch the game. Really, a shut out? I missed that game, and hell, ya know, other than playing video games, Joseph, loves his hockey and his Rovers more than anythin'. He usually yells at me after dinner to watch the hockey game with him. We enjoy the games together. It is nice. Without his beloved video bullshit, I am surprised he did not watch or at least tell me 'bout it. I thought that the home-at-home series began tonight. Ya know, one game here and then up to Boston on Tuesday night."

Doogie tilted his bottle back, drained the last drop of brew from his drink, and then tossed the empty bottle into the trash can.

Doogie's knees cracked as he slowly stood up and said, "Yeah, me too. Yeah, I missed it too and I wanna kick my own ass for missing that game. I can't stand them stupid-ass Boston Bears, but I have to admit that Vance Howard is the best goalie in the league. Maybe the best goalie that I have ever seen."

"Yeah, he is. Hope someday Shambley can be half as good in the net. Say . . . been great chattin' and sharin' the brews. Lemme hustle my ass out of here. Surprised the wife is not blowin' up my phone by now. How much do I owe you for the repair?"

Doogie nodded and scampered off to grab the game console off his "Repaired" shelf and as he walked away Doogie yelled, "Twenty bucks."

"That's all? Geez, Doogie ya gotta make some dough too."

Doogie returned with the game console and he tore off the top copy of the repair ticket and handed it to his friend while saying in a more authoritative voice, "Twenty bucks." Doogie downplayed the time of the repair by adding, "It actually took me longer to find the special tool to take that sucker apart with, then it did for me to fix it. Plus, I goofed off for a few hours while testing it out and playing the game. That might be why I lost track of time this afternoon. I am quite good at playing those games, especially for an old guy."

Arthur fumbled with his eyeglasses on the chain and he adjusted them as they swung upon his chest. He paused to collect his thoughts. Thoughts as to why it was that he still was doing what it was that he did after all of these years.

"Barclay, I don't do this for dough. I do it, cuz, well, I love it and damn, since my wife left this world, things can be lonely as hell. I need to have a purpose in life, and this gives me a purpose and makes me feel useful. But not too much longer, my friend. Anyway, please, tell your son to make sure the paper labels on the game disc don't have tears in 'em before he loads the disc in the game. The game disc is in that envelope taped to the top of the console. Tell, Joseph, that ya wipe out the aliens in the time warp by hitting all the arrows up, then all the arrows down, all arrows left and all arrows right and finally ya gotta hit the, a button and the b button. Do ya have that? Use the x-ray gun, not the proton beam. The proton beam is for pansies, the x-ray gun is for tough guys. Ya blast their alien asses with the x-ray gun and blow the livin' hell outta of 'em. It is fun. Just clean that language up a little for your son."

Barclay smiled at his amazing friend and handed twenty dollars to Doogie. He extended his hand, and while the two men shook hands, Barclay gave a little police advice.

"I think I have it. Doogie, ya the best. Thanks for everything and I will tell him. By the way, one of these punks that I am trackin,' he operates in and around here. Don't leave any dough in the store or in the shop. Especially that cash ya got today. Ya had better not leave that radio on the bench here. Set the alarm and slide that wooden bar across the back door."

"Oh no doubt. I will do it all. The radio is going in the back and inside the safe. The dough goes with me. In a few minutes, we will lock up and alarm the joint, too. Old Doogie is right behind ya. Thank you."

Barclay nodded and turned to walk away when Doogie called out to the good detective.

"Hey, my keys! I have to let ya out and lock up for the night." Barclay stopped, smiled, and waited for Doogie to catch up to him while he fished around in his pocket for the keys and handed them off.

"Yeah, that would help, right?"

"Say, Barclay, this street kid ya huntin' for . . . does he have a name and what does he look like? I always keep my head on a swivel and my ears to the rail. I am old, but still sharp as a tack and I don't miss a trick. Old Doogie grew up on these city streets too."

"Oh yeah, I know that. Sure, please keep ya head up. His name is Mikhail Hosopkov or sumthin' like that. I can't pronounce long foreign names. He is from some country over near Russia or near there. In the mountains. Sorry, my geography sucks. In my opinion, he is in this country for bullshit reasons and for no good. Tall, lean, olive skin tone, black hair, and a long black beard. Around twenty-five years old or so. He always wears a black baseball cap with a cartoon of a ghost on it. He Americanized his name to Michael, but all these street punks use handles. His handle is Ghost because he does his evil deals and quickly disappears. He is difficult to see and track down."

Doogie nodded and patted his friend on the shoulder as he fiddled with the stubborn lock on the front door and he gave in a hard twist to the left with a tiny jiggle of the door handle, right at the end of the twist. Doogie unlocked the door and held it open for Barclay to pass through.

"Gotcha. Sounds like a real joy of a guy. I will listen and watch. Hey, don't be a stranger. Stop at any time. Say hey, to your family and your grandfather and the old man for me. I miss 'em.

"I will, Doogie. Thanks again and you are the man."

Arthur "Doogie" Doogan laughed and yelled out to Detective Millhouse as he made his way onto the busy sidewalk, "That is what the stranger said. That I am the man!"

"Well, Mr. Black knows what the hell he is talkin' 'bout. See ya, Doogs. Take care. Go, Rovers!"

"Yeah, go, Rovers. See ya. Be safe out there, Barclay."

Doogie watched for a few minutes until Barclay disappeared around the corner. He then locked the door and went to gather up his things. He locked the precious radio in the safe, double-checked the coffee maker, made sure his soldering iron was off and made the same checks that he had made for the last forty-three years or so. As he left the store and shop for the day, he fiddled once more with the front door lock, swore that he would repair it one of these days and with a tap of his pocket, he double-checked for the cash from Mr. Black. It was there. All was well, but he would still keep his head on a swivel when he hit the streets. Doogie flipped the light switch off, and the lights flickered and went dark. Doogie closed and locked the door. It closed and locked better than it opened and unlocked.

Yes, indeed, he would repair that lock one of these days.

One of these days.

Tuesday morning broke bright and clear, unlike the overcast gloom of the previous day. The temperature was warmer too, and there was just a hint of spring in the air. It was a glorious day in late March, and a day that found Mr. Arthur "Doogie" Doogan with an extra spring in his step while walking into his shop for a day of work. The extra spring in his step had something to do with the prospect of working on such a fine, old radio from an era, forever molded deep in the heart and mind of the old repairman. A time when everything seemed so much simpler. A time that he missed deeply. Tuesday morning also found Arthur Doogan buried deep into a maze of electronic circuitry. Circuitry that was from an era in time that, to Arthur, seemed so long ago, yet so close to his heart. It seemed as if it was just yesterday when Doogie serviced this exact model radio when they were still under warranty. He recalled that the manufacturer paid him seven dollars to repair them during the warranty period. Seven whole dollars! Those were the types of memories that ran wild within Arthur's mind while he reminisced a bit while servicing the grand radio. From the first moment that Arthur's trusty red-handled nut driver unscrewed the quarter-inch hex head screws (a standard size to Arthur, unlike the crazy screw heads on the "modern" video game) on the back cover of the old radio, he was in awe. Not a bit of dust was inside of the radio, not a speck of dirt. It was indeed, as if the radio was brand new.

Right out of the box.

As his first action of troubleshooting the radio, Arthur replaced the front-end tube in the I.F. section of the radio, even after his trusty old tube tester pronounced the tube . . . good to go. The tester found no gas, no shorts, and no weakness in functions or outputs within the tube. Nothing. The tube looked as if it was brand-new, too. Even the imprint of the original manufacturer on the glass of the tube was as if it was brand new. The tube identification stamps on the glass of the tube still glowed in clarity and in brilliance. Arthur knew his vacuum tubes. He stared into a few thousand of them in his day and he could tell a well-worn tube from a new tube. Despite the supposed age of this radio, the glass of the "old" tube sure looked good to him. The plate of the tube was clean and not pitted. The filament burned brightly; the glass had no dark marks on the side. Yet, on instinct and because he had little else to go on, Doogie replaced the tube.

Luckily, today, Doogie could fully concentrate on the repair of the classic radio. Unlike yesterday, the shop and store had been quiet today. So far, the only customer that he had in the store today walked in around ten in the morning, in order to order a new remote control for his television. His dog chewed the old remote into oblivion. As of late, a few adventurous dogs drummed up some business for Arthur Doogan.

"Maybe, the tube warms up and develops a problem," Doogie muttered his supposition aloud to no one but the walls of his shop and the air within it.

Unconvinced of the tube's faults, the old repairman spent the better part of a few hours digging around in old file boxes in the back area of his shop, while searching for the original radio repair manual and schematic diagram for the radio. When he finally found it, Doogie dug in on test points, voltage checks and alignment readings, even pulling out his old oscilloscope that faithfully sat as a silent sentry did on a cart, awaiting its turn in battle. All the checks were perfect and all the technical specifications of the manufacturer exactly met. As he went through the radio and thoroughly checked it, he marveled at the quality of the point-to-point wiring and the craftsmanship thereof.

There were no loose connections or cold solder joints here. Even under his eye magnifiers, the radio seemed as if it was brand new.

It was a mystery.

Upon an intense examination under the eyes and experience of a master of electronics, this radio was a perfect radio. Other than an intermittent vacuum tube or other intermittent electronic component malfunction, Doogie could not find a reason for this radio to malfunction. Now firmly convinced that the tube was the cause of the intermittent troubles, Arthur rather confidently replaced the rear cover of the radio, plugged the radio in and turned the on and off control to the "on" position and waited for the radio to warm up. Upon warming up, the station located at six-eighty on the A.M. dial once more boomed in with a signal that seemed as if the station was right next door to Doogie's Television and Radio Repair shop.

To Arthur's joy, it was the same radio announcer's voice from the previous day. It was the same quality of broadcast, the same amazing reproduction of the voice.

"In local sports news, the New York Rovers hockey club fell at Bears Arena in Boston, Massachusetts in a dismal defeat at the hand of the Boston Bears. The Rovers lost the game, by a score of six goals to one, in action on the back end of a home-to-home series between the Rovers and the Bears. Watson Shambley, the starting goalie for the Rovers, who just played a remarkable game with his previous shutout of the Bears, was pulled in the third period of the game, in favor of back-up goalie, Andre Lacroix. . .."

Arthur leaned forward on his stool while immersed in absolute astonishment at the words emitting from the speaker of the radio.

The loud and clear words resounded out of a perfectly operating vintage radio.

"No way!" Arthur cried aloud. "The Rovers have not

played that game yet! I am not totally crazy. It is only Tuesday morning!"

Arthur looked at the daily newspaper resting upon the repair bench. A newspaper in which he bought early this morning, and as his mind raced with wild thoughts, Arthur reached for it in order to check the sports section.

As he did so, the radio announcer moved on from the sports news and the speaker on the radio happily spouted out, "Last night's winning numbers in the New Jersey lottery, are . . . first, in the pick-three, the winning numbers are three-three-three and in the pick six, the winning numbers are six-two-one-three-eight-nine. . .."

Rather than reach for the newspaper, Arthur "Doogie" Doogan grabbed the pen from his shirt pocket, grabbed a notepad, and instinctively, he jotted down the numbers. Just when the radio announcer broadcasted the last lottery number, the radio station slowly faded away and a rush of static out of the speaker replaced the golden voice of the radio announcer.

"What the hell is goin' on here? Come on now, old radio, ya just tested out perfectly. What are you doin' to me here?" Arthur asked in shock. He quickly moved over to the radio, he moved the tuning knob a few turns, and a radio station at eight-eighty kilohertz came booming in. That station, Doogie knew very well. It had been on the air forever and it broadcasted from across the river over in the big city. A few turns back down the dial to six-eighty kilohertz, and there was nothing but static. Doogie now leaned in and rather quickly he spun the tuning knob and he watched the dial pointer glide up and down the band. Unlike the previous day, when all the stations faded away, today, the only station gone from the airwaves was the station at six-eighty kilohertz on the dial.

The rest of the A.M. band filled with all the familiar stations. All booming in loud and clear through the glorious speaker in the solid oak cabinet.

Now, with his heart beating rapidly and a few scratches to the top of his head, Doogie slowly approached the newspaper on the repair bench. He slid his eyeglasses over his eyes and peered in on the paper. A quick glance at the date printed on the front page and he confirmed that it was Tuesday, the 27th of March. Arthur's hands shook a little as he flipped rather frantically through the newspaper while searching for the sports page. A few of the pages of the newspaper stuck together and Arthur licked his fingers to grab the thin paper, pull at them and gently separate them. One of the edges of the paper ripped as Arthur grew impatient. Finally, his eyes rested on the sports page and they confirmed what his heart already knew. A heart that felt as if it was going to pound its way out of his chest.

There in bold letters was the headline.

'SHAMBLEY IS THE MAN! A HERO FOR THE ROVERS!' Underneath the headline in a smaller font was a further explanation, 'Goaltender, Watson Shambley notches a shutout and plays the game of his young career as the Rovers shut down the Boston Bears in the first game of a home-at-home series, two goals to zero.'

Doogie did not read the rest of the article. Instead, he steadied his hands and slowly closed the newspaper up, folded it and tucked the newspaper into a corner of the bench next to the cash register.

Near the coffee pot.

Right now, Arthur "Doogie" Doogan felt more like stealing a beer from his refrigerator than he felt like sucking down a cup of coffee. He sat on the stool of his repair bench and after taking off his eyeglasses and resting them on the chain on his chest; Doogie folded his arms across his chest and pondered the surreal situation.

He spoke aloud with his thoughts, "Am I goin' loony bin crazy here or what? However, I know what I heard, and Barclay said the same thing that I did. The Rovers played Monday night, not Sunday. Yet, I knew the score. I knew it was a shutout! Because that radio station announcer told me about it. Ahead of time."

His eyes drifted over to the fantastic radio, and he suddenly had another thought. Doogie rushed in the back area of the shop. He dug around in a storage closet and pulled out a spare radio. A customer left this particular radio after a repair and for some reason or another, never picked the radio up or paid for the repair, despite Doogie's best efforts to contact the customer and collect his money for the repair. Right now, it was the perfect radio for Doogie to use for an experiment, because the radio had a modern digital display and microprocessor-based tuner. There would be no question as to the tuned frequency of this radio. The digital display would be exact, and Doogie intended to tune the display right onto six-eighty kilohertz in the A.M. band. His hands were still shaking as he plugged the radio in and flipped it on. With a few frantic touches on the tuning buttons, the digital display was set to six-eighty kilohertz on the A.M. band. There was nothing there on the frequency but static, the same noise that emitted from the classic radio sitting proudly, but strangely ominous on the repair bench. Arthur left both radios on and turned to his old faithful radio that he usually kept playing in the shop to keep him company, and pulled it out, plugged it in, and tuned the dial to the same frequency.

Static and noise.

All three radios received nothing but static and noise on six-eighty kilohertz.

Pulling the newspaper back out from its hiding spot next to the cash register, he flipped through the pages until he found the entertainment section of the newspaper. A section where there were listings of television and radio stations, programs and a guide to daily programming. There was not a local radio station listed at six-eighty kilohertz on the A.M. band. Doogie was not completely stuck in the past. He could turn on his computer or use his cellphone to perform an internet search, but he felt as if he already knew the answer. His soul calmed a bit more, his heart rate steadied, and when he looked at his watch, he felt the same Deja Vu experience as he did yesterday. The watch hands pointed to five minutes to two o'clock in the afternoon, and Doogie had no idea where the morning went to or how entire day had disappeared today.

He had not even eaten his lunch yet and while his mind wandered; he grabbed the notepad that he had used to jot the announced lottery numbers upon; he tore off the top paper from the rest of the pad, neatly folded the paper, and tucked it in his front shirt pocket.

Slowly, he pulled himself off the stool and stood up. Doogie turned the volume down on each of the radios, maintaining the rush out of the speakers, at just a high enough of a volume for his ears to hear, but not loud enough to be annoying. Deciding to eat his lunch, albeit many hours later, the old radio repairman slowly shuffled to the rear area of the shop to obtain his lunch out of the refrigerator.

His mind still raced with various thoughts, and he remained puzzled as to what was actually going on right now. Perhaps, he *was* losing his mind or all concepts of reality. Losing touch with daily life. Forgetting the time. Are they not the first signs of dementia? Losing touch with the daily flow. Were these short-term memory issues? It sure as hell was not his long-term memory that was faltering. He could still recall his draft number and recite all the tube numbers of a CTC38A television chassis. From the 6GH8As to the 6LQ6 and onward.

Suddenly, he felt as if he was a hundred years old.

As he leaned over to open the door to the refrigerator, the words of the mysterious stranger in black echoed in his head, "The word is that you are the man . . . as they tend to say these days. I am counting on you. In many ways."

Arthur "Doogie" Doogan pulled the brown paper bag out of the refrigerator and he opened it and peered inside. Ham and cheese on rye bread with a light coating of his favorite brown mustard. A bag of low sodium potato chips. He remained conscious of his sodium intake and it seemed as if these days everything had too much sodium. A small cup of fruit and a small cup of strawberry-flavored applesauce. A bottle of ice-cold spring water.

A perfect lunch.

Absolutely perfect.

While walking to the front of the shop to sit and enjoy his lunch at the repair bench, Doogie mumbled aloud, "And you know what else is very weird. The radio announcer never says the station's call letters. I would think that the FCC would get on with them about that. And, when the radio broadcasts, it seems as if I lose time too. Everything is so strange. I think that I am losin' my marbles."

Doogie sat on his stool and slowly undid the foil from around his sandwich. While taking the first bite, his eyes first rolled to the newspaper and then to the classic radio, which now sat mysteriously on the repair bench. The dial lights still glowed with that same glorious warmth and captivating yellow color. The mysterious and ominous static rushing out of the speaker while the radio monitored the now silent frequency of six-eighty kilohertz suddenly gave Doogie a thought. Why has Detective Barclay Millhouse not called yet? He is a huge Rovers fan and so is his son. Did his son dive right into the newly repaired and restored video game and not pay attention to the Rovers hockey game? Perhaps, Barclay was too busy last evening or tonight to realize that the hockey game was already in the books and because of their discussion yesterday over a few beers, they both knew not only the outcome of the game, but the score and exact details too. With another bite of the sandwich and a hard swallow, in order to bypass the huge lump in his throat, Doogie suddenly had a thought that there was a plausible explanation for all of this.

There had to be one.

After another bite and swallow, Arthur realized that no, there was not even one plausible explanation.

Then, after what were seemingly a million different thoughts, and rerunning every detail of the last few days through his mind, rethinking the words of the quiet stranger, and his conversation with Barclay, a wide smile broke out upon old Doogie's face. Suddenly, he thought of an explanation.

Now, it was just a matter of believing it.

Detective Barclay Millhouse sat in a chair in the next to the last row of many rows set up in an auditorium-style, in the largest meeting room within the Paterson, New Jersey Police Headquarters in downtown Paterson. He sat there with many other police officers, detectives, the top brass for the Paterson, New Jersey Police Department, city officials, New Jersey state troopers, representatives from the New Jersey Attorney General's office, federal agents, Secret Service agents, and various United States National Park police officers and park rangers. Even the Mayor of Paterson and some council members sat in the room. Despite the meeting place being the largest meeting room in the headquarters building, there was only standing room left, and some attendees stood around the perimeter of the room. The police chief and the police commissioner, along with some other top officers of the department, all stood at the front of the room, with the police chief at the podium, banging into the microphone to test the audio system.

They were about to be briefed about security, threats, protection and law enforcement for one of the biggest events of the year coming up on Thursday of this week. It was big news here in the city and an exciting event that meant a great deal of interest for and business for the old city. National interest, New Jersey interest, and Paterson interest. Two years before last, the United States Congress declared the Great Falls Historic District in the northern outskirts of downtown to be an official United States national park and part of The United States National Park System. The President of the United States signed the approval and for the first time in a very long time, Paterson, New Jersey, was famous for something other than crime and being an old and typical part of urban America. It was exciting to have such a historic and wonderful place within the city and especially so since; it was so unusual a location. Tucked into the corner of the city, within what was now a rundown area of the old city, the falls had been a source of hydroelectric power for the development of the Mill District of the city where the water powered the abundance of silk, lace, and garment mills that became one of the birthplaces of industrial America. The waterfalls were a spectacular sight and rather breathtaking, being the second highest and largest waterfalls on the east coast. It was just the odd location of them that, in Barclay's opinion, made it all a bit unusual. Since the designation, the federal government had been renovating the Great Falls of Paterson Historic District and turning it into a United States national park, and after over one year of construction, this Thursday was the grand opening to the park.

The grand unveiling.

The word was that there would be many dignitaries in attendance and the ceremony meant an awful lot to the city in not only attention and publicity, but in dollars too. At one point, the President of the United States was rumored to be attending, but now the word was that the Vice President of the United States would attend, along with the Secretary of the Interior, both federal New Jersey senators, all the state senators and the representatives for the House of Representatives' districts for New Jersey. Not to mention a list of celebrities, executives, general big shots and local want-to-be big shots, and other assorted local officials, the Mayor of Paterson and the council members. On and on, the guest list went. It was going to be the event of the year and a grand and honorable ceremony.

Barclay was certainly interested in the event and various details of such, but he knew that the district and park were now, technically, federal land. Therefore, the majority of law enforcement and surveillance details as well as the total jurisdiction of the law would fall under the federal law enforcement agents and other federal agencies. Barclay studied the handout papers, which contained a map, which gave various details of the outlying area, as well as a map of the park and key points from a law enforcement point of view. The good detective studied the handout while the chief spoke out with the opening points of the briefing.

Barclay only half-listened to the opening remarks. He was actually very anxious to return to his previously humdrum and routine internet surveillance of the thug known as Ghost. As of this morning, Ghost's actions and postings on the social media sites turned to a strangely dark side, and it had Barclay's street sense on full alert and tingling. His postings had a new cryptic side to them, with a new code for actions and names that Barclay was not privy to as yet. The replies to his postings came from a new group of persons, and these postings were also cryptic in nature. Slightly radical and anti-American in nature as well as disturbing in content and the hints of violence. Some of Ghost's postings were about, "Having all he needed to do the mission" and "Proving his worth" and "Being ready to step up to the next level for the cause, now." Barclay felt as if Ghost ventured into a new league of evil. That he was no longer a "run of the mill" street thug, but perhaps a tool for something deeper and darker in nature. He needed more time to study it and then he would bring his chain of command in on the actions and his thoughts thereof.

Detective Millhouse sat next to the one detective in the detective's bureau who was close to Barclay in time of service as a detective and the one man in the bureau that struck up a budding friendship with Barclay above a working relationship. Barclay welcomed his assistance and thoughtfulness, especially as it now seemed as if his old friends in the patrol divisions had turned their backs on him. Detective Nate Ingram was about five or so years older than Barclay was, and he received his promotion about eight months or thereabouts before Barclay received his promotion. Nate was still fresh but no longer a rookie, having recently been a key investigator on breaking a high-profile case. He had also been very kind and understanding to Barclay, sort of taking Barclay under his wings and showing him the ropes so to speak, and even though he was still new to the bureau, Nate had sensed Barclay's initial uneasiness at the new position and with making the transition from a street cop to a detective. Nate had more experience on the streets than Barclay did, but he came up through the ranks in the same manner as Detective Millhouse did. Out of the corner of his eyes, Nate looked over at his fellow detective, and he could tell that Barclay was somewhere else and not paying much attention to the police chief droning in front of them. Nate thought how, as a rookie detective, Barclay needed to show more attentiveness. His inattentiveness would not be going over so well in such a high-profile setting, especially if one of the top brass spotted the young detective nodding off or daydreaming. Of course, Nate was not privy to what was floating through Barclay's mind, and how Ghost seemed to be making a move that Barclay wanted to pay close attention to right now.

Nate gently tapped his companion's shoulder and whispered, "Hey, look alive, Barclay."

Barclay snapped out of his daydream and looked over at Nate, and Nate smiled at him. Barclay realized that he was not paying attention, and he nodded, shook off the daydream and sat up straight and true in his chair. Eyes forward and ears up. Feet squared up on the floor.

The police chief concluded his statements and, as expected, the chief yielded the microphone with a closing statement and introduction.

"While we here in the city's police department will have a key role in providing security for this event, of course, the primary law enforcement corps on duty here will be the various federal agencies in charge of protection for the vice president and the other dignitaries attending as well as having jurisdiction over federal land. Therefore, here is Agent John Douglas of the Secret Service for a further expansion and education of our roles, the day's events and the expectations for all concerned. Agent Douglas is in command of the entire event and all agencies report to him through his chain of command."

The agent took over at the microphone, and after a few opening comments by Agent Douglas, a PowerPoint presentation began on the drop-down screen as well as a bullet point outline. Barclay and Nate both settled in for the long haul. Barclay found his attention span still limited, but after listening to the agent speak and begin to roll out the plan, he did finally focus and pay very close attention. Barclay found himself studying Agent Douglas and admiring his professionalism and confidence. Obviously, this was not his first command of a major event. He was a very articulate speaker. He was obviously a seasoned professional and there remained no doubt that he fit the stereotypical image of a cool, calm, and collected law enforcement professional. As suspected, there was little for the detectives to do for the event, other than keep eyes and ears out and be on extra alert. Road patrol officers would have motorcade escort and traffic control duties and the beat patrol officers would have perimeter duties, but much of the inner circle of protection would fall under the various federal agencies. Agent Douglas gave them all a listing of contact information, telephone numbers, emails, and other information for key contacts during the event. Barclay and Nate jotted the info down and programmed numbers into their smartphones. After forty-five minutes or so of a presentation that aside from some daydreaming about if he would someday pursue a career in federal law enforcement, held Barclay's attention, Agent Douglas wrapped it all up with a question-and-answer session. There were a few questions, but now it was pushing four-thirty in the afternoon and everyone began to glance at their watches.

Finally, an ending followed by a dismissal. There was a mass exodus out of seats and chairs, and some conversations began as the groups began to gather for general discussions.

"Hey, Barclay, I don't know 'bout you, but that coffee on the table over there sure smells good to me," Nate said while pointing in the direction of a table set up along the rear wall of the meeting room. A table that held multiple coffee makers, some rows of bottled water, and stacks of cardboard coffee cups.

"Yeah, maybe some decaffeinated coffee, Nate. The high-test will keep me awake like an owl all night."

The two men made their way through the various groups. They were nodding at some officers, greeting others with some handshakes and back pats and saying hello to other persons and then when they finally made their way to the coffee set up and while they prepared coffee, Nate asked, "So, what made you so antsy during the presentation? You were a million miles away there, Barclay. Piece of advice, my friend. When all of this top brass is in one room and you are still a rook under the microscope, ya got to play the role. I know we haven't much to do with this show, but still you got to look alive. I mean, it is the Vice President of the United States coming to our wonderful city. Doesn't get much bigger than this unless the president decided to show. Are you hung up on that punk ya been following on the internet, or is something else eatin' ya?"

Barclay took a sip of the coffee and nodded while saying, "Thank you for the advice and the wake-up call there, Nate. I do appreciate it and yeah, I gotcha, but I kind of knew we were shut out on duties here and while I know how important it all is, I am anxious to get back to watch my guy. Something changed in his actions and rhetoric in the last day or so."

"Oh yeah, how so?"

"He dropped the code word communication bullshit and his postings are more abrupt. More as if his routine is mission oriented. As though, he now has to prove his worth and has a specific task as opposed to just peddling drugs or fencing stolen goods. He is very forceful and almost radical in the postings and they are very frequent. The replies from the usual cast of characters and a few new ones are more like—we are with you type of words. Let's go get them type of stuff. It all sounds like he seems angry at the world type of bullshit talk."

Nate nodded and took a long sip of the coffee out of his cup. He seemed to be pondering the testimony before answering or offering any advice.

Finally, between sips, Nate said, "Interesting stuff, Barclay. A step above the normal street thug stuff. Did ya go see the big boys with an update?"

"Sure did, and Lieutenant Potter did not seem very impressed. He listened and then told me to keep at it and give him an update after the ceremony is over and done. Honestly, he seemed as if he wanted to get rid of me as quickly as possible and jet over here as soon as he could and dive into this."

"I understand that. This is a big deal for these big boys. They are all maneuvering for exposure here and rubbing elbows. Some street punk is not high on their priority list. You keep at it and stay on it. Use your experience and smarts. It does sound as if something has changed and ya had better not discount anything. Especially, with all these big deals and the vice president coming into the city. You heard what Agent Douglas said. Full alert."

Barclay nodded. He took a last sip of his coffee, searched for a trashcan and tossed the cup away, while commenting, "I am on it. You are correct. I guess . . . I understand where Potter's priorities are, but I wish he had listened to me a little more, and given me some honest attention, cuz, this has my street senses on full tingles."

"Then follow your street sense, Barclay. It nailed you a promotion to a detective's position very early in your career, so you must have some good sense. Be sure to use it."

Barclay glanced at his wristwatch and, after realizing the time, said, "Thanks. I will. Say, I have to get home. I will pick the surveillance up in the morning but it is almost five and I will hear it from the wife. I was late coming home last night and can't be late tonight."

"What did ya do? Stop off at Smitty's and toss a few? Come on, I will walk out with ya."

Barclay nodded and turned in the direction of the exit and explained, "No, my old drinking buddies from Smitty's are not quite as accepting of me these days since I made the detective rank. No, our son, Joseph, is a great kid, but he lives for video games and New York Rover ice hockey and his video game console needed repairs. He drove the wife and me, bat-shit-crazy while it was in the repair shop. I stopped off at Doogie's shop on my old beat and picked up the game. Old Doogs fixed it up good as new. I started shooting the shit with Doogie. He closed up the shop. We had a few beers together and before you knew it, I was late."

The two detectives made their way down the main hallway of headquarters and toward the front door.

When they pushed open the front doors of the building and hit the fresh air, Nate said, "Old Arthur Doogie Doogan. Helluva nice guy. Been around forever. Class act. How is he doin'?"

"He *is* a helluva guy. He is doin' okay. Ya know, he lost his wife some ways ago and he seemed kinda lonely, so I hung around with him. He is smart as a whip that guy. I used to stop and bullshit with him when I walked the beat and he knew my old man and my grandfather, too. I owed him the time. Besides, it was sorta police work. That punk, Ghost, works that particular neighborhood hard. Ironically, it is my old beat. That's part of the reason that, Potter put me on Ghost. I know all the haunts and spots he is posting about there on social media. Old Doogie, don't miss a trick. I gave him some inside info and asked Doogie to keep his head on a swivel for me. Other than being lonely, he is good, kinda counting the days until retirement and selling off everything and moving to Florida to be with his kids."

Nate nodded and began to dig around in his suit jacket for his car keys. "Nice of you to spend time with the old guy, Barclay. Bet it is rough losing his wife after all of that time. I wish Doogie the best. Good idea about planting some seeds. Hope they sprout and ya nail this punk and everyone above him too."

They made their way across the parking lot and about halfway across the lot, Nate tapped his friend on the shoulder and rather excitedly said, "Say, ya mentioned hockey and I know you and your son, there are huge Rover fans. How about that game last night? Damn straight. Great game! Shambley stood on his head in the net for us. Taking out Howard and the Bears. I was jumping all over the room while watching it. Howard is great in the net for the Bears, and one of our goals was a lucky bounce off a Bears player, but man, Shambley was awesome. Some saves were unreal. Maybe the season is not down the pipe yet, huh? We are only two points out of the playoffs now."

Barclay stopped walking to the parking area, and he tried very hard not to be puzzled, or at least not to allow Nate to see the surprise flow across his face upon hearing of his testimony of the game. He ran the discussion of the timing of the hockey game and the ensuing debate that he had with Doogie over the game day through his mind, and then he ran last evening's events quickly through his mind, too. He had been late arriving home and his wife let him have it a bit with the usual, "Constantly reheating up dinner" complaint. The kids already ate their dinner, Pearl had many homework assignments to complete, and she fled to her room to finish it. Joseph was so excited about Doogie repairing the video game that he grabbed it and bailed to his room. That would explain why he never alerted Barclay to the game coming on the television. But he thought the game was on Sunday! That is what Doogie heard on the radio and that is why he never gave the hockey game a second thought thereafter. He and the wife watched some television, chatted a bit and hit the hay early. After all, according to the old radio in Doogie's shop, the game was over and in the record books. He even knew the results and the score. Over and done. Already played.

On the other hand, was it?

What in hell was going on here?

Barclay used his police training and kept a poker face while asking, "Geez, what was the score, Nate?"

"Shit! Man, Barclay, don't tell me ya missed that game! Two to zip. A shutout for Shambley in the net!"

Upon hearing the score and his friend's words, Barclay almost staggered, and Nate laughed at the reaction. "Hey, I know ya a big Rovers fan but don't fall on ya ass about one win."

They had reached their detective cars and Barclay did his best to feign his way through it, by pretending he was play-acting at the surprising results of the game. The truth was, he now held onto the trunk of his unmarked car in order to prevent himself from falling over.

"Yeah, yeah, yeah, I missed it. Sucks. The game was last night. Are ya sure, Nate? Not on Sunday night?"

Nate waved and laughed as he stuck his key into the door lock on his unmarked car and said, "Sure, I am sure. If it was on Sunday night, then ya still missed it! Last night, the wife wanted to watch that stupid show where they sing and some stupid, phony, judges who can't sing either, pick the winners. I went and watched the game on the television in our bedroom. Some hockey fan you are. Ya need to stop a little and enjoy life, my friend. This Ghost case has ya all wrapped up and out of sorts. I know it is your first big gig, but ya gotta relax, or this work will kill ya. Hey, see ya tomorrow. Now, don't miss the game tonight. Up in Boston. Home-at-home. Go, Rovers!"

"Yeah, Nate. Don't worry because I will be sure to watch. And I will try to relax. Yup. That is my plan. I will have a few beers tonight, watch the game and relax. See ya. Go Rovers."

With those words, Nate climbed into his car, closed the door, started the engine, waved, and he was off.

Barclay unlocked the door to his car, slowly climbed in, and he closed the door behind him. He sat in the car, running a million ideas through his head. A million justifications and explanations. Despite the fact that he was a detective—he could not think of even one explanation for this strange event. The truth was that, for a few seconds, he was finding it difficult to breathe, let alone to think.

After a slight recovery, Barclay reached for his cellphone, unlocked the screen, and flipped through his contacts. A glance at his watch told Barclay that Doogie was still there. He closed the shop at six o'clock and it was fifteen minutes to the hour. Doogie was a man of discipline. Closing shop early was not on the daily menu. He grew impatient while scrolling through the numbers. Impatient because of the stress and impatient because he knew the number was in here. It had to be.

Finally, he found it and punched in the telephone number for Doogie's Television and Radio Repair Shop.

Arthur answered the telephone call on the second ring. The ringing of the phone shook him back to reality and awakened Doogie to the fact that it was now almost closing time.

"Doogie," the breathless voice of Detective Millhouse was instantly recognizable to Arthur, "I don't know where to begin."

"Hello, Barclay. I guess that you finally heard the score of the hockey game. I figured you were busy all day and would eventually call me when you heard the results and the score."

"I did and there has to be a plausible explanation for this."

"Oh, there is an explanation all right, but I am quite sure that it does not fall into the plausible category."

There was a pause on the telephone, and Arthur waited for Detective Millhouse to gather his thoughts.

"Did you find out what is wrong with the radio?" Detective Millhouse asked, thereby delaying listening to Doogie's offering of an explanation.

At least for now.

"There is nothing wrong with the radio. In fact, it works perfectly. Perhaps, too perfectly. I went through every check and inspection on it. Even dug up the old service manual and schematic for the rig. Spent hours today on checking it out. Every voltage is spot on, every test point, every, single, thing that I checked. I even replaced the front-end tube even though it tested and looked as if it was brand new. In fact, I am not sure that the radio is not brand new."

Another pause.

"Brand new, huh?"

"Yup. Brand, spanking, new. Smells new, operates new, and tests new. There isn't even a speck of dust inside the rig. I know my radios. Brand new."

Detective Barclay Millhouse sat in his car and thought. He had not even turned the engine on yet, and his heart raced as he thought about all of this long and hard.

Thinking, while keeping the cellphone stuck to his ear.

"Okay, Doogs, I am game. Let me hear your explanation. Please keep in mind that I am a detective and I deal with facts."

Arthur answered right away, "Good. I am countin' on that. The radio is just a mouthpiece. A predictor of sorts and this hockey game bullshit and what I heard today is just a method of telling us to pay attention and that. . .."

"Wait!" The detective interrupted his friend. "What the hell do you mean, what you heard today? You mean to tell me that the radio spouted more announcements and stuff from the future. Oh geez, c'mon, Doogie, this is friggin' unreal. It is too far-fetched. I am a detective and I cannot accept this crazy situation being far-fetched."

"And, I am an old man. A man who has been around for a long time. I have seen too much. Seen, my brothers-in-arms blown to bits in war, my beloved wife suffers and dies for no valid reason, and I have spent a lifetime chasing unseen electrons running around inside of man-made devices. I can't see the little bastards, but I sure as hell know they are there. They have knocked me on my ass a few times too when I went stickin' my hands in their world. If someone had told a person a hundred years ago, there would be unseen radio signals and television signals floating in the air and computers and cellphones and all this other crazy stuff we have now, then I am sure they had pretty much the same reaction as we have right now. Bullshit. It is all fantasyland bullshit. This world is full of unknown things. Things we cannot understand or figure out, but that does not mean that they do not exist. Far-fetched, yes, but unreal, no. I think it is all real. Very real. Too real. And yes, the radio broadcasted more information today."

Barclay answered in a barely audible, "Go on."

"Are you driving?"

"No. I am parked at the main headquarters while sitting inside of my unmarked car."

"Good, because I do not want you to run off the road when I relay this info. Yes, to repeat, the radio had a broadcast today. One short, broadcast, after I tested everything and then it went to static land. I am listening to static now on six-eighty kilohertz. There is no local station on six-eighty kilohertz. I checked. The broadcasts come in too early in the day and too loud and clear for long-range propagation to bounce in with distant stations. Another oddity is that the station never states the station's call letters. Announcing your call sign on a timed basis is a federal requirement of a radio station licensee. In addition, it seems as if whenever a broadcast comes in on the radio, the time of the day changes for me. It is all so weird. Very weird. I also have two other radios tuned on that same frequency. Static. All they pick up is static."

Arthur stopped speaking and he could hear his friend breathing on the other end of the phone. Breathing rather heavily.

Finally, Barclay spoke, "Wow. Okay, not easy, but I am following you. I think. What did the radio broadcast today?"

"Please, grab your notepad and write this all down. I want us to be exact and on the same page and ready for when the real mission arrives . . . that we are on our game."

Barclay grabbed his notepad and pen from his suit jacket pocket, clicked his pen and said, "Got it. Ready to copy."

Barclay could hear Arthur Doogan sigh deeply on the other end of the telephone and his words came rather haltingly, but they arrived, "Unfortunately for us Rover fans, the Rovers will get their asses handed to them tonight in Boston. Six to one. They pulled Shambley in the third period and put in the backup, Andre Lacroix. Please, this is what you need to write down. Here are the winning numbers for the New Jersey lottery. In the pick-three, the winning numbers are three-three-three and in the pick six, the winning numbers are six-two-one-three-eight-nine." Arthur listened for as a long pause, came from the detective on the other end of the line, and finally Barclay said, "Okay. I have it all. I guess that if this is all not a dream or some wacky fantasy that we could be very wealthy by playing those numbers, huh?"

"We will be. No doubt in my mind. However, I know we will not because we are too honest and above all of that nonsense. Plus, I would not want to get sideways with Mr. Black or whoever the hell he really is. Something inside tells old Doogie that would be a bad scene and he knows us better than that. He knows we are on the good side. Otherwise, we would not be having this discussion right now."

Barclay did not disagree, but his police sense kicked in and the words flowed loudly and quickly, "Yeah, Mr. Black! Give me that description again. A strange guy like that. I am running his ass through the computer system and finding him immediately. A guy like you describe. . .."

Doogie interrupted Barclay. "You will not find him. Not in any system."

"Why?"

"Because he is a good guy. Maybe, the ultimate good guy. He is not from this world. That much I know now. I doubt that his name is Mr. Black. I think it is a much different name, and he is from a place that we should not guess at or try to surmise."

Barclay placed his notepad and pen onto the console of the car and sighed.

"Not of this world. Where is he from, Doogs? I mean,

what the hell is this?"

"I dunno where he is from, and I rather not even guess at that one. All I know is we have a purpose in all of this and the stranger is a good guy. As I said, he is the ultimate good guy."

"You are correct, Doogs."

This was way beyond his comfort zone now, but he still had no other explanation for any of it.

Doogie began to expound upon his thoughts, "Yeah, I am correct. Mr. Black, or better yet, the quiet stranger in the black hat, planned all of this and he is in control of all of it. Think 'bout it. He dropped the radio off for repair, gave me six-eighty kilohertz as the frequency to listen to, scant other information, except that he was counting on me and other cryptic stuff. No address. No telephone number . . . only trust. Can't ya see, Barclay? The stranger is giving us a mission. A higher cause. Something big for you and me to handle. I don't know why he picked us, but he did so. Maybe, because I am a patriot and you are an outstanding and honest police detective, born and bred from a family of the same. I dunno, but in my heart, I feel that it is our duty to listen and carry out the mission. It is up to us to accept, understand, and to act. I think it has to do with this ghost character that you are chasing. The quiet stranger said, 'I think you have to listen for and find the ghost.'"

Barclay sat back hard in the driver's seat of his unmarked car. He blinked his eyes while his mind whirled.

Now he was in.

All in.

No more doubts.

"That makes perfect sense. Perfect. Michael, or Mikhail, or Ghost or whoever the hell he is, has stepped it up in the last few days. He is turning darker and darker. His posts are deep and threatening, as though he now has completed his street training, proven his worth and is taking on a higher mission. And, the punk is angry. He hates everyone and everything and he especially hates America."

"Well, there you go, Barclay."

"So, what do ya think that we should do now, Doogie?"

"We try not to fall out of our chairs and on our collective asses tonight when our beloved Rovers get the hell beat out 'em by the score of six to one and Shambley stinks up the joint and gets pulled out of the net. Then, we try not to pee in our pants tomorrow morning, when we confirm the winning numbers are the same numbers that I just gave to you. Moreover, I listen to six-eighty kilohertz on this radio. Listen for the next broadcast, which I have a feeling has something to do with Ghost as well as that big event coming up over at the Great Falls."

Without hesitation, Barclay agreed and said, "Okay. You are correct and I agree. I am in. Please, let's stay in constant touch. Use our cellphones for conversations or use texts. I will get in the office early, monitor this Ghost character for his latest moves, and wait. Are you takin' the radio home to monitor it?"

"No. for some reason, I have a gut feeling that this is where the radio needs to stay. I do lock it up every night." Arthur paused for a moment as he considered their plan for tomorrow. "As far as tomorrow goes, that sounds like a plan. We get over the shock of all of this, we believe, we work as a team, we wait and remain steady and alert. Barclay, thank you and please do not try to reach me first thing in the morning. I will be stoppin' off at Saint Peter's Church for early mass. It has been way too long between masses for old Doogie. I was angry with God for takin' my wife to Heaven, but I understand it all now. Besides, something tells me that whoever or whatever the quiet stranger in the black hat is that he will somehow be there too."

Detective Barclay Millhouse smiled and said, "We are not Catholics, but we are all Methodists. I guess right now, it is all the same. Gotta tell ya, Doogs, if we make it through this, ya can bet I will be in church on Sunday. Long overdue for me and us, too. And, Doogs."

"Yes, Barclay."

"I agree with the quiet stranger in the black hat. You *are* the man."

"I am not quite sure 'bout that, but for all of our sakes, let's sure as hell hope so."

Both Arthur "Doogie" Doogan and Detective Barclay Millhouse made it through the shock of the hockey game score and details turning out exactly as the radio broadcast predicted and the two men also managed not to fulfill Doogie's other statement, when they checked and verified all the winning numbers in the New Jersey lottery the next morning.

All the winning numbers were exact matches. Of course, they were, and the coach of the Rovers did pull Shambley in the third period of the game and put the backup goalie in the net. Just as the radio predicted, it all to happen.

It was not the fact that either Arthur or Barclay did not still find all of this amazing, astounding, and remarkable, but it was as if they now understood the situation and accepted their roles within it. Called into action for a special mission. A higher cause.

For Arthur, he did attend the early mass; he accepted the Blessed Sacraments with a humble awakening in his spirit and he knew that he was ready. Ready for what, Arthur was not exactly sure of but the old patriot was ready. Arthur Doogan would do what he needed to do. Arthur had accepted a call to duty once before in his life and in his heart, he felt that if the quiet stranger in the black hat, or God, or his country, or if in fact, someone or something beyond all human understanding needed his service, then Arthur was ready to do what he could do.

He was old, but he was not dead yet.

After mass, Doogie opened his store and shop. He checked in briefly with Barclay and the two men, exchanged more fascination over all the predictions coming to fruition, but they remained grounded and committed. The grand radio remained tuned to six-eighty kilohertz on the A.M. dial, as did the two standby radios, but right for now, the rush of static was somewhat deafening. Not in volume, but certainly in meaning.

All day long, Barclay monitored the social web sites for activity on his suspect and Arthur stood watch over the static. Detective Millhouse rather ominously pondered how Ghost seemed to go silent, and he debated whether to report all of this to his chain of command or not. The top brass remained embroiled in the events for tomorrow, and other than some general discussion with Nate, Barclay decided to keep it all close to the cuff.

Soon enough, something will break. For now, it was a rather nerve-wracking exercise in both patience and vigilance.

At the repair shop of Arthur Doogan, the radio crackled on with the endless drone of mindless static and the old repairman was rather thankful for some action to keep his mind off the situation. A customer brought in an expensive antique lamp that the wiring required replacement, and another customer brought in an expensive and rather large computer monitor with a shorted power supply. Doogie knew the symptoms. Leaky electrolytic capacitors and he had them all in stock. Occasionally, Doogie fiddled with the tuning knob on the old radio and he turned the volume up and down and peered in the rear vent holes on the rear cover of the radio to confirm the glow of the filaments of the array of vacuum tubes, but he did so more out of nervousness rather than need. More times than he wanted to count, he resisted the urge to tune the dial to another station to confirm that the radio set still received stations, but he dared not to do so. Arthur did not want to risk missing a broadcast. He kept the other two radios tuned to six-eighty kilohertz, and those radios now remained watchdogs of static.

Barclay and Doogie exchanged texts, even an afternoon telephone call, and the reports remained the same. Static on one end and dead silence on the other. Perhaps their gut feelings were incorrect and the dedication ceremony of the United States of America's National Park of the Great Falls of Paterson, New Jersey, was not a target of evil intentions and perhaps, it was something else.

Perhaps.

Regardless, the day passed with no strange broadcasts out of the radio, and for Barclay, the silence continued in the postings and activity of his target. Doogie locked up for the day and headed home with nothing to report, and Barclay went home to his family. It almost seemed as if it was just another routine day.

The evening for Arthur Doogan was a very long and restless night. After the thrashing they took in Boston, the Rovers were off for the night, and without a hockey game to catch his interest, Doogie mindlessly flipped through the television channels with his remote control. Nothing held his interest. He tried reading a book, listening to some quiet music on his stereo system, rereading the newspaper articles about the big ceremony for tomorrow, but nothing worked. Around eleven or so at night, Arthur gave in and retired to bed to try to sleep a little. For hours upon hours, he tossed and turned and swore that he saw and heard every tick of the clock. Except for an hour or so of a restless doze, sleep was hopeless. There was a nagging feeling deep inside, a feeling that despite the calm and quiet of the day and no new announcements or broadcasts on the radio, their intuition was correct. Tomorrow was an important and fateful day. Both Doogie and Barclay felt that whatever was going to happen was going to happen around the dedication ceremony for the Great Falls. Around four in the morning, Doogan suddenly awoke from that short doze as if a gun went off and he sat straight up in his bed. He was wide awake, and he knew that he had to do two things. First, he had to attend the six o'clock morning mass at Saint Peter's Church and second; he had to get to the shop and listen to six-eighty kilohertz. His gut feelings were not wrong. No way. Arthur Doogan was going with his gut feelings.

At 7:45 on a cold, but wonderfully clear and crisp morning, Mr. Arthur Doogan turned the key in the door lock of Doogie's Television and Radio Repair Shop, and gave it a good twist. Actually, he gave it a hard twist to the left with a tiny jiggle of the door handle right at the end of the twist.

While speaking aloud, Arthur said, "One of these days, I will lubricate that tricky lock." The lock finally spun free, and the door swung open. The little silver bell, mounted on a bracket on the top of the front door, jingled while it gently swung, tinkling the telltale signal that the door was active. Arthur slowly guided the door back to a closed position, and he pushed his shoulder into the door until he heard the lock snap closed.

The door closed better than it unlocked.

After flipping on the lights, Arthur quickly made his way through the store section of his operation and hurried along. The radio required time for the tubes to warm up and Arthur felt as if the one thing that might not be on their side today was time. Bent over at the spine, but inspired, the old man shuffled along and he set his brown paper bag containing his lunch on the repair bench. He would place the bag in the refrigerator later. Right now, he had to get the radio on the air and ready to receive what Arthur knew would be very important news. Doogie then hastily made his way to the amazing radio. Amazing in many ways. Arthur hustled to the back of his shop, to the door of the safe, spun the dial to line up the correct combination of numbers and the handle clicked when he hit the final number. Swinging the door open, Arthur reached inside and pulled out the precious radio, and he pushed the door to the safe closed with his hip. He carried the radio to the repair bench, plugged it in, and with a flip of the on/off switch, the dial lights glowed once more. Arthur turned around and flipped the two standby radios on and since they did not require any warm-up period, static instantly greeted him. All the radios were set on six-eighty kilohertz. Arthur confirmed it and while the old radio continued to warm up, he picked up his lunch, shuffled in the rear area of the shop, and placed the bag in the refrigerator. Hurrying back, Arthur heard the telltale rush of static through the speakers. He fiddled with the tuning knob, and the volume to make sure he had all the adjustments correct.

He did.

Time to make the coffee.

It was time to warm up the soldering iron and time to do all the same things in a routine that spanned forty-three years or thereabouts. Most days were the same, but this day was going to be different. Very different for Arthur Doogan. He sensed it last evening and felt the power of guidance when Father Guerra served the Blessed Sacraments to him this morning. When the words of the Communion Blessing caused his spine to tingle and a gentle peace enveloped him. Between sips of the coffee, with his cellphone sitting on the bench right next to where he worked, Arthur worked on rewiring the antique chandelier lamp brought in yesterday. It was a tedious process, and since all the old wires were dry-rotted and useless, Arthur carefully used the old wires to pull the new wires through the winding channels of the lamp. It was good busy work to keep his hands as well as his mind occupied.

When the golden voice of the now familiar radio announcer first came out of seemingly nowhere to envelop the room with sound, Arthur froze in place. His spine tingled, and the hair on his head stood on end. His heart pounded and then the calm kicked in. Many years ago, Arthur copied messages while serving during wartime as a radioman. Vital messages of importance. Messages to direct and convey orders, messages to enact strategy and messages to save lives. He did not make mistakes then and he would not make them now. Years might pass, but some things do not change and some things, once learned, never leave you. Doogie instantly grabbed his notepad and his pen and jumped off the repair stool.

He instantly made a note that the other two standby radios remained full of static, with no signals, yet the old radio filled the shop with the loud and clear voice of the announcer. Doogie faced the radio and waited.

"We interrupt our regularly scheduled programming to broadcast an emergency bulletin from our newsroom. There has just been a horrific explosion at the scene of the dedication ceremony for the Great Falls National Park in Paterson, New Jersey. Apparently, right in the middle of the speech scheduled for one o'clock in the afternoon, by United States Vice President Warren Griffin, a powerful bomb detonated underneath the stage where the vice president and many, many dignitaries, local officials, federal representatives and many others gathered for the ceremony. Details are scant, but law enforcement authorities are reporting many casualties, injuries and a horrific scene at the event. Medical teams are on site and more are rushing to the scene, and local hospitals are on full alert to treat victims of the blast. Reports from the scene describe widespread chaos. Law enforcement is on the lookout and now moving into a full-scale search for a young man, who apparently posed as a maintenance mechanic tasked to repair a broken section of supports underneath the stage a few hours before the ceremony began. The man is in his mid-twenties in age, tall, lean, olive skin tone, with black hair and a long black beard. He was last seen carrying a tool chest, wearing a black work jacket and wearing a black baseball cap with some type of cartoon caricature of a ghost on the front of the cap.

Authorities are asking the public to be on the watch for a young man fitting that description and contact local law enforcement immediately with any sightings or details. Once more, the blast has apparently caused extensive damage, many, many casualties and untold amounts of horrific and horrible injuries. Witnesses describe a scene of utter chaos and disruption. A scene of terrible and indescribable terror and tragedy. The fate of the vice president is unknown at this time as is the condition of everyone else on the scene. Please stay tuned for details as they become available. We promise to. . ..”

The voice faded to static once more and the rush of the radio static became a broadcast of ominous silence. A silence embedded in horror. A silence filled with the promise of a menacing evil trying to overcome the good. If it was up to a certain old radioman, that was just not going to happen.

Good was going to win this one.

Arthur “Doogie” Doogan had copied more messages during his naval career and time at sea than he could ever count. He somehow remained steady, focused, and jotted the notes down, and then he glanced at his watch. He tried hard to remain composed when his watch displayed that it now was five minutes past ten o’clock in the morning! Once more, the radio broadcast caused an unexplained time shift. Arthur knew that he was not here in the shop for more than an hour at the most. Regardless, he checked his notes and confirmed what the announcer said. The vice president was to deliver a speech at one o’clock in the afternoon. There was little time to spare!

Doogie picked up his cellphone, flipped the contacts on the screen, and punched the button for Detective Barclay Millhouse. The good detective was sitting at his desk, flipping through the same social media accounts for Ghost. The silence of his postings told Barclay all he needed to know.

It was a silence embedded in terrorism. Detective Millhouse picked the call up within a half-second, when it rang with Arthur Doogan's number. His heart pounded because he knew this was it.

"Whatcha got, Doogie," Barclay said rather harshly, while betting that time was of the essence now. The ring had broken the eerie silence.

Arthur did not delay in relaying the information.

He acted as his training taught him to do so, long ago, "This is it. It is horrific. It is Ghost posing as a maintenance mechanic for a repair to the stage at the Great Falls ceremony. We were correct. It is all about the Great Falls dedication event. The bomb is under the stage. Ghost plants it. The bomb blows everything and everyone in sight to bits." Arthur paused for just a second to catch his breath as well as glance over his notes and then continued, "Heavy casualties, terrific injuries within an absolute horror scene. The bomb explodes right in the middle of the vice president's one o'clock speech. There is not much time, Barclay. Once more, the radio shifted time on me. Most likely to allow Ghost to plant the bomb, but now, we are down to the wire. Your gut feelings were correct on Ghost. He is no street thug . . . he is a terrorist."

Detective Millhouse collected his various parts and pieces, and his training kicked in.

"Got it all, Arthur. I am on it. I will do my best to keep you posted."

"I will watch the live television broadcasts. I am sure there is local coverage. Good luck and God bless you, Barclay. Be careful."

"Thank you. I will." Barclay ended the call with Arthur and immediately scrolled through his telephone for the emergency contact numbers that Agent Douglas provided during the presentation. He punched the first number, and it rang and rang, with no one picking up. He ended that call and went to the next contact number.

Barclay shouted into the telephone, "C'mon, c'mon, someone, pick up! What the hell good are emergency numbers if no one picks up the damn phone?" Same results, and now Barclay's throat closed and his breaths came in deep gasps. Only a skeleton crew was in the building today. He was the only detective and person working in the detective's office today. Even the administrative assistants and Nate were out on the scene. There was no time to play call and wait or email or text bullshit. He needed to get to the Great Falls as quickly as he could. Even with his lights and siren, it was going to be at least a fifteen-minute haul. It was now pushing ten-thirty. He checked his equipment and did his familiar double-check routine, grabbed his keys and jacket, and sprinted to the unmarked car.

Frantically, with sweat pouring out of his every pore, Detective Millhouse drove through downtown traffic with his lights flashing and his siren wailing. Traffic was heavy, most traffic pulled over, and he made his way as fast as he could while remaining under control. He debated picking up the radio microphone and putting out the call, but he knew that might turn into chaos on the airwaves. Furthermore, the total jurisdiction at the scene belonged to the federal agents and federal police. There would be no time for radio chatter and explanations as he wove through multiple radio transmissions in order to explain his actions. That would only delay the situation even more. No, he made his decision, and it might mean his police career, but he knew that he had to get to the scene and find Agent Douglas. There remained no time for any other course of action. Finally, after the longest drive of his young life, Detective Millhouse could see the Historic District and he was within a city block or two of the stage and ceremony scene. This was as close as he felt he could arrive, without all types of roadblocks and explanations. He found a parking lot utilized by an old factory, quickly swung the unmarked into the lot, shut the car down, opened the door and ran as fast as he could while holding his badge in the air.

Barclay was a championship sprinter on his high school track squad and right now, he was going to prove it.

"I am, Detective Barclay Millhouse! This is a dire emergency! I am with the Paterson, New Jersey, detective bureau!" Barclay shouted as he passed groups of stunned police officers, his badge held high over his head and in the air. With one long leap and hurdle, he cleared the wooden barricades and finally arrived at a close perimeter of the ceremony scene and immediately, a battalion of federal agents and officers surrounded the good detective with their guns drawn. The federal officers now protected the breached perimeter, and it was clear that they were intending a fervent defense of that perimeter. Former, championship sprinter or not, he bent over at the waist and barely could puff out the words of warning, but he did so while the agents and officers studied the badge and his credentials. An older, stout, yet powerfully built and rather grumpy federal agent angrily confronted Detective Millhouse. He had graying hair and a face full of lines. His anger at the disturbance and infiltration was readily apparent.

"WHAT THE HELL IS GOING ON HERE! A detective from Paterson city, huh? Well, up your friggin' ass. Come running in here like this, screaming and yelling like some friggin' crazy-ass nutcase! We will kick your ass and have your badge for this bullshit!"

"Ya have to listen to me, please. I have to speak with Agent Douglas. There is a bomb under that stage and it is going to detonate right in the middle of the vice president's speech!"

The stout agent's face grew angrier; he waved to the other officers and agents while instructing them, "Cuff this crazy jackass. This is federal land and you can't create this kind of disturbance here. Take his gun and badge and cuff his ass. You're done, in police work, kid. You look like you just graduated high school, not police training. You'll need to go back to flipping burgers. A bomb! Bullshit! The dogs have already been through three times and a sniffing crew too. Ain't any bombs here. Only lunatics like you are."

As the team of agents and officers threw Detective Millhouse to the ground and stripped him of his weapon and his badge and handcuffed him, Barclay persisted, "Look! I have to speak with Agent Douglas. Youse guys have to bring the dogs back. Please. Do what the hell you want with me. I don't give two shits less. You have to listen. I have been trackin' this guy and I know what he has done. He is a terrorist. Please, please, please listen to me. I might not seem like it now, but I am damn good at my job! The blood of this mess will be on your hands!" Barclay's voice grew wild and loud and he directed his attention and his voice in the direction of the stout agent and then issued a warning, "I am gonna tell you this, if we survive this mess, federal agent or not, once I am free and you uncuff me, I am goin' to kick your ass raw!"

The federal agents and federal police officers stood over and carefully watched over Detective Millhouse as they allowed him to sit up while remaining handcuffed and sitting on the ground. It seemed as if a wave of concern washed over the group as Barclay's frantic testimony and persistence continued. The stout agent softened, and his eyes went over the rest of the group.

He asked, "Why not notify your chain of command? Why come running up here like some wild nutcase while jumping and leaping over perimeter boundaries where you have no jurisdiction? An armed nutcase nonetheless!"

Barclay shook his head and said, "No time. All of my brass is here somewhere. I tried callin' the emergency numbers that Agent Douglas gave us during the presentation, but no one answered. This was the fastest way. The only way."

"You were at the presentation, huh?"

"Yes."

The stout agent nodded. He pointed at another agent standing next to him and instructed him, "Agent Knorr. You have one of the emergency phones. Check the phone for a missed call."

The agent nodded, dug out the phone from his suit jacket pocket and looked at it. He held the screen up for the stout agent to observe.

The stout agent read the screen aloud, "One missed call. Two-seven-nine-three-five-zero-nine. Two-zero-one, area code. Is that your telephone number, kid?"

"It is."

The stout agent's face grew red and even angrier as he handed the phone back to Agent Knorr.

"What the hell, Knorr? Did you have your thumb in your ass?"

Agent Knorr took the phone, shrugged his shoulders, and sheepishly said, "Sorry, Agent Macalister. I did not hear it."

"Hear it, hear it! Geez, friggin' Louise! Shit!" Agent Macalister screamed while he paced and wrung his hands through his hair. He glanced at Barclay and then to Agent Knorr and asked, "Who has the other emergency contact telephone?"

"Agent Douglas does, sir."

Agent Macalister bit his lower lip and his face twisted.

He breathed deeply, looked at his wristwatch and mumbled, "I should've retired last year." He grabbed his two-way radio from his belt, keyed the microphone and transmitted into it, "Agent Douglas, this is Agent Macalister. Code yellow, sir."

No sooner did the radio un-key, and the voice of Agent Douglas crackled through the radio.

"Go ahead, Macalister."

"Sir, sorry to disturb you, but we have a situation. We have a Paterson, New Jersey police detective here, ah, ah," he waved for the agent that held Barclay's credentials and the agent handed them to Agent Macalister while he glanced at them and continued with the transmission, "a Detective Barclay Millhouse. He is beside himself with some wild testimony that there is a bomb under the stage. Claims to have uncovered some terrorist operative. He is a bit frantic. A little crazy. We have him handcuffed here and have taken his weapon, badge, and credentials. He physically broke our perimeter, and he is insisting on speaking to you. He called both emergency numbers but received no response, sir."

This time, there was a longer pause on the return transmission.

"I have a missed call on my emergency contact telephone from an area code two-zero-one number. Is that this detective's number?"

"Roger, sir."

"Your location?"

"In front of the stage. Dead center. You cannot miss us."

"Roger. Be right there. Out."

Within what seemed to be the longest two or three minutes that Barclay could ever imagine, he sat on the ground, wearing handcuffs with his arms and hands firmly latched behind his back. And suddenly, Agent Johnny Douglas arrived. He first looked at Detective Millhouse and then to his groups of agents and finally, his eyes settled upon Agent Macalister. His brows furrowed together, and his eyes narrowed. He still looked to be the calm, cool and collected law enforcement professional, but clearly this scene and news disturbed him. Especially since it was now well past eleven thirty in the morning and time was now down to the last few ticks. The area overflowed with dignitaries, VIPs and officials, and while the vice president had not yet arrived, the motorcade surely was growing close. The initial kickoff of the ceremony was for noontime.

"Details," Agent Douglas barked, while waving his hands in the air to indicate that he needed the details quickly.

Agent Macalister cleared his throat and spoke, "This punk-ass detective here, well, he comes running and screaming up here like some madman and spouting bullshit about some terrorist. . .."

"I need details not spouting of bullshit. Shut up, Macalister. You! Detective! Details! Now!"

"Agent Douglas, there is a bomb under the stage. I bet my life, my career, and everything I own on it. And, if you do not listen to me, it is gonna be horrific. I have been tracking this evil guy on social media for weeks. The last two days he turned dark. We thought he was just a street thug. My task was to flush him out, gather intelligence and nab not only him, but all of his higher ups too. It is not selling illegal drugs or fenced goods. It is a terrorist operation. The drugs and goods were to raise dough and to establish this thug as the man for the job. Ya have to believe me!"

For obvious reasons, the good detective left out the part that there was an old radio in his friend's electronic repair shop that a mysterious man dressed all in black dropped off for repair and the radio broadcasted the future and altered time.

No sense in spilling all the details.

Agent Douglas studied Detective Millhouse, and his eyes narrowed even more.

"Why did you not notify your chain of command?" Agent Douglas asked.

"I tried. No one will listen to me and all of 'em are here. Look, even youse guys will not listen. I am on my ass in handcuffs here, and time is almost gone. But bet ya ass . . . I got ya attention now."

Agent Macalister mustered up courage, and he stepped in front of Agent Douglas.

He ventured back into the conversation, "It's bullshit, sir. This kid has his signals crossed, or he is whacked out of his mind. The dogs have been through three times and the sniffing crew too. All clear and no one has been anywhere near close to the stage since then. Our team has kept the stage and perimeter surrounded and under constant surveillance."

Agent Douglas looked at the good detective and then at Agent Macalister.

Agent Douglas shook his head and said, "Maybe so. However, this detective got through your perimeter and I agree with him because he has my full attention right now."

Agent Knorr cleared his throat, raised his hand, and rather sheepishly said, "Sir, please." Agent Douglas did not say a word, but he pointed at Agent Knorr as if to indicate for him to speak. "Sir, with all due respect to Agent Macalister, his testimony is not quite correct. A maintenance mechanic came in after the bomb sweeping. After the sniffers and after the dogs."

Both agent's eyes widened and their heads snapped around.

"And, what in hell did this guy do?"

"Well, ah, sir . . . he had all the right credentials, and we stood by while he worked on the stage. He had a black case with tools and he repaired a section of the stage . . . a section underneath that was loose and we. . .."

Detective Millhouse interrupted the agent's testimony and screamed, "Let me guess! This supposed maintenance guy . . . he was tall, lean, with dark black hair, and a long black beard. He spoke with a light foreign accent. Maybe Russian or similar and he wore a baseball cap with a cartoon of a ghost on it."

All eyes focused on Agent Knorr, and it seemed as if the

world stopped turning.

"Ah, yes. That is an exact description of him."

Agent Douglas ripped his two-way radio off his belt and keyed the transmitter.

He screamed, "Agent Douglas here! Code Red! I repeat, Code Red! Code Red! Turn the motorcade around! Code red! Clear the stage area! Now! Code Red!" Agent Douglas frantically called out and pointed as agents and federal police officers ran in all directions. "Clear this area! Everyone out! Macalister, get the dogs back here! Get the sniffers and the bomb squads and . . . dammit all! Uncuff that detective and return his weapon, badge, and credentials! We need him more than we need any man on the face of this Earth." Agent Douglas then turned and pointed at Detective Millhouse and said, "Thank you, Detective Millhouse. Your country, thanks you too. My sincerest apologies, sir."

Barclay nodded as a federal police officer bent down and loosened the handcuffs, returned Barclay's items and his weapon. Agent Macalister immediately fled the scene, mostly to take care of business and perform his duty, but maybe to escape the ass kicking that Barclay promised him. Barclay stood up and watched the scene unfold. It was chaos, but he knew that the mission was over. He found a tree to lean upon and he realized that his chest was heaving. Despite the cooler weather of the day, sweat covered his entire body, head-to-toe and his eyes filled with tears. When the dogs pointed, barked, and did what it is that bomb-sniffing dogs do when they detect explosives, the tears flowed harder.

Inside of Doogie's Television and Radio Repair Shop, Arthur Doogan watched the special news broadcast on the television that reported the chaos occurring just a few miles away in the Great Falls National Park. The reporter who was reporting while live, and on the scene, screamed into a microphone and he tried to describe the madness. He reported how the authorities found a bomb hidden underneath the stage, how it was now defused, everyone was now safe, and how . . . it was over. Doogie wiped away some tears from his eyes and he flipped the television switch to off.

Doogie looked over at the old radio. He smiled and then in gratefulness; he bowed his head and prayed.

The static from the radio filled the shop, and it filled Arthur's soul.

Doogie felt that it was a broadcast from Heaven

Detective Millhouse wiped away the sweat and the tears and he breathed deeply and tried hard to recover. It might not be quite as easy as that. Nevertheless, right now, the final score in this game was that the good guys win in a shutout.

He pulled his cellphone out of his pocket, and mumbled aloud, "After this is over, I still gotta find that sour, old, bastard, Macalister and kick his ass."

He then scrolled down the list of contacts and punched the telephone number for Arthur Doogan.

Arthur "Doogie" Doogan stood in the corner of an overflowing conference room in the main Paterson Police Headquarters Building in downtown Paterson, New Jersey. He would rather stand because if he sat too long, his back would stiffen up. It was the middle of April and Doogie thanked the good Lord and all the Saints that it was still cool outside today. Otherwise, this room would be an inferno.

Arthur wore his best suit. Technically, it was his only suit, therefore without question, the suit qualified as his best one. On the jacket's lapel, Doogie wore an American flag pin along with a United States Navy pin.

Arthur beamed proudly and wiped away some tears when the police chief pinned the medals and ribbons on the dress uniform of Paterson Police Detective Barclay Millhouse. His face hurt from smiling as he carefully listened to the police commissioner read the citation aloud to the crowd. Barclay's father and grandfather sat in the front row of the crowd, both of them wearing their Paterson police dress uniforms. Mrs. Millhouse and the two children beamed with love and pride.

It was a glorious scene.

A ceremony for a local hero.

When the ceremony ended, the flashbulbs, endless interviews from the media finally ended, and the greetings and well wishes wound down, Detective Millhouse made his way through the crowd and he walked over to Arthur. The two men shook hands and embraced.

"You know, Doogs, you are the real hero here."

Arthur shook his head and said, "Oh no, oh no. Come on now. We have discussed this at great length. I am not a hero. My hero days are long gone now. Did my duty. Did my time. We are a team. Besides, what would we ever tell anyone? The truth? I don't think so. No, this is the best way. You cracked the case with your incredible skills and outstanding detective work. We fudge around how you found out all that you did, but what the hell else can we do? No, no, no, this is the only way."

Barclay nodded, and he studied his friend's face and eyes before speaking. "I guess. I just feel you deserve something out of this."

"Oh, I have more than you can ever imagine now. I have peace. That is worth more than any medals or ribbons that I could ever receive." Barclay nodded but before he could comment, Arthur spoke once more. "I am glad that you guys nailed Ghost, and all the rest of his cohorts. It would have left too much open and it would seem as if the job was not done yet if that monster and the rest of them escaped."

"Well, I had nothing to do with that one. Nate nabbed his ass and the rest of the bunch. Nate was relentless."

"Fair enough."

"Say, Doogs, are you coming to the ceremony at the White House?"

"Do ya think they will serve Big Boulder beer?"

Barclay's face broke into a wide smile, and he laughed at old Doogie's humor. Still intact.

"I dunno, but I want you there."

"Hell, yeah, I will be there. Would not miss it."

"Great. Ya know, Agent Douglas offered me a job on his staff."

Doogie's eyes widened at the news, and he screwed his mouth up in surprise.

After a short pause, Doogie asked, "Are ya takin' it?"

Without hesitation, Barclay answered, "Hell, no. I love this old city. As gritty and as messy as it can be sometimes, I would never leave it. It is where I belong and sometimes in life . . . stayin' where you belong is the most important thing of all."

Arthur patted Barclay's shoulder and said, "Right on there, Barclay. Good choice."

"I think so. Hey, do you think that the quiet stranger is returning soon, ya know, in order to pick up the radio?"

Arthur nodded and said, "Yes. Soon. I would think that he would return just to fill in some of the blanks for us. Maybe to thank us too. I dunno, but I guess so."

Barclay's eyes wandered around the room and it seemed as if he was hesitating in saying the words that he was thinking. After some pensive wandering, the words finally arrived.

"Who do you think he really is, Doogie? I mean, *really* who he is."

"I do not know, and I think we are better off not knowing that. All I know is that he sure as hell is not from Paterson, New Jersey."

Barclay laughed and said, "Thank you."

"Thank me. Okay, for what?"

"For being the man, Doogs. For being the man."

About two weeks after the glorious medal and ribbon ceremony for Detective Barclay Millhouse, Arthur "Doogie" Doogan was hard at work inside of Doogie's Television and Radio Repair Shop. He was just completing replacing the cord and the plug on Mrs. Gunter's vacuum cleaner.

Again.

Poor Wilhelm.

Arthur already decided that he would give Mrs. Gunter a discount on this repair. He was twisting at the last screws on the case of the vacuum cleaner when the telltale jingle of the silver bell over the front door signaled the activation of the door. Doogie looked up and smiled at the sight of who just walked into his store and shop. He pulled his eyeglasses off and allowed them to dangle upon the chain and rest upon his chest.

The quiet stranger in the black hat had returned.

He watched carefully while the quiet stranger in the black hat stopped a few feet inside of the front door. He spun around, his dark eyes studying his surroundings. It was as if he was confirming his location. Once he stopped studying his surroundings, he made his way to the front of the store to where the shop area began. The clicks of the metal tips of his boots striking the hard surface of the floor tiles echoed throughout the store, and as he approached Arthur, the stranger smiled widely. Even under the rim of his black hat, Doogie could see his piercing black eyes peering out from under the rim of the hat and while his eyes remained dark and piercing, they were not as ominous as they were in their initial meeting. There was a soft glow about his eyes, and his entire face seemed illuminated. Arthur "Doogie" Doogan smiled widely, and he slowly reached out his hand to shake the hand of the stranger. The stranger met the handshake, and the two men shook hands for more than just a few seconds. Doogie felt as if his entire body warmed to the touch of the quiet stranger. After the handshake and greeting, Arthur walked over to where the old radio sat on the end of the repair bench, with the dial still set to six-eighty kilohertz and the rush of static gently filtering out of the speaker. The old radioman gently reached over and he caressed the on/off switch for a few seconds as if he was holding onto a precious diamond. Finally, Doogie clicked the switch to off. The static rush left, and the wonderful glow of the dial light faded away.

"Nice to see you again, kind stranger. Forgive me if I do not call you, Mr. Black. You actually never said that your name was Mr. Black. All you instructed me to write down was the single word, black. I made the rest of the name up, but it was an assumption on my part." Doogie gently unplugged the radio and slowly and elegantly rolled up the power cord. While Doogie did so, his words continued,

"You are too full of the light of this world to have a name such as Mr. Black. Despite your immense size and overwhelming presence, your entire body radiates love and kindness."

Arthur looked over at the stranger while waiting for his response, but the stranger only continued to smile and then he nodded.

"Well, I trust you had a successful trip while you were away?"

Again, no words, but a smile and another nod.

"I know you are a man of very few words. I get that now. You are indeed, the quiet stranger in the black hat and that is all that I need to know. It works for me and for Barclay, too. We both do not need to know anything else. I must say that you were correct about this, how do I put this . . . astounding radio. This radio had some very peculiar . . . tendencies. Particularly in and around six-eighty kilohertz. I checked everything on this radio. I left nothing inside here untouched or examined. I replaced one tube and tested it out. It is in a grand condition now. I think that pesky ghost is gone forever."

Doogie looked over at the stranger, and he smiled again. There were some tears rimming his eyes, and the old radioman managed to wipe them away before speaking once more.

"Your radio is in top notch condition. It is all ready to go now and you can take it home. I also owe you a refund on the deposit," Doogie said while he shuffled over to pick up the repair ticket with the calculated amount of the total cost of the repair on it. Doogie put his eyeglasses back on and studied the ticket. "Yes, I need to get the money out of the safe. I will be right back."

When the stranger finally spoke, and his deep, glorious and melodious voice resounded all around them, Arthur Doogan almost jumped out of his work shoes.

"No, Arthur, please. The radio is yours to keep. You

more than earned it."

Doogie froze in his tracks and slowly turned to face the quiet stranger. Once more, he pulled his eyeglasses off and allowed them to dangle from the chain.

"Oh my. Really?"

The stranger nodded and smiled and pointed first at the radio and then to Doogie.

"Well, okay, very, very kind of you. But, please, let me go in the back and get your money and let me settle the bill and return the balance of your deposit."

The stranger shook his head and said, "No, Arthur. Money really does not mean much to me. Where I come from, money means nothing."

Arthur took a deep breath, and he smiled while his imagination ran wild over the statement.

After regaining his thoughts, Doogie sheepishly said, "Okay, yes, I guess. Never really thought of that until now. Well, quiet stranger, all I can say is thank you. Does this mean that I need to keep the radio tuned to six-eighty kilohertz all the time? I mean, I will, if you tell me to do so. My plan is to sell all of this and move to Florida at the end of the year. However, you most likely know that already. I have to tell ya that I am here if you ever need me again. Barclay too. He is a great man. Destined to do great things, but I am old now. After these past few weeks, I think that I am even older. Renewed in spirit, but older. Yet, old Doogie will always do what I can to help to defeat evil and to glorify God and assist the good of this world. You have my promise on that, quiet stranger. No doubt that I am old but, I ain't dead yet."

The quiet stranger in the black hat shook his head, then he held his hands across his chest, and then he held his right hand over his heart.

Doogie watched in awe as the huge man, lifted his eyes up to the ceiling, and then with his smile still wide and broad upon his face and a marvelous sparkle within his dark eyes, the stranger said, "I know that I can always count upon you, Arthur, and Detective Millhouse too. Yes, you are old, but death, no, no, no, Arthur, you will never die. Your physical body might expire, but death . . . no. Let me assure you that the good of this world will always prevail. Always. There are many more of us than there are of them. No, you do not have to keep the radio on six-eighty kilohertz. Play it, enjoy it and if I need you, then I will know how to get in touch with you. Thank you, and the good detective for the assistance and for the honor. My abilities to intercede are often limited and at times, I count upon assistance from men of goodwill, such as you and Barclay are, to assist me in stirring the waters of the pool. After all, some translations choose to omit the testimony of my stirring entirely. Thank you, Arthur, for being *the man*."

Doogie did not entirely understand the stranger's words nor did he know what to say, but he nodded and once again, the tears began to flow. This time, they ran down his face, and Doogie did nothing to wipe them away or try to hold them back.

The stranger spoke again, and now, his voice was lower in volume and filled with sincerity, "I will always be here. Until the end of all time. No matter where you are, I will be right next to you. You might not see me, but I will be there, hiding in the shadows, watching and waiting for the moments to assure this world and beyond that goodness and kindness will always triumph and evil will always fail. It is my mission, now and forever."

The quiet stranger in the black hat smiled once more. His dark eyes sparkled, and he reached up and tipped the edge of his hat, spun on his heels and turned to walk briskly away. Arthur Doogan leaned in and carefully watched the quiet stranger in the black hat walk away, and he listened to the glorious sound that the metal tips of his boots made as he walked through the store.

The stranger reached the front door, he gently swung

the front door open and the little silver bell, mounted on a bracket on the top of the front door, jingled while it gently swung, tinkling once more with the telltale signal that the door was active. With a quick exit and another quick turn, the quiet stranger in the black hat made his way up the busy city street.

The old radioman hustled as best he could, from behind the repair bench, through the maze of old store displays and to the front door. Arthur pushed open the front door to his establishment and watched as his eyes followed the quiet stranger in the black hat and his ears listened to the click of his boots. Arthur watched and listened while standing silently on the threshold of the front door. He stood and listened as the noise from the tips of his boots sounded loudly and echoed along the city street until the stranger faded from view and the noise of his boots was lost in the madness and noise of the city.

Arthur wiped the tears away from his eyes. He turned to return to the inside of his store and shop, and when he reached for the front door, his eyes met the annoying and troublesome front door lock and handle.

Doogie smiled, and he knew what his next repair was going to be.

While opening the door, Arthur mumbled, "Ya know, I have been puttin' those repairs off for much too long. Gonna call Mrs. Gunter and tell her that the vacuum cleaner is ready. Then, I am grabbing some lubricant, some tools and fixin' that tricky handle. Yes indeed, today is the day. Some things ya just gotta take control of and handle. I am old, but I ain't dead yet."

Arthur slowly shuffled off towards the shop, a little bent over, but with a little bounce in his step.

That is, as much of a bounce as his old body could perform.

When he had a sudden thought, Doogie stopped walking and he stood in the middle of the store. Once again, his words escaped into the air and to the four walls.

"Sure, would be nice if that radio could kinda keep up with the future type of broadcasts. Just once in a while. Might be nice to know ahead of time if the Rovers make the playoffs or not. It would keep my blood pressure down. That Shambley is unreal. One night he is a block wall and the next night he is, Swiss cheese. The guy drives all of us Rover fans, crazy."

He lifted his eyes to the ceiling and perhaps, to Heaven and crossed his chest and held his hand in the air while saying with a laugh, "I promise that if I play the lottery with any numbers that I hear that the dough is going in the collection plate at Saint Peter's Church. I promise. I have to wonder though—if ya got any hockey games and Big Boulder beer up there in Heaven. Now, that, I gotta admit, would be nice. Really, really nice."

While laughing the entire way, Doogie continued his journey to the shop to pick up the lubricant and the tools to fix the front door lock and handle. First, he would make the phone call to Mrs. Gunter, and then he would repair the door lock.

Yes, indeed, today, he would finally repair that tricky lock. Nothing was going to stop him now.

Nothing.

Today was finally the day.

THE END

The Fig and the Thistle

Pastor Kenneth Greene was long since gone. It now seemed as if Pastor Greene lived in a bygone era from several lifetimes ago.

Technically, Pastor Kenneth Greene still was, Pastor Kenneth Greene. It was just that it had been so long since he actually was Pastor Kenneth Greene that it was difficult to recall when he existed. After all, Pastor Rutherford Bartholomew Waxworth was a mouthful to say, but it was so much more of an impressive sounding of a name as opposed to Pastor Kenneth Greene. When the multitudes worshiped you, and bared their souls and opened their wallets, and their bank accounts, upon your every word and you held the power and glory in your hands . . . you just had to forget there ever was a Pastor Kenneth Greene.

It was a Saturday evening and Rutherford stood in the pulpit on the stage of the glorious Golden Cathedral of Praise, all five-hundred-thousand square feet of it. An overflowing crowd of sixteen-thousand worshipers sat in their seats in the arena section of the cathedral, hanging on every word that the handsome, charismatic and overwhelming, Pastor Rutherford Bartholomew spoke from his ornate pulpit of glitter, laced with silver and gold trim. Another audience of millions of dedicated followers, tuned in on televisions and radios across the world to do the same.

Rutherford stared longingly into the television camera with his right-hand man, a longtime friend, and producer, Mr. Lionel Shearing, jabbering away in his earpiece while he gave instructions to the camera operator as well as to Rutherford.

"Once you see tears in his eyes or better yet, tears streaming down his face, zoom in tight and close on Rutherford's face. For now, hold that position you are in right now, the water from the spray bottle that we used for sweat, already dried up and until the tears arrive, hold steady."

"Gotcha, boss," was the camera operator's reply.

Pastor Rutherford Bartholomew Waxworth bought and paid for everyone's loyalty here. From the production staff, to the camera crews, to the sound technicians, to the office staff, to the undercover security persons roaming the crowds. All of these positions paid handsome wages. Leaks of behind the scene information or clues to the inside scoops of the operation did not happen because all the employees knew that even if they did leak inside information, the denials would be swift and the repercussions harsh.

"Time to whip up some tears, Rutherford," Lionel suggested to his friend, but Lionel knew that it was not so easy to do so. Artificial sweat was easy to spray on from a plastic spray bottle, however, producing actual tears required some serious effort. Yet, Lionel had total confidence in Pastor Waxworth's abilities while behaving so passionately in the pulpit. He had seen this act before. A few thousand times or so. With a smile, and the boom microphone from his headset now tucked on the side of his head, Lionel smiled and leaned back in his chair to watch the show begin.

This was going to be a classic performance.

Epic.

Pastor Waxworth leaned into the pulpit of glitter and the emotion switch turned to the "on" position, "There I was! In the gutter of a dirty city street. Face down, with an empty bottle of whiskey in my hands. Drenched in sweat, covered in dirt, and mired in sin. I was oblivious to the world, and now, I fell so far into the depths of Hell that I had no way out. It was then that the Lord spoke to me! I heard his words clearly in my head and a glorious vision of Heaven opened up in the dark sky above me!"

Pastor Waxworth pounded the pulpit with his hand and to Lionel's surprise, a round of magical tears erupted from Rutherford's eyes and streamed down his face. Lionel flipped his boom microphone back in front of his face and flipped the switch to "talk."

"Zoom in now on his face," Lionel instructed the same camera operator.

"Will do," was the prompt reply.

The emotional pastor's voice now boomed into all corners of the arena and it echoed into the rafters of the roof, "Rise up out of your sin, Rutherford! Rise up and I will hold you in my arms and make you strong and powerful! Glorify me and promote the Gospel of truth and praise and I will make you prosper and you will make followers in all corners of the world. I promise you that your flock of faithful followers will prosper too! Your life and the lives of your flock of love will overflow with glory and wealth. The glorious vision of Heaven loomed above me and even though I was only a young man of twenty-two years of age, I knew that this was my only chance at escaping the misery of Hell."

Pastor Waxworth, now, with the full flow of tears streaming down his face, moved out from behind his pulpit and he fell upon his knees on the stage and bowed over at the waist.

Lionel opened the microphone again and advised Rutherford, "Careful now. Remember that is a five-thousand-dollar custom tailored Italian suit you have on with your knees bouncing around there on the stage."

The camera operators and all the crew that were privy to the transmission, all tried very hard not to laugh at Lionel's concern over the expensive suit. After this performance, the dough will roll in and they will replace the suit with ten more.

While lifting his head up and now using his own boom microphone, Pastor Waxworth poured out the fake emotions even more.

"After falling upon my knees in humble thanks, I slowly stood up from the depths of the gutter of despair and sin. I realized that my thirst for alcohol had left my soul and the limp in my left leg from that terrible motorcycle crash that caused me such pain . . . left me too! The Lord healed my body, my soul and poured love into my heart!" While speaking, Rutherford slowly climbed back to his feet, while reenacting the moment of his salvation for the audience to see and to feel, "I stood up out of the gutter, bowed my head, and said, Lord, I am yours! I will do your work and follow your ways and give up my evil and deceitful life." Now, while once more stationed behind the pulpit, he expertly lowered his voice and while the camera panned in on his face, Pastor Waxworth slowly wiped away his tears while proclaiming, "The Lord then commanded me to build this Golden Cathedral of Praise, and to proclaim his glorious works and promises of salvation to the world."

The cameras panned the crowd as many people visibly sobbed and wiped their eyes with tissues that staff and security graciously handed out while they wandered in and amongst the "flock." As they handed out the tissues and made their way through the masses of worshipers, they also held collection plates in their hands. The many wounded and emotionally overwhelmed persons in attendance dropped dollars in the plate while plucking tissues from the box to wipe up their sorrows at the touching story and the glorious and miraculous testimony of the now "saved," Pastor Rutherford Bartholomew Waxworth.

After all, tissues were costly, and they did not exactly fall out of the sky from Heaven.

Sensing that the audience was now ripe for coughing up

a tremendous amount of dollars into the coffers of the empire known as Pastor Rutherford Bartholomew Waxworth's Mission of Love and Hope, and under the constant coaching of Lionel, off went Pastor Waxworth. He began spouting off the closing kill shot of emotions.

"If you are as, I was, and you too, are now down to your last gasp of hope, if you are hitting the bottom, within a wave of misery of despair, please believe me that you must not falter nor waver nor fall farther into a den of sin. You must rise up and follow and God will restore you as he restored me! As we read together earlier in our joyous time of worship, from the great Gospel of Mark in chapter ten, God promises us limitless prosperity and endless wealth and joy when we give freely of ourselves. When we open our hearts and give the fruits of our labors in order to honor God's work, The Almighty Lord our God, rewards us here on Earth and in Heaven. If I wore an ordinary, off-the-rack, department store suit, instead of this designer suit made by the finest Italian tailors, or if I wore an ordinary watch on my wrist, instead of this diamond encrusted watch, I would be failing God. If I preached in a humble wooden church on a rural street corner instead of this glorious cathedral and I drove an old, beat up automobile from my church to a small home instead of the twenty-nine-room mansion that I now live in, I would be doing a disservice to God! I would not be glorifying his works. I would not be showing the world the fulfillment of the proof of his promises. I would be failing in my mission! Do not fail, my fellow followers of the word, open your souls to allow God to enter in, and fill his fountains with the water of wealth so that God may fill yours too!"

Lionel keyed up the microphone and reported, "The word from the call center is that the phones are going nuts. Good work, now you need to wrap it all up. Go to Jess singing a hymn. Cameras swing over to the right. Jess . . . knock them dead. Ya looking amazing! Nice hair, stick that big chest and those amazing twin girls far out there too. For the television crew, scroll the toll-free number and message along the screen. Radio team, go ahead and announce the number now as you fade into the song."

"Now, the other joy and love in my fabulous life, my gorgeous, loving, and faithful wife, Jess Crystal Waxworth, will close our service out with a wonderful hymn of praise and thankfulness. To those faithful worshipers sitting in the far reaches of our grand cathedral, please, keep your eyes on the big television screens. The lyrics will scroll across the big screens for you to sing along, and the cameras will capture the glory of the song and the beauty of my lovely wife. Remember, while our staff and our amazing volunteers flow through the crowd with the collection plates, to give all that you can and your tickets to Heaven and to prosperity will be your grand rewards!"

As the music began, and the magnificent voice of Jess broke into the closing hymn, the coffers overflowed and the calls poured into the call center. The money flowed into the bank accounts as if they were rivers after spring rains and snowmelt.

Tax-free monies, of course, because Pastor Rutherford Bartholomew Waxworth's Mission of Love and Hope was a not-for-profit organization. As the world inside the enormous cathedral exploded into song and music floated into every corner, and while the hundreds of staff and volunteers floated through the crowd with their collection plates, one man stood in a high corner of the arena. He stood watching as the worship service developed and unfolded, and he stood in a row behind the last row of seats, while carefully and silently watching. Others stood nearby him, because the arena had filled every available seat for this service, and they only had standing room available. The local police stood by out on the main road to direct the flow of traffic that soon would crush the local highways and roads as the crowds left the Golden

Cathedral of Praise. This man was in no rush at all. His dark eyes scanned the arena; they narrowed and focused upon the stage and the antics of Pastor Waxworth while he directed the audience and he sang along with his wife to the lyrics of the well-known hymn. The man not only could bring the house down, but he could sing well too.

Not all the actors are in Hollywood and not all the singers are in recording studios.

The man who stood in the row while silently studying the service was an immense man. Towering above all others. Powerfully built, yet tall and lean, the man stood there silently and if you were to ask any person standing or sitting nearby him, they might say that he stood there rather ominously too. He was dressed all in black; he wore a black vest covering a perfectly pressed, black buttoned-up shirt, and his sharply creased black trousers had not a single ripple or a wrinkle in them. On his feet, he wore polished black boots, polished to such a high luster that the lights from the roof of the arena could be seen reflecting in the shine of his boots. There was nothing out of place on this man—nothing at all. He was impeccable, immaculate. His features were dark; he wore on his face, a finely trimmed beard, closely framing a perfectly chiseled face, and he stood silently while watching with dark, piercing black eyes. Dark eyes that focused intently on the stage while ignoring the big television screens hanging over the arena. Eyes that were staring straight ahead, emotionless, expressionless. On his head, he wore a black hat with a wide brim, pulled down to where his facial features were not easily seen, but still slightly visible. No doubt, he was a striking and handsome man.

He was the quiet stranger in the black hat.

Earlier in the service, the stranger had appeared on the radar of the roving undercover security patrol. There had been some radio chatter about his presence and it resulted in a dispatch of one of the security leaders in order to check out the stranger. The security leader needed to see what the calamity was all about and investigate the stranger since the reports referred to his "rather ominous presence." Since the quiet stranger in the black hat stood quietly and did not even say a word, the security leader found no immediate cause for any alarm. Besides, as large and powerful as some men on the security patrol were, the leader could not even imagine having to deal with someone as large and obviously as powerful as the stranger was.

"Assign a single patrol officer to watch him carefully, but leave him alone for now," were the leader's orders on the security channel of the radio. A breathless volunteer finally made it to the high reaches of the rafters and the final row in the grand arena and he worked his way down the rows of standing row only attendees. His collection plate overflowed and a security patrol person followed behind him now, with a small, two-wheel cart as they dumped off the offerings into a bin on the cart to allow more room for more donations. The volunteer was a middle-aged man, with a baldhead and a warm smile. Amongst persons of ordinary size, one would say that the volunteer was a large man, but now, while standing in front of the quiet stranger in the black hat, he looked small. Very small and diminutive. The volunteer paused for just a moment when his eyes met the overwhelming appearance, and then the gaze in the eyes of the stranger.

Recovering, the volunteer smiled and held out the offering plate while spouting off the fine-tuned speech in a rehearsed and happy manner, "Grace and peace, my brother. Give generously of your heart and you will find that the blessings of the Kingdom of God are limitless."

The stranger did not even turn his eyes to the volunteer or acknowledge him in any way. The dark eyes of the stranger remained straight ahead.

"Ah, brother, please, open your heart and give to the cause and the works of The Lord."

There remained no reaction from the quiet stranger in the black hat and now, the volunteer stepped closer and in front of the stranger in an effort to catch his attention and somewhat futilely block his view of the stage. When he did so, the stranger moved and he turned to face the volunteer while now staring down at the man. Every hair on the volunteer's body stood straight up. His skin crawled along his body and his spine shook from the sight of the dark eyes of the stranger. Looking deeply into the stranger's eyes, the volunteer could swear that he saw flames licking within his pupils. Flames as in the fires of Hell type of flames. In shock, the volunteer dropped the collection plate, and it rattled and rolled across the concrete floor. Money floated everywhere. The security person and other worshippers helped, and they all jumped into action helping to collect the fallen plate and the wayward money.

"Oh my, geez, I am so very sorry!" The volunteer shouted at his misstep and the results thereof.

The stranger simply stood there and did not move, react, or say a single word. The security person was now rather annoyed at the stranger's lack of a donation, combined with his inaction while not even trying to assist them in collecting the plate and the money.

The security officer looked at the stranger, pointed at his hat, and said rather curtly, "Men are not supposed to wear a hat in God's house."

The stranger looked down upon the two men and in a low, melodious voice the stranger said, "If I was in God's house then I would remove my hat. While standing within a den of covetous sin, I wear the armor of God."

With those words, the quiet stranger turned and walked briskly away. His black boots made a sharp clicking sound when the metal tips of his boots struck the hard surface of the concrete. The two men slowly turned and watched while overwhelmed with surprise at the words and actions of the stranger. The nearby worshipers stood too, and they all stared in shock as they watched the stranger walk away. They stood and watched for a long time until he disappeared from their view and no longer could they hear the click of the metal tips of his boots on the walkway.

Dr. Warren Ashworth thought while he walked into his office and his eyes glanced over to the young woman seated in front of his desk, 'Mondays are never fun.'

This particular Monday was fulfilling that description rather perfectly.

Too perfectly.

His assistant told the good doctor that the child's mother was in the office, anxiously awaiting an update on Doctor Ashworth's medical examination of her son and the follow-up information because of the examination. The good doctor was nearing retirement. He was a short, stocky man with keen and clear blue eyes. The keen eyes of a skilled surgeon. Besides his reputation for being a skilled and remarkable kidney specialist and surgeon, Doctor Warren Ashworth was famous for his caring heart, wonderful bedside manner and a calm demeanor. His once black hair now was white as snow, yet his handsome good looks remained. The good doctor had been in this position many, many times before, and it is never easy.

He hung up his white coat on the coat hook, straightened his necktie and exchanged the white coat for a suit jacket, which he slipped on, while walking towards his desk. Doctor Ashworth mumbled a low and barely audible, "Hello" and then slowly took a seat in the high-back chair behind his desk. The gentle sigh that the doctor exhaled while taking his seat told Miss Sandra Carrington that this was not going to be the greatest of news. This follow-up was going to be different from all of the previous ones.

Doctor Ashworth cleared his throat and began to explain, "I am sorry but, this is not going to be good news today, Miss Carrington. The situation with Timothy's kidney has taken a regressive turn. I am afraid there is now a complete failure on all functions with the kidney that we have been carefully watching for a long time. Of course, that takes its toll on the remaining kidney because of the functions that the relatively healthy kidney has to assume. All of these issues just compound and it weakens all the processes and the systems of the body and makes for a very ill eight-year-old boy. The dialysis is, of course, keeping Timothy from total renal failure, but I am afraid that at this point, Timothy requires a new kidney. I know we have had this discussion before and tested you and many of your willing family members for a match . . . and we were not successful. Now, we need to move on in our search. It is reaching a critical stage."

Doctor Ashworth stopped speaking and studied the face of the young woman seated on the other side of the desk from him. Since he met her and her son and began to treat the kidney affliction and resulting disease, he had never seen her look so worn. She had come to him, young, dynamic, quite beautiful and shapely in her female figure, but now, her face was haggard and her weight loss had been noticeable. Sandra was still striking in appearance, with a round face, wide eyes with a touch of gray and blue and a long nose, yet a nose that fit her face perfectly. Her mouth formed a perfect complement to her facial features, with full lips that she often pulled up on the lower lip and bit it whenever she was nervous.

She bit it right now.

As a medical doctor, he would be sure to give her advice on taking care of herself, too. The stress was difficult and at times overwhelming, but now it was going to drag her down as well as her son.

This was a case of cause and effect.

His plan was to address her condition and try to help her. Doctor Ashworth admired her fortitude and her love and sincere dedication to Timothy.

"Miss Carrington, with Timothy's blood type and his

particular body types and such, finding a donor kidney is going to be a difficult task. I must be painfully honest with you. It has to be an exact match."

Sandra spoke for the first time and when she did so, she finally let go of the strap handle of her purse, which until now, she had kept the strap tightly in her hands while she nervously fidgeted with it and turned it over repeatedly in her hands.

"I understand, Doctor Ashworth. Your honesty and caring are wonderful and very much appreciated. Is this an impossible situation?"

Doctor Ashworth shook his head and said, "No. It is not an impossible situation, just difficult. Since we have scoured your side of the family tree, we need to move to Timothy's father's side. Of course, we can remain registered in the donor database, hoping and praying for a match, but so far, it has proved futile. By far, the best bet is to concentrate on the potential of Timothy's father's side providing a match. I do not like to pry but I must be frank and honest from a medical situation and standpoint and ask you a very pointblank question. Are you okay with my questioning? I can ask Nurse Sheridan to step in here if you would be more comfortable."

He studied Sandra's face, and she shook her head to indicate no. With a mumble, Sandra said, "No, please, I am fine. Thank you."

Doctor Ashworth nodded his head and continued, "It is just that in all the medical paperwork, the father's name and information are always blank. Timothy's last name is, of course, Carrington. We never pry and remain sensitive to the situations until it is medically necessary to probe deeper. We do need to consider Timothy's father as well as his side of the family to assist us in this situation. Is that a possibility? Please do not be offended, I assure you that these are only medical-related questions, but I assume you know who Timothy's father is?"

Sandra nodded and softly answered, "Yes. I do. The question is not offensive. It is necessary. I understand completely why you asked. I have never mentioned his father to you or any of your staff, and Timothy has not mentioned him because he does not know of him or has ever met him. He was out of the picture right after I announced my pregnancy to Timothy's father."

Doctor Ashworth nodded, but he did not say a word.

"Timothy's father is a lecherous, conniving, and evil man, and I was so stupid to fall for his wiles. Yet, many, many do and still do."

Doctor Ashworth held up his hand to interrupt Sandra, as if to imply that she already answered his question and this was now too much information, but she smiled, waved, and said, "No, Doctor Ashworth, this feels good to get off my chest. You are a medical professional and sworn to secrecy with certain conversations. I need to vent now."

Doctor Ashworth leaned back in his chair and listened. He did not say a word, but the look upon his face told Sandra that if it would help her to feel better that he would listen without any objections.

"I thought he cared and honestly, I was a fool who fell in love with him. He is much older than I am and very handsome, charming, and unbelievably beguiling in his ways. Believe me when I say that untold numbers of persons are under his spell. Yet, all he cared about was having a beautiful young woman and you-know-what on the side, and it led to heartache and pain. He is a man of limitless wealth and power, and he walked away when I told him about Timothy. Out of our lives. For him, love had nothing to do with it. Only lust. The relationship led to nowhere. Except it led to Timothy, and Timothy is my life. He is amazing, wonderful, remarkable, and every other glorious adjective for describing him that I could ever conjure up. He did inherit his father's good looks, and honestly, his intelligence, yet thankfully, his father's evil mannerisms and deceitful ways were not part of the inheritance gene pool. Sadly, perhaps, weak kidneys are. Regardless, Timothy is honest, kind, and loving and we have to do what we can to ensure a long life for my son. I already tried to give my son my own kidney, and I failed. I will not fail him a second time."

Doctor Ashworth leaned forward, placed his arms on the desk, and folded his hands. He was implying and displaying calm. Sandra liked Doctor Ashworth, respected him and, above all, she trusted him.

"Please, you did not fail. Sandra, we will do all that we can for Timothy. Thank you for sharing so much and you must remember that during this time, taking care of your own health is important too. I am a doctor, but a kidney specialist, not a mental health professional, but if you feel you need someone to speak with during this time, I have many solid recommendations that I can make to you for trusted, wonderful professionals. Caring for Sandra is so important. You are not or ever were not a fool. You are an intelligent, beautiful, wonderful person and a great mother. Please, consider help if you need it. This is not going to be an easy time. Do you have a support team? Parents, sisters, brothers, friends, or family?"

"Thank you, Doctor Ashworth. I have no immediate family. I was an only child. My parents, both tragically, died in a car accident a few years ago. There might be some cousins left somewhere but we have little, if any, contact. I have some friends, but honestly, with Timothy being so ill, friends fall away. I apologize for the rant. I will give your offer for counseling some consideration. Honestly, it felt really good to blow that off my chest. Now, I do have faith and trust in God. Life took many of my parts and pieces, but I know that despite the pain, God gave Timothy to me as a gift and I will trust in God to prop me back up. Every day, I pray in the morning and I pray at night for Timothy's health, for God to send me a sign, send me some hope and to send me some help." Sandra waved in the air to dismiss the rims of tears in her eyes, and she quickly wiped them away. Recovering, Sandra said, "Thank you for this, doctor. It is certainly above and beyond, and I know that you are a busy man and others require your time. I do feel better. Sorry to have burned your ears up." Sandra almost laughed, but she withheld it and instead managed a weak smile.

"No apologies are necessary. Please. I am sorry to hear of the loss of your parents. Yet, I sense that your faith and just blowing off some steam here is providing you with some much-needed strength and comfort. Therefore, we move to the next question. Can you try to get in touch with Timothy's father?"

Sandra took a deep breath while her mind raced with the thoughts of doing what Doctor Ashworth just asked of her. Could she attempt to contact Timothy's father? She could, and she would, even while knowing full well the potential implications of doing so. The agreement that she signed with Timothy's father specified a permanent cease and desist clause for any further communications or contact.

That is, as in, cease and desist forever.

It was explicitly clear in the legal document that she should never reveal to Timothy who his biological father was, and she should never contact him ever again. Contacting his father, even for an emergency such as this, might mean the end to everything. The end to the money, the medical benefits, their home, their daily lives as they now know it, but Sandra knew what she had to do. She would go find a job and work day and night to make it work out. Some kind of job. The stress washed over her face and when she exhaled; she realized that Doctor Ashworth was carefully studying her face for her reactions. He was emotionally caring for her as well as medically caring for Timothy, and Sandra appreciated his dedication and his kindness.

"For Timothy, I will do anything, including, contacting his father."

When she left the meeting with Doctor Ashworth, that is exactly what she planned to do.

Pastor Rutherford Bartholomew Waxworth sat behind his desk in his luxurious office, located deep within the labyrinth-like maze of the back of the house of the sprawling Golden Cathedral of Praise. The luxurious office suite was not for the use of the general parishioners. When you are as close to Heaven and reside on a high and mighty level, as did Pastor Rutherford Bartholomew Waxworth, well then, you cannot lower your position for visits from the dull creatures of this world.

At least, that is what Pastor Waxworth told the architect when he designed the building. In exactly those same words, too.

The office suite was beyond exceptional. The best of everything as far as furniture, flooring and finishes go. Deep pile carpets with the occasional high-end Turkish throw rugs here and there. Deep, oak, wooden finishes fit and crafted by the finest carpenters lined the walls, the baseboards and the trim work. You will find no "home improvement store" quality fixtures or finishes here. Only the best of everything. Elegant light fixtures, decorative low-lights glowed in soft blue, red and yellow hues. On the walls were paintings and photographs of modern art and landscape scenes and just in case that a random visitor ventured in here, there were a few token art pieces displaying Bible scenes and stories. After all, this was a ministry dedicated to the glory of God.

Rutherford sat in his high-back leather chair and fiddled with a computer mouse while he scrolled the latest accounting sheet with the updated figures of the gross receipts from his powerful broadcast of last Saturday's night service. It required a few days for his team of accountants and bookkeepers to tabulate the figures, but usually by midmorning on Tuesday, the financial spreadsheet arrives in the in-box of his email. It was midmorning Tuesday and the distinct "Ding" of the message alarm on his computer announcing the email was wonderful music to his ears.

This music was especially glorious.

A smile broke across his lips because the figures were astounding. Lionel had correctly predicted the success of Saturday night's service. His right hand-man knew that the sermon and Pastor Waxworth's performance was exceptional, as he passionately bared his soul with the tale of how poor Pastor Waxworth rose from the ashes of despair to be enlightened by God. Lionel was correct. Now, Pastor Rutherford Bartholomew Waxworth was on top of the world. In his mind, and in the eyes and the minds of his millions of worshipers, he was only a step away from Heaven. Leaning back in his chair, he glanced at his watch and saw that it was now just past ten in the morning. Perfect time to celebrate the success that the blessed spreadsheet revealed. His eyes caught the wall where his wet-bar sat neatly hidden behind a movable wall. It was the perfect time for a cocktail. It was time for his lips to taste some very expensive bourbon. The best batch just arrived from his private supplier in Kentucky.

Only the best batches shipped to Rutherford Bartholomew Waxworth.

Pastor Waxworth reached for the button underneath his desk and felt to make sure it was the button for the doors, for the wet-bar and not the panic button for calling his security officer. The last time that he had too many drinks, he missed the mark and his bodyguard and driver, Mr. Claude Buxton, came dashing over in order to save Pastor Waxworth from the clutches of evil.

This world is full of many, many hidden ironies.

With just a simple push of a button, a motor flipped on and the motors and gears, seamlessly moved the heavy oak wood door and it glided across the wall, while revealing a fully stocked wet-bar of the highest quality, whiskies, wines, cognacs and other alcoholic delights. Delights hidden from the prying eyes of those who would think such extravagant indulgences were not proper behavior for a man so close to Heaven as was Rutherford Waxworth. Yes indeed, the movable wall hid everything that the admired and important Pastor Rutherford required in order to bring him that one precious step closer to Heaven.

Inside of a modest three-bedroom home located in a neighboring town about fifteen miles from the Golden Cathedral of Praise, Sandra Carrington nervously fingered the buttons of her cellphone. She was not even sure that this phone number; she had scrawled across a piece of notepaper many years ago, was still valid. Sandra was sure that Timothy's father might change his cellphone number quite often. It was worth a shot, perhaps; he rotated numbers, and this one was now active. In her heart, Sandra knew that her nerves were only creating various suppositions to stall in the inevitable pushing of the buttons. When Sandra and Timothy had returned home from the doctor's appointment yesterday, Sandra dug around in the fireproof lock box that she kept hidden in her bedroom closet for *the* papers. The legally binding document that she signed about seven years ago, in which Sandra received a large monthly stipend for Timothy until he reached the legal age, in turn for her silence and other stringent conditions. There were a number of them listed here, but out of all of them, two conditions remained the most troublesome. The first was never to contact Timothy's father for any matter or for any reason, and the second was that Timothy, and anyone else, were never to know, meet, or understand who his biological father was. If Sandra voided any of these conditions, then the monthly stipend and flow of money would stop and quite possibly, Sandra would face a counter lawsuit for voiding the conditions of the agreement. Yet, Sandra did not care. Instead, she pushed the buttons and with a deep breath; she put the phone to her ear and waited.

In his office, Pastor Waxworth leaned back into his office chair and put his feet up on his desk. He put the glass of bourbon to his lips and took a long and glorious sip of the heavenly distilled liquid. As the liquid chased down his throat and warmed his soul, he smacked his lips, smiled and placed the drink glass on a gold coaster on his desk. The coasters were custom fitted in order to fit the faceted glass from his wet-bar. The coaster had his initials cast into the surface of the gold and the glass had those same initials imprinted onto the glass.

The scintillating taste of success lingered upon his lips and tongue.

No sooner did the glass land on the coaster, did Pastor Waxworth's cellphone jingle and buzz and the dial lit up with the numbers of a local telephone number. Rutherford stared at it for a second or two, trying hard to figure out whom it was that was calling him. Very few individuals even had this number, and those who he programmed into his contact list would indicate the name as well as the number on the screen. This was a random number . . . local, but random, and there was no name associated with the number. It was then that he recalled the gorgeous blonde woman. A gorgeous blonde who sat in the front row on Saturday evening. Young, tall, lean, with an amazing chest, wide hips, and a gorgeous face. A young woman with religious needs in her heart, hidden lust in her soul and admiration for the work of Pastor Waxworth filling her mind. He had told Claude to slip her this number. This was how it initially worked. This is how he lured the innocent and admiring women into his lair and then after attending to their "religious" needs, and once he hooked them under his charm and spell, he told them that their love and bodies were gifts from God and they needed to share them. Share them in order to fulfill the desire that God instilled in their hearts. In order to prosper, of course. Yes indeed, share their bodies with him. It was a formula of success that had always been successful for him in his various conquests. Now it was time to lay the groundwork for another conquest. A smile flowed across his mouth, and wonderful visions of undressing the young woman and then enveloping his body with the gorgeous young woman entered his mind as he pushed the green button to answer the call.

While he did so, he spoke in his best, seductive and melodious voice, "Hello, this is Pastor Waxworth."

His smile faded and his heart stopped for a moment as he instantly recognized the voice on the other end of the line. It was a young woman, and it was a conquest, but it was not the conquest that he had in mind for today.

Or any other day.

It was a voice and a reminder from the past that he thought was gone forever from his life.

"Rutherford," the voice spoke haltingly and laced with some panic, "I am very sorry for bothering you, but it is an emergency. I do realize what I am risking by calling you, but I have to call. It is Timothy . . . he is very ill and I am afraid that without help from you . . . it would be. . .."

Pastor Waxworth interrupted her and yelled into the phone, "Risking! Risking! Hell, yes, you are not risking. I assure you it is now past risk. You have broken the rules. I do not care about Timothy, or you, or anything else to do with your world. You were a nice piece of ass for me and Timothy means zilch to me. I paid for your silence and you just screwed it all up! Better, pack your bags, honey, and get ready for eviction because the gravy train just stopped. The next contact you will receive is from my lawyer!"

Pastor Waxworth angrily pushed the end button on his cellphone and then tossed it onto his desk. He picked up the glass of fine bourbon and downed the remainder of the liquid in one shot. No more savoring of fine whiskey. No more smiles. No more basking in the glory of financial spreadsheets. Instead, he hit the speed dial button on his desk telephone for his attorney.

Attorney Gordon Aldrich picked the telephone call up on the first ring. Everyone who worked for Pastor Rutherford Bartholomew Waxworth picked up his calls immediately.

"Gordon! I am coming over to your office. Right now!"

Gordon paused and thought for a second before answering. He surmised the worst. With Rutherford that was always the best way to handle things. Assume the worst and work backwards from there.

"Okay, I am here. Do you want to tell me what is going on with you? Why are you screaming at me?"

"Hell, yeah, I want to tell you! Hell, yeah, I am going to scream. I am mad as hell. The bitch just called me. Out of the friggin' blue."

Gordon cleared his throat and because he was his trusted attorney, Gordon could say certain things and get away with the words and statements that other persons could not say to Rutherford.

"Okay, which bitch?"

"Don't be a smart-ass, Gordon!" Pastor Waxworth shouted into the telephone.

"I am not. I assure you that it is a legitimate question. I know certain things about you. One of which, is, well, let us just say that you are not so good at keeping certain things contained within your pants."

Now, it was Pastor Waxworth's turn to pause on the line and ponder the words of his attorney. In his heart, he knew that Gordon was correct in his statement.

With a deep breath and now under better control,

Pastor Waxworth explained, "Yeah, well, okay. Point made. Carrington called me. Just now."

"I see. Why, in the name of hell, did you answer the call? I have constantly told you to screen all your calls. It gets you in a world of shit and I can only do so much to pull you out of these situations."

With a nervous cough and while picking up his empty glass and heading for the wet-bar for a refill, Rutherford admitted, "I thought it was this hot chick that was at the Saturday evening service. I told Claude that she was in my sights and for him to give my cell number to her. Man, Gordon, her body is amazing."

The attorney sighed on the other end. His conscience told him that this man was just simply no good; yet, his bank account told him that he needed to endure his distaste for the man and his evil ways. Dealing with this level of a wretched example of a human being was just not what he envisioned when he went to law school. Mustering up some words was not easy after listening to his most lucrative client's statement, but somehow Gordon did so.

"Well, it is exactly that sort of thinking that put you where you are right now and will continue to do so. I can only do so much to cover your tracks. Stop thinking with your male body parts and use your mind a bit more. What do you want to do with Miss Carrington?"

Pastor Waxworth poured his bourbon. This time, it was a generous pour. Almost to the brim of the glass.

Without further hesitation, Rutherford instructed his attorney, "I want to cut her off right now of all support, all money, the housing, the medical benefits . . . everything! She broke the agreement!"

Gordon loudly sighed again and then with great effort, he managed some words, "Yes, please, come over so we can talk this out some more. We should have these types of conversations one-on-one and only in private. Before we hang up, tell me, did she say why she even called?"

"Oh, some kind of bullshit about an emergency and the stupid kid being ill. I cut her off before she went on with any information."

As soon as he said the words, a slight pang of guilt crept into Pastor Waxworth's heart. Even for his corrupted heart and soul, the words stung with their incredible coldness and meanness. After all, the boy was his own blood son. Quickly shaking off any influence of sympathetic thoughts, Rutherford listened for his attorney's reply.

"Are you not curious about the emergency?"

"No! I am not. The kid is just the product of his mother having the body of a goddess, an untrustworthy condom, and my wayward sperm. Curious . . . no! I wish the kid stayed in my sack!"

As soon as the words left his lips, Rutherford tilted the glass and took a long sip of the bourbon. He felt the numbness of the drink creeping into his soul. He needed the numbness now. For some reason, after listening to Gordon's question, his mind whirled with guilt and he never felt guilt.

Ever.

"Okay, please come over. We can discuss this. I think there might be an emergency clause in the agreement. I will pull the documents and review them while you are riding over here."

As soon as Pastor Waxworth heard the attorney's word, he felt his blood boil over and while he did not scream into the phone, it was very close to a scream, "An emergency clause! You better hope there is no emergency clause or you can kiss your sorry ass goodbye!"

"Calm down, Rutherford. You reviewed the document, approved it, and signed it. I only drafted it."

Rutherford did not answer Gordon; instead, he slammed the telephone down into its cradle without any further words. He then sank into his chair and his body heaved with the heaviness of the conversation and the thoughts overtaking his mind. He grabbed the glass once again, took another large sip, and followed with a burning swallow of the potent bourbon. Now the previously smooth bourbon took on a harsh and powerful burn. Strangely, it was not an ordinary burn, but now, the whiskey felt as if the distiller plucked the liquid from the flames of Hell as it burned all the way down his throat and, seemingly, to his toes. Rutherford picked the cellphone that he previously tossed aside, dialed up Claude's number and punched it on the dial.

When Claude answered, Pastor Waxworth instructed his driver to, "Pull the car around. We are going to Gordon's offices."

When he ended the call, the rest of the bourbon was history. When he slammed the glass into the custom golden coaster, with his initials emblazoned upon it, all that remained in the glass was a swirl of brown liquid.

Sandra Carrington sat in her chair and hung her head while staring at the number fading away on her cellphone. She could not withhold the tears. Everything was so wrong. How did she allow this to happen? To be so stupid to fall for the evil ways of such a vile man. A man who told her she was beautiful, who said that God smiled upon their relationship, that he was not married to Jess Waxworth and this was all part of God's plan. His charm swept her off her feet at such a vulnerable time, and she really believed that it was true love. Yet Timothy was born out of the relationship. God granted a gift within her misguided disguise of love. Timothy was her entire life. Her entire world. Now, her sobs and her grief came hard and heavy. Her entire body shook.

It was a product of the pain leaving her soul.

Timothy was watching television in the other room, yet his mother's sobs were so loud, the young boy heard them and he climbed to his feet to see what was wrong. He knew that he was very ill. He had been ill for as long as he could recall. Despite his weakness and his sickness, the young boy's soul was full of love and kindness. He walked into the room, put his arm around his mother, and gently comforted her.

Thinking that it was his illness that caused his mother's pain, Timothy said, "Please don't cry, Mother. I will get well. I will feel better soon. I will pray to feel better. God will hear me praying."

Sandra leaned over, embraced her son, and whispered, "Yes, Timothy, God will hear our prayers. God will never abandon us. Ever."

Pastor Rutherford Bartholomew Waxworth stomped and plowed his way toward the open rear door of the polished black limousine. Fueled by the potent whiskey and enraged by the call from Sandra Carrington and the sudden turn of events, his anger consumed him. His personal bodyguard, driver and loyal employee, Mr. Claude Buxton, stood stoically beside the open door of the limousine waiting for his boss to arrive. Yet in the wild frenzy of activity since Pastor Waxworth received the phone call and then with no prior warning or notice, summoned Claude; both men did not see that there was another man present. It was as if the strange man appeared out of nowhere. An immense man, an ominous man, and Claude, although taken by surprise, held his ground and did his job. His fierce loyalty to Pastor Waxworth and his steady and lucrative paycheck were both about to be tested. When the strange man appeared and stood next to the driver's door of the limousine, Claude reacted. He held his hand up to Pastor Waxworth to show for him not to walk any closer, and then Claude turned and confronted the man. As he did so, he felt his chest rise and fall. Claude Buxton was a large and powerful man. He was a fearless veteran of combat action in the military, a man who was in the gym every day, a man who other men would not tangle with or even entertain the thought of crossing. Yet, the sight of this man caused Claude to freeze in his steps. Claude's eyes scanned and studied the man standing in front of him and he felt sweat instantly break out and roll down his back. His custom-fitted black suit felt ten sizes too tight and instinctively Claude tapped his left shoulder to make sure his holstered weapon was still there.

It was still there.

While studying the stranger standing close to him, Claude recalled some radio chatter and testimony from the security crew during this past Saturday's worship service, when they spoke of and confronted an immense stranger at the services. A stranger dressed all in black. A stranger wearing a black hat with a wide brim on his head. Claude could not help but to think that this was the same man, and this was trouble. Despite Claude's large size and powerful build, the stranger standing in front of Claude made him look small. The man towered over Claude. His frame and build were powerful, yet tall and lean, and the man stood there silently and ominously. He was dressed all in black; he wore a black vest covering a perfectly pressed black buttoned-up shirt, and his sharply creased black trousers had not a single ripple or a wrinkle in them. On his feet, he wore polished black boots, polished to such a high luster that the sunlight reflected brightly in the shine of his boots. There was nothing out of place on this man, not a wrinkle, in fact, nothing at all. He was impeccable, immaculate; he wore on his face, a finely trimmed beard, closely framing a perfectly chiseled face, and he stood silently while watching with dark, piercing black eyes. On his head, he wore a black hat with a wide brim, pulled down to where his facial features were not easily seen, but still slightly visible.

Standing in front of Claude Buxton and in the path of Pastor Waxworth was the quiet stranger in the black hat.

"Look, pal, this is private property and Pastor Waxworth does not meet fans without appointments or sign any autographs. I am going to have to ask you to leave," Claude said while poking his finger in the direction of the stranger.

The quiet stranger did not react, nor say a word, or move a muscle. He just stood there while staring ahead at them with his piercing dark eyes burning holes in their souls. Rutherford sensed some sort of danger with the presence of the ominous stranger. He ducked behind Claude, and he kept his hand on the top of the open rear door of the limousine. Pastor Waxworth debated his options. He thought that he could dash back into the building and allow Claude to handle the immense stranger, or a better option seemed to be to duck into the vehicle, close and lock the door and escape the potential action. Yet, his curiosity as to why the strange man was here, and his trust in the skills of his loyal bodyguard, kept him from escaping right away.

"I don't want to have to tell you again or escalate this to another level, or use some other type of influence, so once more, pal, I am gonna ask ya to leave. This is private property. Get your big ass out of here!"

Suddenly, the air all around them turned cold and grew colder and colder until it reached the point of a deep freeze. The quiet stranger in the black hat stood there in and amongst the cold air, still staring straight ahead without moving his eyes. Claude and Rutherford stood shocked, while shaking and holding their arms around their bodies in a vain attempt to warm themselves. Claude worked his arm free and worked his arm across his frozen chest while reaching for his weapon. His hand reached for the handle of the holstered gun and just before he could wrap his frozen fingers around the gun's handle, the quiet stranger held his hands in the air and the freezing air immediately dissipated and the temperature returned to normal. The quiet stranger stomped his right foot upon the ground and the ground shook and quaked as Claude and Rutherford held onto the vehicle to prevent their bodies from toppling over and falling to the ground.

Finally, the stranger spoke, "I am not your pal. Do not bother with your weapon. It will not help you, nor will your weapon fire. I have no quarrel with you, Claude Buxton. Yet, you stand in the way of good and you choose to protect evil. Your courage holds your feet to the ground, so I will move you, but I will try to not injure you."

Since he no longer shook in frozen fear, Claude drew his weapon, pointed it at the stranger and pulled the trigger. The weapon did not fire. More frantic pulls and squeezes to the trigger proved the stranger correct. The gun did not fire. With one quick move, and with Claude resisting in futility with all his power and strength, the quiet stranger in the black hat picked Claude up as if he was a feather, held him high in the air and with one toss, threw Claude across the asphalt of the parking lot. A now horrified, Rutherford moved to jump into the vehicle and slam the door closed, but the stranger was too quick and Rutherford too slow. The stranger pulled at the door of the limousine and the door came off the hinges as if the stranger was tearing tissue paper in his hands. The stranger tossed the door aside, and it bounced and landed hard on the parking lot.

Claude rolled around on the ground and made a vain attempt to get to his feet, but while his mind might have been willing, his strength to do so was gone.

Rutherford sat inside the vehicle, with his hands held up over his face, quivering in fear and trembling in utter horror as the stranger loomed over him.

While the stranger pointed his finger in the direction of Pastor Waxworth, the words came out powerfully and melodiously, "I could wave my hands and turn you and this empire of evil into ashes, but you have a mission. You need to once more, become who you really are. From here on and forever, Pastor Kenneth Greene, until you return to your original vows, until you do what is right, what is good, and what is just, you will only know one Bible verse. It will haunt you, day and night. It will be all you see and envelop all that you do. For you cannot pick a fig from a thistle."

"Who are you? What are you?" Pastor Waxworth asked with a voice laced in horror and shock.

"I am who you could never imagine that I am."

The stranger pointed once more at Rutherford. He turned and he walked briskly away. Rutherford held his chest as his heart felt as if it was going to pound right out of his chest and Claude slowly picked his battered body off the ground. Both of the horrified men remained in shock. They watched the stranger walk away, and they both listened as the metal tips of the quiet stranger in the black hat sounded loudly across the ground. They watched until he went out of sight and they could no longer hear the distinctive sound of the metal tips of his boots hitting the ground.

Pastor Rutherford Bartholomew Waxworth lay wide-awake in his bed. Fear overwhelmed him, and the dark eyes and words of the stranger haunted him. As soon as the words left the stranger's mouth, Rutherford immediately recognized the stranger's biblical quotations. He might be a fraud now, but at one time, he was a man who feared God, and he knew, and still knew, the Bible inside and out. He knew what the scripture said, and he knew the implication of the words. He had no idea who or what the stranger was, but he had a feeling that where he came from was a place beyond his wildest imagination.

Unlike many of his same type of fellow televangelists and preachers of the Prosperity Gospel, Mr. Kenneth Greene was a highly educated and an ordained pastor. Rutherford Bartholomew Waxworth was a fraud. Kenneth Greene was a man who came from a long line of ministers of the word, his grandfather, his father, and now, he was ashamed to admit, the last in line was the fraud known as Pastor Rutherford Bartholomew Waxworth. Right now, everything about his life and his world was a fraud. Jess was not his wife. Not on paper, nor in real life. Jess was a singer and professional actress. That was another charade. A pretend marriage for the success of the mission. Mr. Lionel Shearing arranged for Jess to be Pastor Waxworth's "television wife" as Lionel had arranged most of his success. Until he met Lionel, Kenneth Green had been a humble preacher with a gift for charismatic sermons and for captivating his audience, but his intention at that time was honest and good. He wanted to be a pastor and continue the family legacy of preaching the good word. His grandfather and his father were Presbyterian, but Kenneth chose the nondenominational path with an organization that retained some vague Presbyterian ties, but still, his original intentions were solid. His handsome good looks and captivating words and ways propelled him to the forefront during a mission overseas. A mission where he met Mr. Lionel Shearing. Lionel convinced Kenneth that they could conquer the world, and they did. Somewhere along the way, Pastor Kenneth Greene was lost, and, in his place, the evil creation known as Pastor Rutherford Bartholomew Waxworth took over his mind and his body. He knew that even from Heaven his grandfather and father must look upon him with terrible disdain.

Now all he could see and hear was what the quiet stranger in the black hat foretold to him. That verse from the Gospel of Matthew that the stranger extracted the words from in order to haunt him in both his vision and in his ears. The words of the biblical verse floated in front of his eyes, and the powerful voice of the stranger resounded repeatedly in his head. All he could focus upon was the verse. A verse that warned the world to be wary of false prophets. A verse that now constantly echoed within his mind, unceasingly since the words left the lips of the stranger.

Gordon had called rather frantically when Rutherford and Claude did not arrive at his offices. Rutherford told him the strange tale of the encounter with the ominous man dressed all in black. At first, Gordon chalked it up to the excessive consumption of the prized bourbon that Rutherford drank, as did Lionel too. They accused Claude of dipping into the booze too, and Gordon and Lionel dismissed the encounter and testimony to drunkenness. That is until Rutherford and Claude showed both men the damage to the limousine. That is when some doubt crept into the bizarre event, the validity, and the circumstances of the stranger's visit. Claude verified the story in all of its entirety, showed them the bruises and cuts on his body from the toss of the stranger and without any further hesitation, Claude handed in his resignation too. Lionel, of course, not wanting to allow anything to stop the wheels of the gravy train, simply downplayed the entire event and chalked it up to a fanatical follower of Pastor Waxworth's ministry. He emphasized that all of this was the result of an encounter with an unusually powerful and strong individual, as well as a touch of booze to cause an exaggeration of the events, and moreover, to a jammed and malfunctioning gun.

Rutherford sat up and while on the edge of the bed, he reached for the switch on the lamp that sat on the nightstand next to his bed. He flipped the switch on and then opened the drawer of the nightstand next to this bed and after opening it; he removed a copy of The Holy Bible from the drawer. Nervously, Rutherford fingered the well-worn cover and then, after a deep breath and mustering some courage, he opened it. The shock when every single page had the same verse printed upon it was not only overwhelming—it was incomprehensible. His eyes nearly popped out of his head, as he frantically flipped each page of the Bible and every page had the same verse repeatedly printed upon it. Page after page. From Exodus to Revelation were all the same. The Gospel of Matthew, Chapter 7, Verse 16.

His Bible had no other words.

None.

As of that very moment, Pastor Rutherford Bartholomew Waxworth ceased to exist, but instead, Pastor Kenneth Greene returned. Pastor Greene carefully closed the Bible, and he reverently replaced it into the drawer. He flipped the light off and then in the darkness; he fell upon his knees and prayed until he sobbed for repentance and forgiveness. He prayed for a new life. He prayed for those he deceived, for those that he hurt, and for those that he took advantage of in this world. Mostly, he prayed for restoration of his soul and for the guidance to do the right thing.

Out on the street in front of the mansion where Kenneth Greene sat praying on his bedroom floor, a moonlit shadow danced across the street. It was the shadow of a man. An immense man, and the only indication that he was actually there, was the fact that the boots that he wore upon his feet made a distinctive clicking noise as the metal tips of the boots sounded loudly upon the pavement. The noises from his boots echoed, rose, and seemed to float in the air everywhere, until the sound faded away into the darkness of the night.

It was a Saturday evening and Pastor Rutherford Bartholomew Waxworth was nowhere within the Golden Cathedral of Praise. In his place, Pastor Kenneth Green stood in the pulpit on the stage of the glorious Golden Cathedral of Praise, all five-hundred-thousand square feet of it. An overflowing crowd of sixteen-thousand worshipers sat in their seats in the arena section of the cathedral, hanging on every word that the handsome, charismatic and overwhelming, Pastor Greene said while he stood in front of his ornate pulpit of glitter, laced with silver and gold trim. Another audience of millions of dedicated followers, tuned in on televisions and radios across the world to do the same.

What none of them realized was that Pastor Rutherford Bartholomew Waxworth no longer existed.

Pastor Greene stared longingly into the television camera with his right-hand man, his supposed longtime friend, and producer, Mr. Lionel Shearing, jabbering away in his earpiece while he gave instructions to the camera operator as well as to Kenneth. The camera operator might have been paying attention to the gibberish of words, but Pastor Greene was not.

All that Pastor Greene could do was to focus his eyes upon the Teleprompter in front of the stage. A screen that displayed in big, bold, block letters, The Gospel of Matthew, Chapter 7, Verse 16. He knew that particular verse was not what the teleprompter was supposed to be displaying, but a force beyond anyone's control or wildest imagination was now controlling their entire world.

Pastor Greene smiled and then he began to speak, "I would please ask for everyone seated here to open your Bibles and for those tuning in on television and listening in on their radios to open their Bibles too. Please turn to the Gospel of Matthew, Chapter 7, Verse 16."

Lionel was puzzled as to the change in the program, and his co-producer, as well as the teleprompter operators all chimed in on the headset, asking as to what was happening.

Lionel keyed his transmit button and asked, "Ah, Rutherford, what the hell are you doing here? Follow the script now. There is no time for preaching extra bullshit."

Pastor Green did not answer.

There was no Rutherford here.

"You will read here in your Bibles that this verse tells us of the horrors of following false prophets and God warns of the wolves hiding within sheep's fur. Well, I, my weary friends, am such a wolf. I am a scoundrel of the lowest kind. I am a deceiver and a fraud. I am here to repent and to tell you that I am a false prophet. My name is not even Rutherford Bartholomew Waxworth. I am Pastor Kenneth Greene. However, what I really am, is a man of deep sin. A man of fraudulent ways, and a man, who asks for your humble forgiveness. There is no prosperity for any of you for following my evil ways and for following me. There is only despair. I am a wretched and despicable human being. As the verse tells us . . . you cannot pick a fig from a thistle."

The audience sat in shock and Lionel almost fell out of his chair in the production office as his headset exploded with the staff erupting in shock too. Lionel screamed into the headset microphone as the cameras whirled and twirled in all turned in all directions and they shut down Pastor Greene's microphone.

"Cut it! Cut it! Go to a commercial! Bring Jess out to sing! Tell Jess to announce that Rutherford took ill, and he is feverish! Shit! TELL THEM SOMETHING!"

A week later, Pastor Kenneth Greene lay in a hospital bed. The tubes hooked to a needle stuck in the vein of his left arm pumped some pain medication into his system, but there was still some pain throbbing within his body. Despite the pain, his soul was warm and his mind was clear.

Pastor Kenneth Greene now only had one kidney, and right now, Pastor Greene never felt better in his entire life. His eyes focused and despite the intense levels of pain medication in his system, he spotted the lovely Miss Sandra Carrington standing next to his bed. He smiled at her, and Sandra smiled back.

"How do you feel?" Sandra asked.

"I feel renewed. I feel wonderful," Kenneth answered. "How is Timothy?" He asked.

Sandra smiled, and she gently took Pastor Greene's hand in hers and held it warmly.

"He is doing amazingly well. He is beyond fine. Doctor Ashworth is thrilled. Your kidney, or ah, the new kidney, already produced urine. Doctor Ashworth said it is a miracle for that to happen so soon. A miracle, for which he has no explanation."

Kenneth studied her beautiful face, her eyes filling with tears, and he knew the truth. It *was* a miracle. All of this was. God's plan evolved in front of their eyes. He closed his eyes and prayed quickly and silently in his mind, 'Thank you, quiet stranger in black. Whoever you are.'

"Thank you, Kenneth. Thank you for you. Doctor Ashworth said that Timothy's life span just doubled and then some and with the technology evolving so rapidly, his hope for a longer life is very good and we think that. . .."

Pastor Greene interrupted Sandra and said, "He will live a long and wonderful life. Together, we will make sure that it is so."

"Together?" Sandra asked, while her eyebrows narrowed a bit.

Kenneth nodded and said, "Yes, together. If you will forgive me, I would like to be a part of Timothy's life. Perhaps, even a large part of your life too. Start anew. It will not be easy. I am mostly penniless now, but God will watch over us. I will work hard. We will pray. I will find a new church. Find my way. I hope you can understand and forgive me. Can you search your heart and do so?"

Sandra emphatically nodded, and she gently leaned over and kissed the cheek of Pastor Kenneth Greene.

"I forgive you and I know that God smiles upon you, Pastor Kenneth Greene, and that God will empower us to move on. Always and forever to move on."

Pastor Greene smiled widely and asked, "So, does this mean that, I . . . or rather, we . . . have a chance to be a family. To love?"

"We have more than just a chance. I feel your profound repentance and I feel your love. Moreover, I know what I feel in my heart right now. Besides, I think it is God's plan."

Out in the hallway, an immense man stood near the nurse's station on the floor where both Timothy and Kenneth were recovering from their surgeries. He stood waiting for a nurse to walk down the hallway and arrive at her post. At first, the nurse was aghast at the size of the ominous man dressed all in black. However, when she took a deep breath and studied the man, her entire body relaxed. In fact, she felt an incredible warmth overtake her body while she studied his handsome face and amazing features. The man was dressed all in black, he wore a black vest covering a perfectly pressed, black buttoned-up shirt, and his sharply creased, black trousers had not a single ripple or a wrinkle in them. On his feet, he wore polished black boots, polished to such a high luster that the lights from the hallway could be seen reflecting in the shine of his boots. There was nothing out of place on this man. Not a wrinkle—nothing at all. He was impeccable, immaculate.

His features were dark; he wore on his face, a finely trimmed beard, closely framing a perfectly chiseled face, and he stood silently while watching with dark, piercing black eyes. On his head, he wore a black hat with a wide brim, pulled down to where his facial features were not easily seen, but still slightly visible.

He was the quiet stranger in the black hat.

The nurse could not help but to think how remarkably handsome this stranger was, yet it seemed as if he magically appeared from a bygone era.

Recovering, the nurse smiled and asked, "Can I help you, sir?"

The stranger smiled back and said in a glorious, deep, and melodious voice, "Yes, please. Would you be so kind as to give this to Pastor Greene when he is awake and feeling better?"

The stranger handed the nurse a small piece of paper, unsealed, but neatly folded in half.

"Yes, of course. In fact, if you wait a few minutes, you might be able to see him soon. . .."

The nurse stopped speaking when she noticed the stranger shaking his head to indicate no.

"I see. Well, then, why, yes, of course. I will make sure that Pastor Greene receives it. If I might ask . . . who, shall I tell him, left the paper?"

The stranger's eyes wandered around a bit, and the nurse marveled at how his dark eyes sparkled and seemed as if they were full of glory. The nurse could not help but to think that in all of her years she had never seen a more handsome man, or more captivating eyes.

"A friend. Please, tell the good pastor that a friend came by to see him one, last, time."

The nurse studied the stranger's face one more time, and she smiled and commented, "Ah, yes, a friend. However, for the last time? Are not friends forever?"

"They are. So is God. So is love. So are hope and joy

and peace."

The nurse smiled, nodded, and said, "Indeed. Yes. I will be very happy to take care of this for you."

The stranger smiled. He leaned over and tipped his hat to the nurse, quickly spun on his heels and began to walk away. As he did so, the nurse listened to and admired the sharp sound that the metal tips of his boots made upon the hallway floor.

She decided to sneak a peek at the content of the paper. Something inside of her told her to read it and that it was perfectly fine to do so, too. The nurse gently opened the paper to see a Bible verse emblazoned upon it.

Revelation, Chapter 3, Verse 20.

The nurse smiled because she knew her Bible verses.

Many nurses do.

They tend to come in handy in their critical line of work.

While the good nurse leaned over the desk to watch the exit of the stranger, the words fell from her lips, "I stand at the door and knock. . .."

She recited the rest of the verse, watched, and listened, until she could no longer hear the sound of the metal tips of his boots as they struck the floor and the stranger slowly and gloriously disappeared from her view.

THE END

Echo of a Requiem

Mr. Alastair Sterling Cocklefield sat rather stoically in a guest chair opposite the desk of his manager within the manager's office. His manager sat in his executive chair, nervously fiddling with random pieces of paper on his desk. Alastair recognized the nervous attempt to shuffle nonsense as a hapless attempt at diversion.

This was going to be bad news. Just another cog in the bad news wheel. Sadly, bad news and wide elements of despair had become almost ordinary within the life of Alastair. As of late, he almost expected it, and this news was not going to be much of a surprise. When his manager spoke the words that Alastair knew he was going to say, the words became a blur. Almost as if the manager was speaking in another language. There was little to no need to pay very much attention to them. After all, the young man currently sitting opposite of Alastair was the store's fourth manager in about three years. The business ate them up, spit them out and funneled in the next victims in what seemed as if it was some bizarre assembly line of managers with business degrees.

"Let's face it, Alastair, this business keeps changing and the retail world is under tremendous pressure. Most businessmen simply do not wear suits to work any longer. Blah, blah, blah, blah."

The words all ran together while lost in a maze of rhetoric. His words sounded as if they were gibberish because his mind could not endure the pain of capturing all that the manager was conveying.

Alastair breathed in deeply, and then he exhaled and felt his body relax. Some pain left his body. He grew impatient and just wanted the young man to get to the heart of the matter and then they could move on with the next phase of their lives.

"I am sorry to tell you this. I know the last six months or so have been very difficult for you. However, we. . .."

'Difficult?' Alastair thought, 'hmm . . . that might be immensely understated yet, the one word does sum it up. Difficult. Or tragic, or painful, or devastating.' All those words work rather well, too.

"We have little to no need any longer for an on-site tailor or a custom-fitter for men's suits and an expert here at the store to make immediate alterations. The business just is not there. The traffic does not drive the expectations to have immediate alterations. We can send the few suits that we sell out for alterations and have them back within a day or so. I am afraid your position is, well, from a bygone era. Your English heritage and proper behavior, impeccable dress and amazing skills at fitting and alterations has been a huge asset for the store. I heard the stories of the years and years of businessmen, coming here to Hanley's Department Store to see the gentle and kind man with the English accent that made their suits fit so perfectly. You have done so much for the store's reputation, but I am afraid that part of this business is long gone now. The modern era brought so many changes and casual business attire overwhelmed our sales. We need to retool the area where we have suits and radically condense it. Afterwards, we need to bring in something chicer, more fashionable. You know, how management is under pressure to maximize the retail square footage of the store." Finally, the young man's eyes wandered around the office and he paused in his rambling explanation. Alastair could not help but notice how difficult it was for the manager to make eye contact with his eyes. Therefore, he knew the young man felt the pain and difficulty of the conversation and his actions. Alastair could also not stop his eyes from noticing the manager's attire. He, too, dressed casually, and in Alastair's professional opinion, it did not suit his appearance very well. The old tailor and fitter sighed while recalling how the store manager used to dress in the finest suits that Hanley's Department Store sold and how Alastair fit the proud men into their suits, so they looked as if they were movie stars rather than store managers.

Perhaps this young man was correct. It was now a bygone era.

Alastair's eyes followed the young man's mouth, and he thought, 'Oops, okay, he is speaking once more.'

"I am so sorry. Today, will be your last day here, Alastair. There is a generous severance for you based upon your amazing thirty-seven years of service with the store. I wish you all the best and please, do not hesitate to contact me if I might help in any manner."

Alastair leaned back, breathed in deeply, and exhaled in a long, painful dispelling of pain as the rest of the manager's words hung in the air as if they were icicles hanging off the edges of frozen cliffs of solid rock. The rest of the manager's words sounded just as they did a few minutes earlier, "Blah, blah, and blah." Then, in a collapse of all emotions, the final word reverberated in the air and it sounded just as all the rest did.

"Blah."

All the words shook Alastair to his soul and stole what remained of his heart.

The long and agonizing walk to where Alastair parked his car in the parking garage was a walk of despair. Pieces of his heart littered the asphalt and concrete pathways and the shards of shattered memories unmercifully pounded within his mind.

Each step was painful.

Each step came with a reminder of lost times and the reaping of what was sown by a cruel fate out of Alastair's control. Yet, as of late, there were so many things out of his control. So much desperation that remained out of his ability to reach or correct. It was almost unfathomable.

Just when Alastair thought that, it could not become much worse . . . it became that much worse.

Alastair Sterling Cocklefield was sixty-two years of age. Almost six months to the very day that his longtime employer bid Alastair farewell, he lost his beloved wife to a long battle with the horror known as cancer.

They had been together since they were sixteen years old. Since they were love struck teenagers in their homeland of England, and those glorious memories of when they were so young, followed Alastair wherever he went.

They married at nineteen and everyone around them and in their lives told them that they were too young. It was a mistake, and that the marriage would not last. Forty-five years or so later, they proved everyone wrong. Alastair and Meredith only had one child, a precious little girl, who died shortly after childbirth, and the heartbreak of the loss of their little Annie, would not allow them to have another child. Ever.

And so it goes, and now, Alastair found himself alone, stuck somewhere between the dead and the living and the uncaring. At this point of his life, that was not where Alastair ever thought that he would be. The loss of his wife tore his heart apart, unceasingly and relentlessly gnawing at his soul. The pain and loneliness worked at him, day-by-day, piece-by-piece, and it was beyond agonizing.

He left nothing on the table in an effort to save his darling Meredith. When the medical insurance ran out, he spent all of their savings on her medical care. He sold their house, sold the newer car and bought an old bucket of bolts of a used car, he cashed in savings bonds, drained their savings account, and he turned in his pension fund savings to the medical care. Even their possessions were not safe; first, he sold their large screen television, precious jewelry and family heirlooms and other household possessions. Desperation set in rather quickly. The catastrophic finances proved to be an embarrassing and degrading experience, especially so for a man of pride and for a man such as Mr. Alastair Sterling Cocklefield was. He remarkably managed to pay most, if not all, the debts off, with just some lingering bills that the hospital agreed to allow Alastair to pay off on a term payment plan. He worked hard for all of his life and he always took good care of all of his responsibilities. Alastair would have done anything to save her; Meredith was his true love, his guiding light, his reason to live. Onward the struggle went for a very long time. Too long. The doctors would say that she was over the hump and gaining, and then it all went crashing down. Now, Alastair felt it was all unrewarding, and now, he recalled kicking mindlessly at the spent flowers on the edge of his wife's grave on the day that they buried her, in an effort to quantify and to understand all the madness of the battle.

The battle of daily life. Of the sense of it all.

Now, as he climbed into his old car, and prayed that it would start, he glanced down at the bag containing all of his personal tools of his trade, and he tossed the paperwork the human resource manager for the store gave to him, along with an envelope containing his severance check. Five-thousand dollars is nothing to sneeze at, except when you do not know where your next paycheck is coming from, the rent is due on the one-bedroom apartment he rented, or you needed to buy food, and spend money on all the other bills that haunt our lives. Mercifully, the old bomb of a vehicle started and Alastair put the transmission lever into drive and off he rolled into the sunset of his career. Five-thousand dollars for thirty-seven years of service with the store. And now, Alastair drove off for the last time.

Returning to his small apartment, Alastair filled the

teapot with water and flicked the flame on underneath the teapot. At least he still had some tea bags in the cupboard. When they run out, who knows if he will have money to buy the one pleasure that this world had not stolen from him. His eyes met the calendar on the wall of the small kitchen, and he saw that the rent was due next week. Thank goodness, he already had set that money aside, as well as some grocery money. The apartment was a seedy place, fitted with sparse, leftover furniture, from their house sale, what no one else wanted when they sold all the remaining possessions. Seedy apartments in seedy neighborhoods are all that you qualify for when your reputation and credit is less than perfect. Unfortunately, the electronic credit reports do not have stamps with explanations nor with the emotions of medical hardships that remain out of a person's control emblazoned on them.

Now Alastair had to search for a new position. He knew there is the demeaning acceptance of unemployment benefits, but that would simply be another blow to his already destroyed ego, and for a proper and prideful Englishman, just another step closer to the edge of the precipice that had become his life. Mr. Alastair Sterling Cocklefield was a garment fitter, an expert tailor, an expert at alterations and in transforming ordinary appearances into movie star appearances. Now, at sixty-two years of age, he needed to find work and rebuild his life from the shattered remnants of despair.

Yet, the question remained as to exactly how he would do this?

The young manager had correctly summarized the current conditions of his trade . . . there was little to no demand for his services. The few shops around that did tailor work and alterations were mostly single-staff operations and performed many other services in order to stay in business. Alastair knew of one such shop in his own neighborhood a few blocks away from his apartment. The shop offered dry-cleaning as well as performed laundry services along with a fold and wash service and there was a sign advertising custom alteration of garments. The establishment was a family operation, owned and operated by a Vietnamese family and when Alastair dropped off a stained dress shirt for some intense cleaning services, he noticed the small sewing machine and tailoring operation neatly tucked in the corner of the store, and his assumption was that a family member performed the tailoring services. Because of the influence of his circumstances, his heart harbored a defeatist type of attitude, the old tailor felt as if no one would hire him, and if the management of such an establishment did so, it was going to be a part-time opportunity at a very low wage or on a piecework basis.

The teapot screamed a warning of the boil within its belly and Alastair shut off the flame. While drowning a helpless tea bag in the steam and the boil, he could not help but to think that, perhaps, we live too long.

A few years into their marriage, a very young Mr. Alastair Sterling Cocklefield and his precious Meredith traveled to America in order to chase a dream. England had been very good to them, but the men of the Cocklefield family were all in the garment business. In the aftermath of World War 2, the war-ravaged mills and factories, and other businesses in England, were slow in rebuilding and rather than remaining in the business of manufacturing of garments, instead, the Cocklefield family moved into the retail end of clothing sales. Where they lived, in the Midlands of England, the larger retail stores were few and far between, and when a distant uncle told the family of the vast opportunities that America and the Metro-New York City area presented, off the family went.

His grandfather was a tailor and a fitter, as was Alastair's father and all their uncles and cousins too. For many years, America provided exactly what they expected. Some of the dreams came true until they all shattered.

Now, it was time for intense self-examination and time to pick up the pieces.

With a slow sip of the comforting tea, Alastair felt the calming influence of the magical liquid and he knew that despite the despair and the pain, there was still something left in his soul to pick up the shattered remnants of his life and continue onward.

With a glance of his eyes toward Heaven and with another sip of tea, Alastair mumbled, "My darling, Meredith, I plow ever onward."

Stocking shelves at the local grocery store was not, in Alastair's mind, exactly the definition of moving ever onward. However, when all the other options dried up, it was the only employment opportunity left. He took the wretched unemployment benefits, and when he was a few weeks away from the expiration of the checks, Alastair received a telephone call from the manager of the grocery store. The caseworker at the unemployment office kept very close tabs on his applications, and Alastair knew that he had little to no other options available. He had to take the job. "Ever onward" had landed Alastair back to the ground in a resounding "thud." Yet, despite how far away this position landed Alastair from his former job, he managed to look on the optimistic side of his current employment. The job produced a meager, but steady paycheck; it also offered medical and dental insurance as well as a retirement plan. Alastair laughed when he studied the pamphlet detailing the retirement plan because he would have to live to be close to one-hundred years of age to receive enough money to live. In between the bills and the obligations, Alastair managed to survive. The store was close enough to his apartment that he could walk to it, therefore; he saved money on fuel and maintenance on his old and slightly unreliable vehicle, and he managed, somehow, not to use all the severance money from his former job. A few thousand dollars lingered in a bank account and slowly, Alastair even paid off the last of the medical bills. Upon close and honest examination, he might have to admit that he was moving ever onward. It was a slow creep, but there was a movement.

True, he could take his government retirement benefits early and try to work part-time, but when he did the math, it was not worth it. In addition, hanging around that seedy and ragged apartment would drive Alastair crazy.

On a whim, about eight months after he lost his position at the department store, Alastair stopped by the local store in the neighborhood that performed the alterations and he introduced himself to the owners. A husband-and-wife team owned the establishment; Mr. and Mrs. Nguyen were very kind and welcoming to the offer that Alastair provided for his expertise of tailoring services. Mrs. Nguyen did most of the alterations and tailor work, but here and there, Mr. Nguyen called Alastair in for some occasional overflow work or a difficult alteration. Alastair enjoyed the occasional work because he allowed him to keep his hands in his lifetime trade.

It was a Monday morning and Alastair diligently worked on stocking shelves of canned goods in the canned food aisle. It was almost a year since his layoff and when he caught the date on the paperwork that detailed the new plan-o-gram arrangement for impulse items at the end cap of the aisle, Alastair realized that tomorrow, he would turn sixty-three years of age.

'Ha! A birthday,' he thought, 'Well, the way that his back ached from lugging the heavy hand truck full of canned goods around the store and how much his feet hurt from standing for so long, perhaps, he was better off celebrating his funeral as opposed to a birthday.'

Alastair turned to pick another case of canned tomatoes off the cart and he immediately dropped the case back onto the pile of goods and took a step back. Shock ran throughout his body as he caught sight of a man standing right next to his cart. Alastair had not heard the man approach; it was if he magically and suddenly appeared. Alastair's eyes grew wide as he studied the man standing next to him. The first thought that ran through Alastair's mind was that this was the largest human being that he had ever seen.

Immense was the word that worked the best for a description.

Mr. Alastair Sterling Cocklefield was a man of a slight build and medium height, yet this man towered over Alastair. His frame and build were powerful, yet tall and lean, and the man stood there silently and ominously. He was dressed all in black; he wore a black vest covering a perfectly pressed black buttoned-up shirt, and his sharply creased black trousers had not a single ripple or a wrinkle in them. On his feet, he wore polished black boots; polished to such a high luster that you could see the reflection of the lights of the supermarket in the shine of his boots. There was nothing out of place on this man—nothing at all. He was impeccable, immaculate. His features were dark; he wore on his face, a finely trimmed beard, closely framing a perfectly chiseled face, and he stood silently while watching with dark, piercing black eyes. On his head, he wore a black hat with a wide brim, pulled down to where his facial features were not easily seen, but still slightly visible.

Standing next to Mr. Alastair Sterling Cocklefield was the quiet stranger in the black hat.

As his former career and lifelong work overcame his thoughts, Alastair's eyes once again scanned and studied the strange man's attire and appearance. Mr. Cocklefield was aghast, in awe at such finery, such craftsmanship, such remarkable clothing. He immediately noticed the thread lines, the immaculate work, the fit, the artistry of the woven fabrics on the stranger's body. And the hat! And his boots! It was the finest attire that Alastair had ever encountered, and he immediately wanted to reach out and touch the clothing to feel the material in order to test it to determine if it felt as fine as it appeared. Alastair took a deep breath because suddenly, he was deeply jealous of the master tailor that had created such a masterpiece. Honestly, he wanted to run out of the front of the store and find a sewing shop in an attempt to recreate it. His mind captured all the details of the stranger's attire and appearance. And then, Alastair recovered, and he genuinely felt foolish at his reaction.

"Oh, my, I am quite sorry, sir, at my strange reaction." Alastair's gentle English accent laced his words while stumbling through an explanation for his behavior. "I am sorry, but you startled me . . . I did not hear you arrive."

The stranger did not speak, but a smile broke across his face. Alastair relaxed as he enveloped in some strange warmth and kindness from this immense stranger standing before him. The old tailor could not help but to admire the remarkable sparkle in the stranger's dark eyes.

Piercing eyes, but eyes full of wonder and magic.

"I also must admit that I deeply admire your attire . . . what now seems as if it was a lifetime ago . . . I worked in men's fine suits and fashion and I have never seen such fine clothes. You have my compliments, sir, as does, whoever is the creator of such finery."

Once again, the stranger only nodded, and Alastair thought how this man was certainly a man of very few words. Then again, when you looked as he did and were as large as he was, words might be optional.

"Please, may I offer some assistance, sir? Do you need to find something in the store?" Alastair asked, and as he did so, he was aware that the stranger held a small bag in his hand, a plastic bag emblazoned with the logo and name of the grocery store.

When the quiet stranger in the black hat spotted Alastair's eyes dart to the bag in his hand, the stranger held the bag out in front of his enormous body and nodded in an indication for Alastair to take the bag. Mr. Cocklefield had a puzzled look on his face at the bizarre actions and encounter, but he nodded and took the bag from the hand of the stranger. When he handed off the bag, the quiet stranger finally spoke in his deep, gloriously melodious voice.

"Happy birthday, Alastair Sterling Cocklefield. I bought and paid for the gift. The store manager is aware of this."

Alastair was shocked at the words and while remaining deeply puzzled, he opened the plastic bag, reached in, and removed a package of birthday candles. Candles such as a person would place upon a birthday cake while celebrating a birthday.

"Why, sir, my goodness, how nice of you, but I must ask, how did you know it was my birthday? Do I know you?"

The stranger did not answer, but instead, he first pointed at the nametag on the uniform shirt that Alastair wore. A tag that proudly broadcasted, "ALASTAIR" in block letters. Then, the stranger pointed to a store sign pinned to the wall behind the customer service desk that announced employee milestones and celebrations for the month. Anniversaries with the company, retirements, wedding anniversaries, and yes, birthdays. Sure enough, even without wearing his glasses, Alastair could see his name on the list as well as the date of his upcoming birthday.

"Oh well, how foolish of me. The sign is right there, and I never noticed it before now. Moreover, I imagine that it was quite easy to find the only, Alastair Sterling Cocklefield in the store."

Alastair waited for a reply from the stranger, dressed all in black. But by now, he knew he might only receive a reaction. Sure enough, the stranger only smiled and nodded. Anxious now, to figure this unusual situation out and to discover why this random stranger decided to give him birthday candles, Alastair continued to stumble through a conversation.

"Well, thank you for your extraordinary kindness, ah, ah . . . sir. Beg my pardon, but your name?"

"What comes to mind for my name?"

"Ah . . . Black. Mr. Black."

Alastair waved his hands in the air in order to encompass the entirety of the stranger's presence.

"Honestly and sincerely, I just made that up but everything about you—broadcasts black to me. Perhaps, it is my old trade calling me from the grave."

The stranger nodded and smiled.

Upon seeing the stranger's reaction and pondering his own words, Alastair's eyes grew wide once again, and he almost laughed, but held back the emotions.

"Good guess, eh? Well, anyway, thank you, but I am not sure why you gave me a birthday gift, perhaps, that is a mission of yours to spread some joy in lonely people's lives."

As expected, the stranger did not speak, but this time, he did not even react. He simply stood there with his dark eyes reflecting the warm magic contained within them.

Alastair felt awkward at admitting his loneliness and remained puzzled as to how this immense stranger could feel his emotions, but inexplicably, he felt the need to speak once more, "Mr. Black. I guess that it is quite an appropriate name. You know, it was exceedingly strange, but just before you arrived, I was thinking about how I might not celebrate a birthday tomorrow. Instead, I feel as if I need to celebrate a funeral. The way that I feel right now, instead of singing, 'Happy Birthday to You,' I need someone to sing or play a glorious requiem."

The stranger's eyes grew even darker, and it seemed as if they reflected all the lights in the store or even all the lights in the world. Alastair held tightly onto the rail of his handcart in order to steady his body and, to a certain extent, his mind too. The deep, melodious voice of the stranger returned, and it resounded in the heart and mind of Alastair.

"Then, do so. Celebrate a funeral. Afterwards, bury the

past and move ever onward. Sing a requiem and the echo of a requiem will forever inspire you towards a new life. We have to die in order to live again. Each sunset brings a new day. Therefore, celebrate a new day, rather than just a birthday, Alastair. You will find it more than worthwhile. It will be glorious to your soul."

The stranger smiled. He leaned over and tipped his hat to Alastair, and then he quickly spun on his heels and began to walk away. As he did so, Alastair heard the noise that his boots made when the metal tips of the boots struck hard against the surface of the floor tile of the store. He remained puzzled as to how he did not hear the noise previously and the stranger silently appeared. However, nothing about this strange encounter was ordinary.

Muttering aloud, while wiping his forehead of a few beads of sweat, Alastair said, "And, he knew my catch phrase too. Ever onward. My goodness. Who are you, Mr. Black?" Alastair stood and listened to and admired the sharp sound that the metal tips of his boots made upon the store's floor.

Alastair stood in amazement and enveloped in puzzlement until he could no longer hear the sound of the metal tips of his boots as they struck the floor and the stranger slowly and gloriously disappeared from his view.

He then tucked the birthday gift in the pocket of his uniform shirt.

On Tuesday, there was no birthday celebration in the small apartment of Alastair Sterling Cocklefield. Instead, there was a funeral celebration, and the echo of a requiem resounded throughout the walls of the small apartment. It was time to move on.

Alastair used the birthday candles as funeral candles.

Alastair had an idea.

A glorious idea, inspired by the words as well as the appearance and attire of the quiet stranger in the black hat. Alastair sipped a cup of tea while sitting at his kitchen table, and he sketched a pencil design on a sheet of white paper and then measured and figured out the materials that he required in order to make this idea a reality. Black pants of the finest materials, a perfectly tailored vest, the black shirt, the boots with the metal tips, and finally, the wide-brimmed, black hat. It will cost some money to create, perhaps, a large chunk of his savings, but he knew that he could do it.

His confidence abounded, and it overwhelmed his soul.

The next day, Alastair burst rather exuberantly through the front door of the Nguyen's establishment and with a wide smile of his face, proclaimed, "Mr. Nguyen. Mrs. Nguyen. Good morning. I have a business proposal for both of you to consider. . .."

Three years later, Mr. Alastair Sterling Cocklefield stood proudly in the center of his store, "Fine Fashions by Alastair" and he carefully watched one of his young assistants measure a handsome young man for his custom fitted attire. The young man had opted for the latest variation of one of Alastair's classic designs and one of his original successes. The outfit, originally named, "Mr. Black," now had the title of "Mr. Black Returns." The new design added just a hint more of the distinctive red line design that Alastair added to the original design. The hat also had a matching red design, as did the original hat, but this design was slightly larger and decidedly more intricate.

Alastair created all the designs. He proved that you are never too old to use your mind and to rebuild your life.

"Now, remember what I taught you, Samuel. Ask this young man to take a deep breath when you measure his chest and then exhale a little. Let's make sure he does not have too tight a vest over the top of the shirt," Alastair reminded his young assistant as he passed on a lifetime of experience at measuring all types and sizes of bodies. Samuel nodded and carefully instructed the customer as he grabbed his tape measure and wound it around his chest. Alastair smiled at the reaction and the satisfaction of developing an entire new generation of tailors and custom-fitters. It began as a dream and with one custom creation of the outfit known as Mr. Black. They placed the outfit on a mannequin display in the front of the Nguyen's store, and that is when all the magic occurred. One order led to ten and by the time that he split the proceeds of the first sales with the Nguyens, they had orders for ten more and Mrs. Nguyen and Alastair could not sew fast enough to keep up with the orders. The Nguyen's daughter jumped into help and before you knew it, together they had built a little fashion empire in their neighborhood. Eventually, the Nguyens sold their store and retired very happily. Alastair continued onward and now, even as his age slowly approached the ripe age of seventy, he had little intention of slowing down. He might not sew, cut, and measure as much as he once did, but his fingers and his mind were involved in all the operations. Not all the suits and outfits were black, there were so many designs and many colors now, and while he would like to think that his store on a fancy section in the downtown section of the city, did not establish a cult fashion statement, his sales told the true story. One of the famous men's fashion magazines even featured a story on Alastair, and before you knew it, the big companies began calling in an effort to buy his designs and convince Alastair to mass-produce them. He refused, and all his designs received trademarks. These creations would only ever be custom-fitted and created by master tailors and seamstresses, and while they fetched top-dollar, there remained little doubt that they were worth it.

Movie stars, star athletes, powerful businessmen, politicians, and other high rollers, all purchased custom outfits and suits so they too could proudly claim that they wore a, "Design by Alastair Sterling Cocklefield."

Even the store manager from Hanley's Department Store came by one day and purchased a suit. Alastair laughed when the manager commented how wrong he was that custom-fitted suits and men's fashions were part of a bygone era.

Mr. Cocklefield no longer lived in a seedy apartment in a seedy section of the city. He no longer drove an unreliable car, and his cupboards held wide selections of the finest teas.

The door to the store opened and in walked an immaculately dressed man. An immense man, a strikingly handsome man, and while everyone in the store turned, looked and held in a gasp, at the sight of the man, Alastair only smiled widely. The metal tips of the stranger's boots echoed across the entire store, and it seemed as if the sounds penetrated your heart and soul.

It seemed as if time now passed so slowly, and Alastair had been waiting for this meeting and this moment since he first sketched that original design on his kitchen table. Alastair walked across the floor of his store and extended his hand to meet the hand of the quiet stranger in the black hat, and the old tailor tried his best to hold back a tear. One look into the stranger's dark, piercing, yet radiant eyes, told Alastair what he needed to know.

"Greetings, my dear, Mr. Black. So nice to see you again. Honestly, I knew we would meet again, and I have looked forward to this moment."

Of course, the quiet stranger did not speak . . . the stranger only gave that now familiar nod of his head. Alastair and the stranger shook hands and Alastair stumbled once more to find the right words.

"You would think that I would be better at saying what I need to say here. I have rehearsed it enough times. Perhaps, I need to take a clue from you and say very little except for a genuine thank you. I hope you did not mind my making a fashion statement of your attire, but in my meager defense, I did add my own touches to your design." The stranger still smiled, but remained silent. Alastair spun and pointed at Samuel and asked, "Would you like a new design? The new variation of Mr. Black, adds more of a touch of red. I can have Samuel measure you. No charge of course if you would like to. . .."

When the stranger stood silently while shaking his head to indicate no, Alastair stopped speaking and he held his hands up to indicate that he understood.

"Of course, of course. Please forgive me. I am rambling a bit. I know wherever it is that you come from that you do not need much more than what you wear right now. I just want to say, Mr. Black, you were so correct in the fact that you have to die and have a funeral in order to live again. Why, I even met a lovely woman, who keeps company with me. Meredith smiles down from Heaven on our relationship and perhaps, someday, despite our ages, we will marry, but time will tell. You have taught me—that there is always time to begin anew."

The stranger nodded again and his eyes scanned the inside of the store, and when his eyes stopped on Alastair's face, the stranger finally spoke.

His gloriously melodious voice boomed throughout the store, "This is all so glorious. Wonderful. A new day dawned and a new life began. When you bury your pain of the past and open your heart, then each day, will bring you closer to where you need to be in this world. Closer to joy, closer to our hearts, and more in touch with our souls. Never lose the echo of a requiem within your soul, Alastair. Never give up again and never feel as if you are ever alone. You are never alone. I am always watching and waiting in the shadows to stand beside you. To stand beside this weary world. No matter how painful life can be, there is always hope, there is always love, and there is always a chance at a new day."

Alastair nodded and mumbled, "Ever onward, Mr. Black, or whoever you really are."

The stranger smiled. He leaned over and tipped his hat to Alastair, and then he quickly spun on his heels and began to walk away. As he did so, Alastair heard the noise that his boots made when the metal tips of the boots struck hard against the surface of the floor tile of the store. The stranger tipped his hat, smiled at Samuel and the customer as he opened the door, and disappeared into the light of the day.

"Whoa, a super cool dude, Mr. Cocklefield! Never saw such a huge man! Geez, he must be six-feet ten or something like that!" Samuel exclaimed as the customer nodded his head in fervent agreement. "Did you sell that suit and outfit to him? It is awesome! A little different from ours, but supercool. I love the metal tips on the boots. We ought to do that to all of ours."

The customer nodded, and he agreed and then proclaimed, "Hell, yeah! I want metal tips on my boots with this suit."

Alastair smiled and said, "No, Samuel, I did not sell that suit. It is an original. As far as the boots go, so shall it be. We can add the metal tips for you."

The old tailor opened the door to his store and leaned on the doorframe while listening and watching as the quiet stranger made his way into the maze of downtown activities.

Samuel was puzzled and he first looked at the customer who shrugged his shoulders and then Samuel looked at Mr. Cocklefield and asked, "An original, what?"

"An original, Mr. Black, dear Samuel. And sometimes, there is no substitute for an original."

When Alastair finally lost sight of the stranger and he could no longer hear the metal tips of his boots striking upon the sidewalk, the old tailor slowly closed the door, and pensively walked through the store.

As he walked, Alastair muttered, "Ever onward. I am quite sure that in the case of Mr. Black, there is in fact, only one original. Yes, I am not sure of too much in the world anymore, but of that, I am quite sure indeed."

THE END

If Only for a Pause

Sitting in the open air on the patio of this neighborhood bar and restaurant, while sipping some red wine, was quite an unusual experience for Mr. Mark Holiday.

He was more of a seltzer water and cola type of guy.

Red wine was not his bag. Even though this restaurant was within walking distance of his residence, and it was a fancy and exclusive dining location, this was the first time that Mark ever visited the establishment. It was Saturday evening; the restaurant was full of high rollers, dropping major coins and dollars for drinks and dinner, and even though Mark Holiday could afford it, he thought how he should have ordered a mug of their cheapest beer. However, when the cute, little server came floating by to take his order, her beauty and perkiness and amazing spirit caused his mind to sputter and for some reason, a glass of red wine popped into his mind. Now, he felt awkward and out of his element. Yet, here he was . . . out and about sipping red wine and watching the activity on the busy city street in front of him. For Mark, busy city streets were in the same category as red wine was.

Not his usual bag.

In fact, he was more of the stay at home in front of his sprawling and extensive computer gaming system type of guy. For Mark to be out and about at all was a major behavioral change. Some people, especially his mother and his father, labeled him as a recluse. Other people simply knew he was a gamer, and that is what he did with his life. Interaction with other human beings was not required when you could push a few buttons and the entire world, and a few worlds more, were at your fingertips. Yet, something inspired Mark to go out this evening. To shut down the worlds he frequented and let the power supplies cool down. Take an evening off to relax his fingers as well as his mind.

Mr. Mark Holiday was out on the town and it was very unusual.

Monumental might be a better description.

Mark Holiday was one of the world's greatest video game players, if not the greatest of them all. Usually, the so-called experts that track such things rated Mr. Mark Holiday, the number one all-around player in the world across a variety of different games, with his position alternating from number one to an occasional two or three depending upon his recent activities. A world of fantasy enveloped his life within a computer-generated world where aliens routinely invaded the Earth, where warriors and wizards tangled as one, and time meant little, if nothing, to anyone. Mark could be in ancient Rome one day fighting invaders from the east, and on the surface of the Planet Mars, fighting alien inhabitants the next day. There were no boundaries to his make-believe world, and that was perfectly fine to Mark Holiday. The "real" world was an angry, deceitful, and difficult place and Mark had seen just enough of it to know that he was perfectly happy to reside within the fantasy world of his video empire in order for him to stay happy, safe, and secure. His apartment housed his empire. The apartment was on an upper floor of a nearby apartment building, a building that was an upscale and affluent apartment building and located just a few short city blocks north of where he sat. As it is in any old city, there are areas that ebb and flow, and areas of sadness and areas of joy. Mark liked to think that this section of the city where he lived and currently sat sipping red wine on the patio of a fancy restaurant was one of the areas of joy. Inside his apartment, the best, custom-built gaming computers that money could buy blinked and constantly whirred with the magic of modern electronics and the world of fantasy and gaming. His business was very successful; millions of gamers read his newsletter, and he earned quite a large sum of money playing games in competitions for prize money, working within his own world, testing and reviewing games for prestigious manufacturers and developers of video games, and publishing his news and notes. For such a young man to be an entrepreneur in a business that he thoroughly enjoyed was enough success for Mr. Mark Holiday to relish and enjoy.

Mark Holiday was young in age and long in some type of fantasy world experience, however, it was, somehow, a strangely relevant amount of real-life experience. At twenty-nine years of age, he had seen enough of the world to know that there was not too much there to interest him. Mark was tall, lean and in a decidedly different manner, very handsome. His wavy dirty-blonde hair hung long over his collar. It was a hairstyle that most people would consider out of fashion, but Mark Holiday did not worry too much about style or locking in step with the latest trends. Mark's drum was a different type of drum to tap upon, and the drum, the drummer, and the drumsticks existed in an entirely different world.

Mark was not exactly sure as to what the sudden motivation was for him to wander out of the safety and security of his gaming world, and into this world of calculated reality, but, between sips of red wine, he carefully sat and studied it. If he was part of it, then so be it. If he was separated from it, well, then that was fine and well and good too. It was an exceedingly pleasant early summer evening. The air was dry; the wind was calm, and the temperature was cool, but not at all, chilly. It was the type of evening where you might want to wear a jacket, but in the interest of going unencumbered, you preferred not to do so. Mark Holiday was an unencumbered type of guy and therefore, he sat without a sweater or a jacket. Instead, he wore a short-sleeved tee shirt sporting the logo of his video game company. He ran an empire of electronic mayhem and Mark was the king of it all.

Mark Holiday was famous in electronic gaming circles, chat rooms, competitions and networks, computer monitors, and gaming consoles worldwide. Or, more specifically, the gaming handle of Mark Holiday was famous worldwide. "Winterkill" was famous . . . Mark Holiday . . . not so much.

As Mark sat and slowly sipped the red wine, and a touch of the wine influenced his bloodstream, it seemed as if the humdrum world would simply pass before his eyes. The restaurant sat squarely in the center of a downtown setting. A busy city street was directly in front of Mark and all the hustles and bustles associated with a busy city street sat in front of Mark, too. The traffic darting up and down the road in front of his eyes, the obnoxious taxicab with its horn blaring, a touch or two of the squeal of vehicle brakes. It was all so predictable.

The years of gaming provided Mark with cat-like skills of anticipation and reflexes to match. He could see the scenes of his video game occurring long before they flashed upon the screen, and he could easily maneuver the buttons of his hand-held game controller to wipe out enemies while simultaneously escaping to another world. His skills at doing such were what made him one of the world's greatest game players and all of his co-players and critics agreed that Mark skills were far and away above most others. He was as if he was the seasoned professional football quarterback, dropping back, studying a defense from the pocket and within a few seconds, throwing the football to a spot and threading the needle into his receiver's arms for a completed reception. Or, Mark was the ice hockey goalie, carefully watching the puck glide across the ice and anticipating a play or shot just a half-second before it occurs.

Yes, indeed, compared to the world of gaming and whirlwind speed and action of video game competition, the real world was a tad boring to Mark Holiday and oh so, predictable.

At least, to a point it was.

On the other hand, perhaps, this real-life world was not quite as predictable as Mark previously calculated, because, suddenly, an intense element of unpredictability crept into it.

He leaned forward in his seat and carefully studied a man. Not an ordinary man. No, there was nothing ordinary about this man. It seemed as if the man appeared out of nowhere. One second, the entrance to the outdoor patio area of the restaurant was vacant, and then when Mark blinked and looked over once again, this man stood there. He was without a doubt the largest human being that Mark had ever seen, but it was not only his size that caught your eye. It was his attire, his presence, the way he stood, the way he moved his eyes. Mark could not help but to think it looked as if the man had appeared out of a video game.

"Whoa . . . super cool dude," Mark spoke in a voice just above a whisper. "How cool is this guy? Not even, super cool, more as if he is mega-cool. He would be an awesome character in a game."

Winterkill took over the controls of life for Mark Holiday, and while he lifted his glass to his lips and took a small sip of the red wine, he carefully studied the man and his thoughts wandered as to whom he actually was and where he came from. The man stood stoically next to the hostess station, waiting for the hostess to return and to seat him. Winterkill sat, studied, and enjoyed the scene. Indeed, he could place this within a video game and not in reality. It was very easy for Winterkill to do so. The hostess returned and she, too, seemed slightly overwhelmed by the man's appearance and size. The man towered over the hostess. His frame and build were powerful, yet tall and lean, and the man stood there silently and ominously. He was dressed all in black, he wore a black vest covering a perfectly pressed, black buttoned-up shirt, and his sharply creased, black trousers had not a single ripple or a wrinkle in them. On his feet, he wore polished black boots; polished to such a high luster that you could see the reflection of the lights strung around the perimeter of the outdoor patio in the shine of his boots. There was nothing out of place on this man—nothing at all. He was impeccable, immaculate. His features were dark; he wore on his face, a finely trimmed beard, closely framing a perfectly chiseled face, and he stood silently while watching with dark, piercing black eyes. On his head, he wore a black hat with a wide brim, pulled down to where his facial features were not easily seen, but still slightly visible.

Standing in front of Winterkill at the hostess station for the restaurant was the quiet stranger in the black hat.

"Just one?" The hostess asked with a wide smile as her eyes studied the handsome face and the outstanding features of the stranger in black. The stranger did not speak, but he nodded. "Is out here, near the street, going to be okay for you?" The hostess asked as she waved in the general direction of the tables sitting near the edge of the patio, next to where Mark Holiday sat watching the scene unfold.

With his initial analysis of the stranger completed, and his imagination stopped whirling in a fantasy world, Winterkill yielded to Mark.

Once again, the stranger only nodded, and the hostess took a menu and she waved with her hand for the stranger to follow her toward the tables. It might have been Mark's imagination, but the hostess added an extra wiggle to her hips, a jiggle of her large chest and a seductive sway to all of her body, while she slowly led the handsome stranger to the open table. As he downed the last of his red wine, Mark smiled because he thought how the hostess did not wiggle that way for seating him. Then again, Mark did not exactly have the same appearance as the immense stranger dressed all in black did. He thought that most likely, no one did. As soon as the stranger began to walk and follow the hostess, a loud clicking noise resounded all around the patio area. All the patrons seated in the patio area of the restaurant turned to look and identify where the unique noise was coming from. Mark leaned forward because he quickly realized that the noise came from the metal tips of the boots that the stranger wore. His polished boots struck hard against the surface of the patio, and the echo of the metal tips added just another element of mystery to this dark stranger's persona.

"Man, oh, man, I gotta find a game designer to create a character like this dude. His boots are so cool," Mark said with a smile of admiration locked across his face.

"Here you go, tall, dark, and wonderfully handsome man. I love your boots. So cool," the hostess said with a wave as she pointed to the table and chair set directly next to Mark's table. "Here is the main food menu, our wine list, and the drink menu. Hailee is your server for tonight, but please do not hesitate to ask me for anything."

The hostess leaned in while the dark stranger pulled out a chair and worked his immense body into the chair. She slowly and seductively placed each of the menu cards on the table, doing all that she could to allow the moment spent seating the stranger to linger just a few seconds longer.

With a wink and a low growl in her voice, the hostess said, "And I do mean, anything."

She left the stranger with a wide smile and still, the stranger never spoke or said a single word. He only nodded, reached up, and tipped the edge of his wide-brimmed hat at the hostess. The hostess moved along and

Mark almost laughed at how she swayed and bounced away, yet the stranger in black never even moved his eyes to follow her. The hostess had all the correct parts and pieces to sway and bounce with and there were more than just a few male eyeballs following her as she walked away. But the stranger's gaze was not included in the waves of lust.

"Whoa . . . such a mega-cool-dude. That hostess is a knockout, and she does not stand a prayer of a chance with him. This dude is awesome," Mark said again in a low whisper and he was just going to track down Hailee when his server magically appeared with her cute smile and perky behavior. Other men, well, they might consider Hailee to be cute, but just an ordinary type of woman. However, to Mark Holiday, there was something special about her. To Mark, Hailee was anything but ordinary. Mark found her extraordinary.

Mark smiled and lifted his empty glass and held it in the air and said, "Perfect timing. You read my mind."

In one quick motion, Hailee scooped the wine glass up while saying, "Ah yes, a perfectly read mind. That is what I do, you know." A wide smile appeared on her face, and the lights of the patio sparkled for a brief moment in the golden earrings dangling from her ears. "I wait tables and read minds. Careful now as to what you are thinking because I can see into your mind. I will be right back. Going to grab this gentleman's order too." Hailee took two steps and spun and pointed to Mark, and with a voice laced with exuberance, Hailee said, "Ha! Now, I have you thinking, right?"

Mark laughed and said, "You do, yes, you do. I have to tread very carefully now. This world is full of mysteries and potential mind readers are now at the top of my list. Only pure thoughts allowed." In jest, Mark put his hands to his temples and narrowed his brows, as if to pretend that he was forcing thoughts from his mind. While he watched

Hailee move effortlessly to the table where the stranger sat, Mark thought, 'The hostess might ooze sexiness, but Hailee oozed love and life.'

It might have been just a touch of the red wine running through his veins, but right now, he could only think how he would pick love and life over sexiness any day. Sexiness can fade, but love and life never do.

He watched as Hailee stopped by the table next to his and she flashed the same cute smile, poised her petite body to the side, and said, "Good evening. Welcome, sir, to Silverado's Restaurant. My name is Hailee and I will be your server tonight. Might I start you off with a drink of some sort?"

The stranger smiled, and even from his vantage point a few feet away, Mark could see his dark eyes sparkle and reflect the nightlife all around them. With a nod, the dark stranger finally spoke in a deep, melodious voice that resounded strongly throughout the night, above the low music playing in the background and above the noise of the city street a few feet away.

"Please, a double pour of your finest Scotch. Neat."

Hailee nodded, and she asked, "Would you like to place a food order now?"

The stranger nodded his head sideways, this time to indicate no, and he gathered up the rest of the menus from the table and handed them to Hailee, along with another flash of his dark eyes and a smile.

Hailee took them, tucked them under her arm, and said, "Thank you, sir. Double pour. Finest Scotch. Neat. Coming right up."

Hailee turned and winked at Mark, and his heart melted a little. While he watched Hailee hustle off to the bar, Mark thought how the stranger in black did not say too much. He gave a new meaning to the old cliché of a, "Man of few words."

The hostess caught Hailee as she whizzed by the

hostess station on her way to the bar and Hailee handed off the menus. The hostess smiled, the two women whispered, and when the hostess fanned her face with the menus, Mark knew that the handsome stranger dressed all in black was the subject.

Since Hailee was beyond excellent in her server skills, the petite woman returned in a flash. She dropped the red wine on Mark's table and leaned in and said, "I will be back soon. I am loaded down with tables, but this table is my favorite one tonight." She tapped her free hand on the table and said, "Please, let me know if you need anything." Mark nodded and smiled as he watched Hailee spin around, and then she gently dropped the glass of scotch on the table of the dark stranger. With that same irresistible smile on her lovely face, Hailee said, "Please sir, if you change your mind on the food, let me know and I will be back to check on you in a few. Gorgeous evening tonight, right?"

The stranger nodded and tipped his hat and followed with a smile. Mark admired Hailee from his table. She was not the bombshell, Hollywood type of knockout, that the hostess was, with a huge chest and luxurious hips and a perfect backside. No, Hailee was different. Petite, yet perfectly shaped, her body oozed with genuine wholesomeness, and Mark admired the rear view of Hailee as her tight black pants clung to her body in all the right spots. Her hair was a mix of brown and touches of auburn and she wore it cut in one of the latest hairstyles of a medium length with a layer of longer hair flowing across her face. Hailee tucked the dangling length of her hair behind her ears and off she went to the next table.

'Ordinary in appearance? Hell no,' Mark thought, 'he found her gorgeous and captivating.'

Mark only occasionally dated women. His hermit-like way of life and dedication to video gaming and his business did not exactly allow for meeting many women.

After all, this was a rare day and evening. For the most part, Mark slept during the days and worked the games circles all night long. A lot of game action from the world's top gamers came from overseas and he needed to work the time shifts. Those hours did not make meeting women very easy. He did have a longer-term relationship with a woman that he met at a gaming convention, but it was a long-distance relationship and those types of relationships only succeed when it is true love.

That particular relationship was not true love.

Not by a long shot.

Mark once more transformed to his alter ego of Winterkill and his mind whirled with how cool a character the dark stranger would make in a video game. He directed his focus on the dark stranger seated next to him. In a moment frozen in time . . . Winterkill found the eyes of the dark stranger focused hard upon him! With the red wine glass in his hand and precariously close to his lips, the sparkling, dark, and piercing eyes of the stranger locked in on his face. It felt as if they were able to see right through him and caused a shudder to roll up and down his spine. Winterkill imagined this is where he would take the game controller and, in a game that allowed him to do so, he would hit the pause button. On the other hand, he might push the proper buttons to make his Winterkill character turn and run away. Winterkill's anxiety eased when the stranger's face broke into a smile and he lifted his glass in the air as a toast. Mark was back down to Earth, so he smiled and lifted his wine glass in the air, while they each timed a sip together.

"Cheers! Beautiful evening, huh? Cool, but not chilly. No humidity. The sunset was very cool and now the lights of the city and the activity on the street are an amazing backdrop," Mark said as he took another sip.

The stranger also sipped his whiskey but not surprisingly, he did not say a word, he only smiled. Mark took that as a statement of agreement.

Mark leaned in over the edge of the table a little and looked around and in all directions for the whereabouts of Hailee, and when he spotted her a number of tables away and not within earshot, Mark commented, "And the gorgeous young women are awfully nice scenery too. Especially Hailee. She is very cute and seems like she is so full of love and life."

The quiet stranger in the black hat nodded and smiled again. He lifted his glass of Scotch to his lips, and this time, he took a long sip. The glass was almost empty, and the stranger held the glass up to the lights of the patio as if to study exactly how much Scotch whiskey remained in the glass.

Once again, the stranger spoke in his golden, melodious and powerful voice, "I believe that she is full of love and life and you are, too, Winterkill. You just need to realize it. I think the blurred line between your games and the real world is much closer than you could ever realize. Perhaps, the time will come, very soon, where you will need to hit the pause button and some other controls too. Hailee and many others will be counting upon you and your skills." The stranger stopped speaking and stared at Mark . . . or was it . . . Winterkill?

Mark tried very unsuccessfully to hide his astonishment over the fact that the dark stranger knew who he was, and while stuttering, he recovered and managed to ask, "Ah, you know who I am?"

The stranger nodded.

"I see. Something tells me it is best not to ask you how you know me. Seems as if you are the kinda dude that knows an awful lot of things."

Another nod from the stranger and a hint of a smile.

"You know, not all games have the ability to hit a pause. It is tricky. The pause button works only if you are playing versus the computer's artificial intelligence . . .

kinda of a one-on-one type of thing."

The stranger picked up his glass, and he finished it off in one last sip. He slowly set the glass on the table, reached into one of the pockets of his vest, and pulled out a roll of money. Even in the rather dim light of the patio, Mark could see that the bills were all one-hundred-dollar-bills. The stranger peeled one of the bills off and carefully set it under the edge of the empty glass. The stranger pushed his chair out from under the table and he stood up. Mark took a deep breath and continued to stare at the stranger. His immense size was a little overwhelming, and his presence encompassed everything and everyone.

"Then, when the time comes, be sure to play it one-on-one. Sometimes, Winterkill, this weary world comes down to one man being courageous enough to take it all on one-on-one. Sometimes, it requires a pause. It requires a reboot, and it needs a man of courage, superior intelligence, and a man possessing the skills to do so. You are such a man. Please, do not abuse your gift. Use it and your skills for Hailee, for this world, for the cause of good, when the time arrives. Good wins, evil loses, if only for a pause. Please, keep it in mind."

The stranger smiled. He tipped his hat at Mark, spun on his boot heels and turned and walked briskly away. Neither Mark, nor Winterkill, had the slightest idea what he meant by his outlandish words and his rather bizarre statements, but they both sat and watched and listened as the metal tips of the boots of the stranger struck hard against the surface of the patio. The mysterious stranger passed by the hostess station and the wide-eyed hostess waved and smiled and mouthed goodnight, but her moue on her beautiful face when the stranger brushed past her without even looking her way was all too noticeable. Mark sat, watched, and listened until the stranger disappeared from his view. The noise from the tips of his boots sounded loudly and echoed along the city street until, gradually, the noise of his boots was lost in the madness and noise of the city.

Hailee walked over and she first looked at Mark and then to the table where the stranger sat. She plucked the empty glass off the table and smiled when she saw the crisp bill left as payment and a more than generous tip. "Wow!" Hailee smiled as she folded the bill in half and tucked the bill into her server's apron.

"I know, right? Strange dude, strange words, but man, oh, man, was he just the coolest dude that you have ever seen?"

Hailee smiled, and for a second, she posed in front of Mark. Her right hip stuck out as she leaned into Mark, and her hand rested on that same hip. Her beautiful green eyes sparkled, and she flipped the dangle of hair that fell across her face and grabbed the hair and tucked it behind her ear.

"Oh, I guess, but I kind of think the guy sitting right here in front of me, is just as cool. Maybe even a lot cooler. Not as mysterious, not as strange, but I think just as handsome, if not more so! Now, please, don't get me wrong, the man in black was incredibly handsome, he was very cool and stylish, and our hostess was ready to faint when she met him and she was ready to propose to him when he left, but he was just not my type. You see, I think the guy in front of me right now, is just the most adorable man that I have ever seen."

Mark smiled widely, his heart melted, and the first thought that he had was how he wished that he did have a game controller with a pause button that controlled the real world. Because if he did so, he would push the living hell out of it right now to hold this scene forever in his mind and within his heart.

If only for a pause. . ..

"So, can I hang around and maybe when you finish up your shift, we can go and catch a drink together?" Mark asked as Hailee stopped off at his table and dropped his check off. He looked at her rather longingly, and hope was all over his face as well as embedded in his eyes.

Hailee smiled and said, "Well, no offense here, but you seem as if you are a lightweight when it comes to drinking wine. Did it all go straight to your head? Anyway, another drink might be the last thing that you need right now. I was going to suggest a cab for you if you are driving. You had, ah, more than just a few glasses of wine and I suspect that your head might be swimming a bit."

"I do not drive much and that might be because I don't even own a car. Really, I have no need for one. I walk all over the city or I take the bus or the train. However, I don't usually go out too much. This is an unusual night for me. In so many ways." Mark stopped speaking, and all that had happened tonight flashed in his mind. The words of the dark stranger echoed in his head for a few pensive moments before he was able to speak once more, "Anyway, I walked here and will walk back . . . I play all the games that I play—by the rules and drinking and driving, don't make the cut. It's not far at all, because I live in the big red apartment building right over on the next corner from here. The one with the black canopy in front of it and the iron window boxes on all the windows." Mark blinked a little and said, "Admittedly, I am a bit of a lightweight as far as alcohol goes."

Mark nervously fiddled with the nearly empty wine glass on the table, and then he ran his fingers through the thick mop of tousled hair on his head.

Now it was Hailee's turn to have her heart melted a bit.

She meant what she said earlier that he was just the most adorable man she had ever seen. From his incredibly long eyelashes, to his unkempt hair that stuck out in all kinds of directions, in no actual style, to the plain black tee shirt that he wore on his lean frame. A tee shirt, with a logo of some kind of video game company emblazoned upon it. He was beyond adorable, all the way from his head down to the worn, black canvas sneakers on his feet.

Hailee forced her mind back to reality and, with a great effort, managed to say, "Good, good, so glad that you are walking. That apartment building is so cool. Oh, well, there is more to you than meets the eye. The high-rent district, an exclusive address and a very fancy building. I know the building that you mean and I admire it all the time. It looks so historic . . . and expensive too. But, yes, I would love to have a drink and spend some time with you." She took a big gulp of air and tried as hard as she could not to look too nervous as she dropped the bomb that usually chased away most of the guys that she met as of late. Hailee did not want to chase away this guy in front of her. The little pitter-patter that her heart was making right now told her not to chase him away, but honesty was always her priority and so were her responsibilities. "Not tonight, though. I can't because I have to get home to, ah, relieve my mother. Mom is watching my little girl while I work. I am a single mom. This is my second job. My mother is on babysitting duty while I am working here." As soon as she finished speaking the words, she studied his eyes for a clue as to his reaction to her honest pronouncement that she had a daughter to provide for, and that she was a single mom. Quickly, she prayed that he was not as all the others were as of late and that he did not immediately lose interest in her. To her relief, his face broke into a wide smile, and he seemed as if he remained interested in her.

In fact, he seemed to be more than just interested in her. . ..

His exuberance proved captivating.

"Wow! A little girl. That is so awesome. You work two jobs, and Mom pitches in. Wow, awesome . . . you have my admiration even more now." He winked and said rather coyly, "Not just a beautiful face, huh? By the way, I am Mark Holiday and you are, Hailee, ah, ah, please, could you tell me your last name and your daughter's name too?" Hailee reached out, she grasped Mark's outstretched hand, and Hailee gently shook it. His hands were large and his fingers were very long, but his touch was gentle and, with the sharing of the touch, comforting warmth filled her with joy.

"Hi, Mark. It has been my pleasure. I am Miss Hailee Nathanson. Ingrid is my daughter's name." Hailee's eyes grew wide and excitement filled her voice as the very proud mother explained, "Ingrid has red hair that I tie up in a yellow or a white bow above her head and she has the greenest, widest, most beautiful eyes that you have ever seen. Her spirit is so special and kind and she is full of love and life."

Mark paused for a second, while he recalled the exact same words that he shared with the mysterious stranger in black.

"Full of love and life."

Recovering a bit, Mark said, "Amazing. What a joy. And, I bet she is just as cute, amazing, and wonderful as her mother is. I would love to meet Ingrid . . . someday."

Their eyes locked and for a few seconds they studied each other's gaze. It was as if their feelings were budding gardens in the springtime, ready and waiting to burst into full color on the first warm spring afternoon. Hailee picked up the empty wine glass from his table and she ran her finger around the rim of the glass, trying to break the gaze but retain the feelings of the moment.

While still toying with the wine glass, Hailee admitted, "I would love you to meet her too."

"Look, I understand that you need to get back to work. Here, please, take my business card and send me a text message when you have time. I own my own company, and there are many aspects to it, but mostly, I am just a geeky gamer. We will go out somewhere. When Mom has, Ingrid and you have time. Where . . . we can share a few drinks, some laughter, and some fun. And . . . then we can walk. No rules broken. Ever."

Hailee took his card, nodded her head and said, "Yes. The boss is giving me the evil eye right now. I will text you. Soon. No broken rules. Honest. Thank you so much."

"Honest," Mark said with a wink. He handed her the money for the tab, along with a very generous tip too. She took it, smiled, pushed that amazing dangling length of hair behind her ear and scampered off. Hailee read the business card, stopped, and studied it for a moment, before placing it into her server's apron. The card was simple. It was black with a logo of a computer and video game controller and the name of a company called, "Winterkill Enterprises, followed by Mr. Mark Holiday, President." The card had an email address, a social media site address and a telephone number.

"Interesting," Hailee mumbled as she made her way to the waiting table. "In order to live in that fancy apartment house, he must earn a ton of money at this gaming stuff. A video gamer, huh? I must say that he is a very cute one too."

From a few feet away, Mr. Mark Holiday admired the glorious view of Miss Hailee Nathanson from the rear, and he took a deep breath. Standing up without wobbling might be tricky. And yes, his head was swimming. It was due to a bit too much wine, however, a certain, very cute and amazing server made his head swim too.

"On your feet, now, Winterkill. The night is still young and there are bad guys to take care of and worlds to control with your fingers, your eyes and your skills," he joked as he stood up, caught a deep breath of the cool night air and propelled his feet in the direction of the street. Actually, he did his best to stay steady, upright, and propelled while making his way to the exit, which was just past the edge of the bar and the hostess station. He performed his best, "I am not at all tipsy type of walk" but his wobble and his glassy eyes gave his true condition away. The hostess smiled at him as he passed by.

She gave a wink and added, "Be careful out there, precious, and please, be sure to come back and see us again really soon. I know that Hailee will love that. Are you sure that you are okay to make it home? I can call a cab."

Mark surmised that all the staff knew he was half-in-the-bag, but that he was walking home. "I am fine. It would be the shortest taxi ride in history. I am only going to the red brick apartment on the corner."

The hostess nodded and smiled.

"See ya darlin'! I will be back. I promise," Mark answered with a wave and when he arrived at the edge of the sidewalk of the busy city street, he stopped, spun around, caught his bearings and pointed his feet in the direction of home. The night was still cool, and the air was gloriously clear, crisp, and inviting. Mark felt as if his head cleared considerably when he hit the city street.

He walked up to the nearby street corner, to the busy intersection with the crosswalks and traffic light, glanced up at the pedestrian crossing sign and in his foggy mind, he swore that the sign instructed him to "WALK" in its typical yellow glowing letters.

Mark needed to cross the street. An everyday and ordinary task for a city dweller. Especially a city dweller living on a busy city street.

Yet nothing about this particular day was proving to be ordinary.

Mark stepped off the curb and onto the sidewalk, took two or three strides into the street and to his horror, he heard the loud blaring of a car horn and he looked up to see a car hurtling towards him at a blinding speed.

Mark Holiday's mind spun with what he assumed were the last thoughts that he would ever have.

Remarkably, Hailee was a large part of them. Strangely, everything from that moment on became surreal, as if it moved in slow motion. The car still hurtled toward Mark at a blinding speed, but his mind could slow the distance and the evolution of time. While processing the scene and his actions, Mark thought, 'Well, this sure sucks. Just when I met the woman of my dreams. I guess this is what it is like to die in one of my video games. I wonder how much this is going to hurt?'

Realizing that impact, pain, and potential death, loomed only a mere half-second or so away, Mark did what he always did when he was in his world of make-believe.

A fantasy world.

On the other hand, was there some truth to the words that the quiet stranger in the black hat just spoke to Mark? The words, when the stranger told him that the lines between the two worlds were much closer than any person ever realized?

Mark held his hands and his fingers outward as if he was holding his video game controller and playing one-on-one against the computer.

Against the world.

Mark closed his eyes, and he hit the imaginary pause button that he held in his hands. To his surprise, there was no impact. No pain. No death. When Mark slowly opened his eyes, he blinked a few times and stood there in shock and awe.

The pause button worked.

The car stopped only inches away from his body. The driver of the car, was a middle-aged man. A man who was gripping the steering wheel in a death grip. His eyes were wide open and his mouth was wide open in horror too.

Mark touched his body and felt all around and up and down his body. It was intact. Perhaps this is how it feels to die and he was in some heavenly state of limbo. He attended church as a small boy but had drifted away from organized religion when he became a man. God, he believed in, it was all the stuff that mankind made up that Mark had issues with. So, okay, had God intervened and sent him to Heaven, anyway? Slowly, he lifted his feet and stomped on the ground as if to test the surface beneath his feet.

"Maybe it's a cloud and I will fall through it," Mark spoke his thoughts aloud.

No, it was the street. His canvas sneakers confirmed that fact. Suddenly, Mark was as sober as he was on the day of his birth.

Wine? What wine?

He blinked about ten times, opened his eyes wide open, and looked around the scene. Not only the "death car" paused in place, but everything else paused too. All the traffic remained frozen in place at this busy main intersection in the street. The corner of Long Street and Main Street. Buses, cars, taxicabs, a pickup truck, or two or three, a few people walking down both sides of the sidewalk on each side of the street.

The traffic lights, the noises of the city . . . everything!

Paused.

Just as if Mark hit the pause or home button when he was playing a video game. One-on-one. The stranger's words echoed once more in Mark's head as if they were some words of guidance now! Mark versus the computer brain inside of a microprocessor. A calculated algorithm flipping electrons against one of the world's greatest video game players. Despite the shock of what had happened and was happening in front of his eyes and his efforts at pressing his brain to try hard to understand all of it, a smile forced across the mouth of Mark Holiday. He smiled, because he knew that the computer never won when he played it.

Never.

Mark looked back over his shoulder and he stared into the patio of Silverado's Restaurant. He could only see the hostess standing next to her podium at the entrance. Her beautiful face remained paused and frozen in time while she was smiling at some guests leaving for the evening. A man and a woman, frozen in their greetings and in their steps. Mark tried but he could not see Hailee anywhere inside the patio. But the bartender was pausing within the mid-pour of a mug of beer from the beer tap. In fact, the beer paused in midair too.

'Astounding. Remarkable. Beyond belief. Hell, yes,' Mark thought while he looked around and gauged exactly what this was all about that evolved in front of his eyes. Then his mind filled with the vision of the unusual and peculiar quiet stranger in the black hat. How he seemed to have stepped out of the main role as a character in a video game into the real world. Right now, Mark was not too sure what the real world was. Who, or what the hell, was, or is the quiet stranger in the black hat?

Mark could not even guess and he was not about to try, but the words of the stranger echoed in his mind and the chills went up and down his spine as the meaning of the words raced around his mind, "Sometimes, Winterkill, this weary world comes down to one man being courageous enough to take it all on one-on-one. Sometimes, it requires a pause. It requires a reboot, and it needs a man of courage, superior intelligence, and a man possessing the skills to do so. You are such a man. Please, do not abuse your gift. Use it and your skills for Hailee, for this world, for the cause of good, when the time arrives. Good wins, evil loses, if only for a pause. Please, keep it in mind."

Another smile broke wide across Mark's mouth and his eyes lit up.

"Holy, guacamole! I really am, Winterkill! Whoa, this is friggin' awesome! The stranger is out of this world! Literally!"

When the words left his mouth, he leaned in, tapped the hood of the potential "death car" and the hood sounded loud and clear. Yes indeed, it was a metal car hood. Mark ran across the street and he stood on the opposite street corner on the side of the street where he lived.

After taking in the scene one more time, Mark held his hands and fingers out in the same manner as he did before, and he worked the buttons of the imaginary game controller that he held in his hands and with what he could now, seemingly control the world.

Mark hit the pause button again and he could not help but shout out the words, "Okay, world, here we go. Right now, I am Winterkill. Sorry, Mark Holiday, but go and take a short break from your usual world. I have a real world to control and save. Resume!"

And . . . the world instantly sprung into life.

Mark watched and held back a smile and a laugh, as the driver of the "death car" shook his head, rubbed at his eyes as if to gauge whether he was losing his mind, and he tried to figure out where the guy who he was about to make a pancake out of, went off to. After looking around and spotting Mark on the opposite street corner, the driver rubbed his eyes once again, and Mark waved and smiled. The confused and stunned driver must have thought that Mark was the world's fastest sprinter. The driver waved a feeble and puzzled wave in return as a car's horn loudly blared from the car waiting behind the "death car."

The world was no longer in pause mode and we all know that the city never really sleeps. Impatience and obnoxious drivers never sleep either.

The driver continued on his way, making the right turn and Mark watched as his taillights disappeared out of sight. The noises of the traffic and of the city returned, and the cars, trucks, taxicabs, and people all moved about, just as they normally did.

With the wide smile still plastered across his face, Winterkill grabbed his phone. He picked the ear buds off his chest and popped them in his ears. After dialing up his favorite tune, Winterkill put his hands in the pockets of his jeans and listened to the music while strutting down the street to his home. Between his newly discovered gift of pause from the stranger, his meeting with Hailee, and the remnants of wine floating around inside of him, Mark was feeling more than just a little cocky. He was on top of the world.

His body swayed to the beat, and the sway combined with a brash hop and bounce to his steps.

Between songs, Winterkill spoke aloud, "Okay, I get it dark stranger, you need Winterkill for a mission of some sort. Picked me because of my skills and the fact that I might just be a video gamer geek, but I am not afraid of jackshit. You picked me because in my world of video make believe, it is very easy for me to believe in a real world of make believe too. Easy transition. Once I know the rules, then Winterkill can play any game. You saved my life with a gift and a demonstration of the power of it, and now we need to take care of something evil. Something, very big. Something, very important. Well, stranger, whoever you are, you can count on me. Especially, if Hailee is involved. Too bad for the bad guys out there, because Winterkill never loses a game."

Winterkill snapped his fingers to the beat of the song playing in his ears and swayed his body even more.

Above the music, Winterkill announced to the world, "I love this song. It is one of my faves. Look out bad guys out there in the evil world, beware because I am coming and whatever you are planning—I am going to stop you. I am giving you fair warning. Real world or video world, I am coming and yes indeed, Winterkill never loses a game. Ever."

Greg Vander Waal was a career criminal. He could not help it; it was a part of his makeup and his mind set. It began in his youth, with petty shoplifting in stores and then it progressed as a teenager to stealing cars. Despite his high intelligence level, Greg never finished high school, and he found out that a life of crime was easier to deal with than finding a job was. His mother deeply cared for her son, and to give her credit, she tried everything that she could do to reform Greg and convince him to change his life. However, rather unexpectantly, a little girl came along and with more mouths to feed, there is only so much that you can do when you work three jobs to make ends meet. The city was unforgiving, and in many ways, it was relentless.

Greg never met his father. Neither did his little sister.

However, in being factual that might have presented a difficult challenge, because all Greg's mother knew of their identities, were that they were not the same man.

Eventually, Greg did a short stint in prison for stealing too many cars. After serving about eight months in prison, Greg went through the standard psychiatric mental health profiling examinations and verbal interviews, the rehabilitation, and the mandatory court-ordered mental counseling. A psychiatrist who wore his glasses on the very tip of his nose, who was late for a rendezvous for lunch and cocktails with his mistress, and had a wall full of endless degrees, pronounced Greg cured of his penchant for committing crimes and that he was now ready to assume his place in society and contribute in positive ways. The doctor never lived on a city street. The doctor never knew desperation, nor did he ever live in a world outside of what some university classrooms portrayed to him. They released Greg Vander Waal from prison, and within hours, he had a shiny new set of wheels. A top-of-the-line model. The car was a luxury ride. There was no vehicle title or bill of sale for the vehicle, no money exchanged, but it was an exceptional set of wheels. The motor purred like a sleeping kitten and, as an bonus, the air conditioning was extra cold. As if it was icing on the cake, the vehicle even had low miles too.

Quite the deal. Greg did not intend to keep the car, despite all of its fine attributes and the extremely low price. Instead, the car would serve quite nicely as a fundraiser.

Perhaps the doctor required a few more degrees, because he sure as hell needed to go shopping for a new luxury automobile.

Now Greg moved up in the world. Cars no longer satisfied his criminal itch, and they did not bring in enough money for Greg to live the life he wanted. The doctor's high-class wheels brought in a nice paycheck, when he pawned it off to the right "collectors." The car funded an apartment and bought some weapons and other assorted items that Greg needed for his step up the crime ladder. Recently, Greg recruited a bunch of street thugs that he knew for a long time and whom he trusted. They looked up to Greg as their leader and after pulling off a few very brazen armed robberies of some local stores, and some after hour break-ins, the gang found that the paydays were becoming more lucrative. Greg's plan was to step up to a bank robbery or two and then a few more armed robberies and once he packed enough cash, he would drop some money off for his mother and his little sister, flee the city and never look in the rear-view mirror. Once he was somewhere far away, he would straighten his life out, maybe go to a technical school, learn a trade and begin anew. He was not stupid, and he knew if they became too greedy, their luck will run out. So far, his stash was large, his buddies were happy with their cuts and he knew that eventually, he would quit, but first, he needed the larger paydays, and after looking around at his arsenal and the assorted items that he required for pulling off a bank robbery, Greg turned his attention to the banks along Main Street.

It was time to scout it all out and use that intelligence. It was time to formulate a plan. It was time to rob a few banks.

Up on the sixth floor of the red brick apartment house on Long Street, inside the Command Center for Winterkill and the headquarters for Winterkill Enterprises, the monotone hum of multiple computers droned ever onward. The heat was on too and the apartment's air-conditioning system always struggled to offset the heat emitted from the multiple power supplies powering the huge wall and desks full of monitors, computers, smart cell telephones and gaming consoles that blinked and buzzed as the multiple worlds of Winterkill transformed from reality to numerous fantasy worlds. The electrical utility usage every month was astronomical in cost. The apartment house management had agreed to put in a larger electrical load center, in order for Winterkill to power his worlds, as long as Mark Holiday paid for it.

Mark did, and then some too. Critical systems had many back-up power supplies and even utilized a generator that sat out on a concrete pad on the side of the apartment building. At this point, after so many improvements, Mark's plan was to someday plunk down cash and buy the apartment building. It would be an investment.

It was now the Wednesday after the fateful past Saturday where Mark Holiday took a sabbatical and Winterkill took his place. Where the world turned upside down in so many ways for both Mark and for Winterkill.

Not only a day where he met the amazing quiet stranger in the black hat and a day where he received an extraordinary gift, but also a day where Mark was sure that he fell in love with a wonderful woman named Hailee. Hailee and Mark had exchanged numerous texts most every day since Saturday. They had a meeting and a date planned at Silverado's Restaurant for this coming Saturday. Hailee arranged for her mom to stay with Ingrid and the plan was to meet at Silverado's Restaurant and then go out and hit the streets for a quiet place to chat and, in Mark's mind, to fall deeper in love.

Now, Winterkill could not think of too much more other than Hailee, the stranger's words, his amazing powers and when, where, and what the mission was that Winterkill knew he would eventually need to undertake. A mission of such an importance that sleeping, eating, and his normal daily work as well as his life were all disrupted and uneven. Winterkill had changed his daily schedule up since Saturday. He no longer slept during the day; in fact, he found it difficult to sleep at night, too. His new gift was a little difficult to fathom and to understand, even for a young mind that dwelled within the fantasies of video games.

He was on full alert now, his eyes scanning the monitors with his numerous websites, and sponsored games and competitions were all flashing before Winterkill's eyes. One of Winterkill Enterprise's websites with his famous tips was getting hits that were off the charts. The advertisers will be thrilled with the numbers and the revenues for Winterkill Enterprises will be off the charts too. Winterkill had placed first in a gaming competition on Monday evening. He found his skills to be razor sharp, and he trounced the number two and three players in the world and his skills were the talk of all the gaming forums, enticing the hits on the websites and promoting his already immense popularity and fame. Winterkill could no longer answer the emails coming into the main mailbox . . . the numbers were too large. Emails full of praise and adulation from fans. Adulation was no longer a priority, but this one game in front of Winterkill was.

Since yesterday morning, his one gaming console had taken on a mind of its own. The usual game that Winterkill was playing in order to review it and analyze it for the gaming programmers was absent from the screen. Now it was another game. A game that Winterkill never saw before, or he ever played, and a game that Winterkill suspected that the quiet stranger had a hand in and his influence allowed the game installation to infiltrate his sophisticated systems and firewalls. It was a game where a team of heavily armed robbers terrorizes an entire city. Robbing banks, holding up stores and gas stations, taking hostages, gunning down innocent people and the goal of the game was to stop them. Yet, when Winterkill picked up the handheld controller, he found that he had no weapons, no body armor, no way out, and no defense at all. He only had the ability to pause the game. That fact alone told him that this was the prelude to the mission, and the stranger was somehow controlling this situation. The other fact that he made very careful note of was that he could only pause the game for ten minutes and then it would automatically resume and his pause button would not work again until he lost the round and the bad guys won. Winterkill never lost so many video games in a row—until now. First, he needed to understand the rules of the game and his capabilities. Then he had to learn how to engage the enemy before he could play the game and have any hope to win it. There was no doubt in his mind at all; the stranger controlled this game and the situation.

Somehow.

As the stranger said, the line between reality and fantasy was very blurred. Winterkill felt as if the stranger was now utilizing the strange game for prepping him, teaching him, and coaching him until providing Winterkill with a real-life situation to handle.

One monitor above the head of Winterkill constantly scrolled live, local news reports, another monitor had world news, and one remained tuned to social media sites. High technology existed not only in the world of governments or law enforcement, or in the evil hackers within the dark web, but it existed proudly and strongly in the worlds of high-tech gamers such as Winterkill and his dedicated network of followers and fellow gamers. Winterkill knew that if he needed to, he could unleash a fury of electronic allies and mayhem that would bring some of that evil to its knees. From a seventeen-year-old mathematical genius gaming in England to an eighty-year-old retired chemical scientist gaming in the Outback of Australia, to a retired long-haul trucker gaming out of Los Angeles, a world of knowledge and skill was at his fingertips. Winterkill knew that help was out there, and all he needed to make was a call to duty.

He waited while ready to do so.

The monitor with the mysterious game sat in front of him. The game was in pause mode. It had been for about three minutes or thereabouts and he did not know what the next move was, but he sat with the game controller in his hand and his eyes glued to the screen. The armed robbers were ready to assault a bank and, with no other defenses available to him, Winterkill stopped and hit the pause button for the game when the robbers charged the front door. He sat, studied, and waited for the next move.

A local news report caught the eye of Winterkill as the noon news update told of a brazen armed robbery of a local store located on a main street in the city that occurred last night. The gang got away with an undetermined amount of money, and there were no leads. The video of the robbery showed the typical hold-up scene with three men, brandishing weapons, ordering store clerks around, cleaning out the cash registers, all while wearing ski masks to cover their faces. He leaned in with such interest at the news broadcast that the game controller he held fell to the floor and he made no effort to retrieve it. No sooner did the news report end and an instant message bubble popped up on the screen that monitored all of Winterkill Enterprises' social media sites.

There was no name on the message bubble to indicate the identity of the sender, but Winterkill did not need one to know who sent it. The message was ominous and all in caps.

"A BANK ON THE CORNER OF SPRING AND MAIN REQUIRES A PAUSE AND GAME INTERACTION FROM WINTERKILL."

Winterkill's heart pounded in his ears and immediately beads of sweat broke out on his forehead. This was a reality. Game action was simply training now. He looked down at his attire. His lean, long, lanky, and skinny frame packed into a tee shirt and black jeans. His trusty black canvas sneakers were on his feet and he was sure going to need them now. He was the most unlikely hero in the history of the superhero world. No cape, no cool insignia on his chest and little to no muscles. Nevertheless, he did have special skills and a special friend dressed all in black.

That was all he needed.

The corner of Spring and Main Street was one block south from the stoop of his apartment building, and Winterkill did not wait for the elevator. He grabbed his apartment keys from the gaming table and off he was. He took the stairs three at a time and before he knew it, his eyes were squinting from the bright sunlight and he was in a full sprint down the street, dodging pedestrians, eyes up, gaming senses on full alert, while scanning his surroundings and remaining ready to use the pause command at any moment. Winterkill's chest heaved in anguish, while he drew in full breaths and sweat flowed as if it was a river from his face and what seemed as if it were every pore of his body.

"That's it. If I have to run around these streets like some kind of crazy-ass superhero, then I am signing my dead ass up for a gym next week," he swore aloud to the world as he continued to sprint down the street.

The First National Bank sat on the corner right in front of Winterkill, and he braked to a halt and swore that the soles of his canvas sneakers were on fire. It was a warm day and the heat on the sidewalk was intense. Within microseconds, Winterkill used his superior gaming skills from his numerous fantasy worlds in order to process the reality scene. There were many reasons that the quiet stranger in the black hat picked Mr. Mark Holiday and his alternate identity of Winterkill as an ally. Foremost, there was the fact that there was no one better than he was at processing information quicker than he could. Countless battles and years of gaming had turned Mr. Mark Holiday into Winterkill, who was a fine-tuned human machine of micro-processing both evil and danger. Within microseconds, friends and foes were on the radar and identified.

Winterkill's keen eyes scanned the entire scene in front of the bank. An elderly couple struggling to walk along the sidewalk to the front door of the bank. The woman was using a walker, and the man's eyes were of concern at the failing health of his beloved wife.

They were innocent bystanders.

Next, his eyes landed upon a young couple walking briskly along the hot sidewalk with a baby in a stroller in front of them. The man pushed the stroller and the woman's face glowed in dual love. The woman loved the baby and her husband with all her heart and she wore all of her love on her sleeve.

They were innocent bystanders.

With a baby.

A balding, middle-aged businessman with a large belly stood at the bus stop on the corner. He held his suit jacket over his folded arm, beads of sweat pushed from his forehead and his finger scrolled the screen of his cellphone.

An innocent bystander.

Winterkill was sure of his designations—even though—criminals pose in innocent costumes. Not this time.

Winterkill thought, 'There was no damn way that innocent people and an innocent little baby were going to come in harm's way with Winterkill on duty. No. Damn. Way.'

There was a four-door sedan parked in front of the bank. The vehicle had out-of-state license plates, and two men sat in the car. One man was driving, and he scanned the area nervously and the other man was in the rear seat, leaning forward with his eyes glued on the front door of the bank. That was the transport car, and those men were part of the robbery team.

Guilty and targeted.

Parked on the side street was another car. It had in-state plates, but it was an old, rusty, and rag-tag car. No one sat in it. It was a getaway car. Despite the appearance, Winterkill was betting that the car ran like a charm. As if it was a brand-new vehicle. An unreliable getaway car was not going to work out too well. On the other side of the street was a pickup truck with a toolbox in the rear. Could that truck be a potential backup getaway vehicle? The toolbox might be a decoy. Then Winterkill spotted the lead bank robber. He was standing just to the side of the front entrance to the bank, hugging the wall along the side street. He dressed in a tee shirt and jeans. Not unlike Winterkill's own attire, except that on his feet, he wore military boots, and he wore a jacket. A jacket on a hot summer's day. A jacket, in order to conceal weapons.

Guilty and targeted.

The young couple with the baby stroller now folded up,

and with the baby in the husband's arms, entered the bank. The elderly couple finally made it there, too. When the man lurking on the side of the front entrance to the bank, who was still wearing the jacket, reached inside of his jacket and took out a black ski mask, Winterkill focused intensely on the scene. The man in the jacket quickly slipped the ski mask over his head. His assistants jumped out of the sedan, and they did the same thing with their own ski masks.

"Bingo," Winterkill said after his earlier observations of separating the bad guys from the good proved correct. The head henchman took a few running steps to the front door of the bank, and Winterkill assumed his gaming position. He knew that it was time and he closed his eyes and he hit the imaginary pause button that he held in his hands.

"Pause!" Winterkill yelled out at the top of his lungs. He immediately glanced at his watch and made a note of the time. Something told Winterkill that this reality utilized the same rules as the video game did and he only had ten minutes to pause the scene. Ten minutes and the world would resume and he could not hit the pause button again until . . . the bad guys won the round.

The lead robber had already made it into the front entrance of the lobby of the bank, and the other members of his evil team were on his heels. They all had their hands inside of their jackets and appeared to be in the act of pulling out their weapons.

The world froze.

The traffic along the street and the entire world paused.

Winterkill ran past the motionless businessman and the businessman's fingers were paused on the screen of his cellphone. Winterkill ran through the maze of the pause, he ran into the bank, pushed the door open and his eyes quickly surveyed the situation.

Winterkill stopped and studied the lead bank robber. He was pausing while frozen in his steps, his hand inside of his jacket as he reached for his weapon. The elderly couple paused while the husband was wrapping his arm around his wife in what appeared to be an effort in order to hold her up. The young couple with the baby paused in place, the father gently reaching down to place the baby back into the stroller while Mom looked on, her loving smile frozen on her face. If not for the pending doom looming all around the young family, Winterkill could not help but think how it was a bucolic scene.

The armed security officer for the bank and the primary line of defense was a handsome young man, with dark features and bulging muscles underneath his uniform. The security officer was walking across the front of the lobby floor. In his pause mode, his head turned to the side, and he was smiling at a teller who was a beautiful, young woman. From the look on their faces, they were in love. Winterkill sighed deeply, and for the first time, this new power gave him some pause of his own. He knew from playing countless video games that without intervention or protection, the handsome young security officer was a dead, handsome young security officer.

He did not stand a prayer of a chance.

His ample and overflowing muscles would mean jackshit right now because his head was not in the game. It was an ambush, and he was oblivious because he was in love. The robber would gun him down immediately because he was the first line of defense. The teller would scream at the sight of her dead lover, and the rest of her life would be hell. She would never get over it. However, it was not going to happen because Winterkill stood in the way and Winterkill never lost a game. He might have lost a round here and there, but he never lost a game. His wristwatch was down to about eight minutes.

He did not intend to lose this one.

Winterkill stood and studied the scene. The video game that took over his world a few days ago on the screen back in his apartment was a conundrum for him, because other than controlling the pause, his controller was useless. He was confident that the stranger sent the game as a training tool, a manner to make Winterkill think of how to handle the "real life" bad guys. Now, here he was, right back in the same situation as he was in the mysterious video game. Stuck in pause mode. To test his powers, Winterkill held his imaginary controller in his hands with his hands and fingers outstretched toward the scene in front of him. He pushed all the buttons that he would normally use in a game. He knew the placement of all of them by heart. No joystick control, no ability to move anyone, no weapons, no target screens, no defense or operations at all. Nothing. He scratched the top of his head in thought and then he pulled his tee shirt up over his chest and wiped the sweat off his face. Apparently, the air conditioning systems in the bank paused too. Winterkill was sweaty from his sprint in the heat, anyway.

Suddenly, the air conditioning systems gave him a thought.

Winterkill spoke aloud to the paused world all around him.

"Okay, think, now, Winterkill, you need to learn what you can do and what you cannot do here. What are the rules of this game? Not only have all the people in my little world here moved into the pause mode, but maybe much more than just the people are paused. It seems as if all the mechanical and electrical systems are paused too. When I resume, they return to normal operation. So, I need to figure it out . . . can I move stuff on my own?"

Winterkill ran over to a trash pail in the corner of the lobby, and he reached down and picked it up. It moved as it normally did. While studying the lead bank robber, Winterkill walked over and tugged at his ski mask to pull it off his head in an attempt to reveal his identity. No good. The mask would not move. He reached inside of the jacket and sure enough, the lead bank robber had his fingers on the handle of a handgun. A handgun that he was in the middle of pulling out of his jacket when Winterkill hit the pause button. Winterkill tried, but he could not remove the handgun from the hand of the criminal. Winterkill had a rudimentary knowledge of handguns and he tried to eject the bullets from the gun. But once more, nothing worked. He tried to pull a wallet out of the robber's pocket to identify him, but the effort proved futile. He wrapped his arms around the waist of the lead bank robber, tugged, and pulled at him to see if he could move him from his spot, but he could not. His first idea was to disarm the criminal, and when that was a no go, he thought that he could drag him out of the building and at least get him out of the bank.

No good.

Down to six minutes.

"Well, this sure is a bomb. Not going to be very easy. I have no defenses, just a pause. But I do have my brain."

He already knew what the results were going to be, but when he spotted the handcuff pouch on the belt of the security officer, he had to give it a try. If he had handcuffs, then he could simply handcuff the lead bank robber, and at least he was out of the picture. Tugging at the little clip of the pouch confirmed what Winterkill suspected. No good. However, he could move objects and the air conditioning systems were stuck in the pause mode, but he was sure that they would turn back on when he hit the resume button.

"Okay, cool. How about other systems? Such as fire alarms and burglar alarms. Will they work? And how about my stuff? Can I use my stuff?" He recalled that he grabbed the apartment keys, and he reached in his pocket and, yes, he had them in his hands. How he wished he had a rope, or three pairs of handcuffs, instead of these stupid keys.

Winterkill now knew the rules of the game, and he had to play this round with what he had available to him. Next time, if there was one, he will be better equipped.

Winterkill spotted the fire alarm pull station on the wall near the front door of the bank and he smiled. He ran over and tugged on the handle of the pull station, and sure enough, it locked down and into the alarm position.

"Cool, when I hit the pause button again in this, ah," Winterkill almost used the word, game, but he swallowed hard when he realized that as bizarre as all of this is, it was not a game, "the fire alarm will be blaring and the fire department will roll this way. One point for Winterkill." He then ran around to the rear of the bank teller's posts and gently squeezed in next to the tellers, and found the panic buttons for the silent burglar alarm. These were push buttons and he could not lock them into the "ON" position. However, this was Winterkill, and he played all kinds of games in a million different situations and in those games, he used all types of tricks and devices. It might have been a fantasy experience, but it was going to work in real life too. Winterkill found a paperclip on the desk and strategically bent it, pushed the button in and wedged the clip between the button and the body of the mount. The button was now in the "ON" position.

"Two points for Winterkill. Bad guys zero," Winterkill mumbled.

A glance at the watch told him he had about three minutes left.

Down to three minutes to resume.

The sweat now poured from his face, and he wiped the sweat away from his eyes as he tried to focus. Since he could move things, Winterkill pushed a table that held deposit slips and other paperwork, and he placed the table in the path of the robbers to block them into the nook of the entrance to the bank. He pushed a few chairs over and strategically placed those, too. Anything to stall them for a few seconds.

"Three points for Winterkill. Bad guys zero," Winterkill mumbled.

Almost out of time. Winterkill did not want time to expire on its own; he rather set himself into position and resumed the situation on his own command. He had nothing left, but he was a courageous young man. Winterkill decided to stand pat and resume the world while he was next to the lead bank robber. He might end up going down in a hail of bullets, but he was going to try his best. Winterkill noticed an umbrella stand in the bank's lobby that was holding one lonely umbrella, he pulled the umbrella out of the stand, and he decided that since it was all he could find and time was running low that it was going to be his weapon. At least it had a sturdy wooden handle.

"Geez, c'mon now, in my video world, I have laser beams, ray guns, tanks, bombs, machine guns, virtually every weapon known to mankind and to fantasy, and now, all I have is an old umbrella that someone left in the lobby of a bank." He placed the umbrella at his side, held his hands out, and closed his eyes as he hit the imaginary pause button.

"Resume!" Winterkill yelled, and as he did so, he picked up the umbrella, opened his eyes and swung the sturdy wooden handle as hard as he could at the head of the lead bank robber.

The world returned to life.

The fire alarm blared and screamed, and the umbrella hit the crook right across the neck and it splintered into a hundred pieces. The robber stood stunned, the force of the blow and his astonishment at the fire alarm blaring and the wall of "stuff" blocking his way, caused him to draw his weapon out of his jacket, but then he fumbled the weapon, and the handgun fell to the floor at the feet of Winterkill. Quick as a flash, Winterkill kicked the gun, and the gun flew across the floor. How he wished that he did not have canvas sneakers on his feet.

"Four points for Winterkill. Bad guys zero," Winterkill

said with a smile.

The criminal held his neck in pain. He spun in all directions and his eyes met Winterkill's eyes. He pointed at him and then yelled, "I will find you and I will kill you for this! Abort! Abort! Out!"

The lead robber waved his hand in the air to signal a retreat, he yelled directions to his team of robbers and quick as a flash, they ran out of the bank as the security officer jumped into action and with his gun drawn, he commanded everyone to hit the floor. People screamed, the elderly couple held each other in a bear hug, the father dove over the stroller to protect the baby and he pulled his wife close. A general wave of bedlam broke out and, in the distance, the wail and screams of a fire truck and police cars' sirens grew closer.

Winterkill called out to the fleeing gang, "Good luck with that! Fair warning . . . I swing a mean-ass umbrella."

Through the large windows of the bank that were facing the streets, Winterkill watched the fleeing robbers as they jumped in the truck with the toolbox that was parked on the side street next to the bank. Winterkill kicked at the floor as he slowly went down to the prone position.

"Okay, well, shit, I missed the truck, so the bad guys get one point, but hell, I still won this round."

The police detective tilted his head a little and wiped his forehead of a bead of sweat.

Once again, he picked up his notepad and pen, and the police detective asked Winterkill, "So I get it now. I think. You could not see any faces, because they all wore black ski masks and you suspect there are no fingerprints on the gun or anywhere else, because of black gloves."

"Yup, all high-quality tactical gear too."

"No offense, but you do not look as if you are ex-police, or law enforcement or military. How do you know this stuff?"

Winterkill waved and laughed while explaining, "Hey, my gaming world uses the same stuff the real world does. The line between reality and my world is vague, and it is certainly blurred."

The detective shook his head, and his eyes examined Winterkill once more. Obviously, the detective had no idea what Winterkill meant, but before he could comment, Winterkill continued with the details of the adventure. "The head guy is a husky dude. I am six-three, he was as tall as I was, and I would guess his weight at least, two-twenty. Deep voice too."

"Okay, well, it is not much, but they are all good observations, considering the stress of the situation and the speed of which it came at you. Let me get the rest down pat. You hid behind the robber and he did not see you, so you swung the umbrella and cracked it across his head. Right?"

"No, Detective Dalton, I hit him in the neck."

"Okay. The neck. Gotta tell ya that ya are a courageous guy, Mr. Holiday. A hero. But once again, how the hell did this table and the chairs get here?" Detective Dalton pointed at the assorted items that Winterkill pushed into the path of the potential bank robber. "And who pulled the fire alarm? And why did you have an umbrella? It is hotter than hell out there and clear as a bell."

Winterkill thought quickly, and he pointed at the muscular security officer who was standing next to them with the beautiful bank teller on his arm. Next to the teller and the security officer was the wide-eyed and smiling manager of the bank. Winterkill noted how the bank manager wore the most ridiculous and awful comb-over-haircut on his head that Winterkill had ever seen. It was difficult for Winterkill to suppress a laugh at the hairstyle.

"Ah ya, know that loudmouthed weatherman on channel six . . . he said there was a chance of thunderstorms. That dude is always wrong. However, I tell you that, oh no, I am not the hero here. The security officer here is the real hero. I might have pushed the chairs over, when the bad guys were looking the other way, but the officer here pulled the fire pull station, pushed the silent burglar alarm and pushed the table over there. I mean, look at the size of him and those muscles. The guy is huge, but believe me . . . he moves like a cat. Never seen anyone move that fast! My goodness, I am just some skinny guy with an umbrella. A sturdy-handled umbrella, or at least, I used to have an umbrella, but I am weak as a feather in the wind. I am just a geeky video gamer dude. There is your hero!"

Winterkill pointed at the security officer, who puffed out his huge chest and flexed his numerous muscles, while the bank teller swooned at her hero's efforts. The elderly couple, as well as the young couple with the baby, all shook their heads in agreement and they clapped for the security officer's heroism. Blurred reality, indeed.

"Well, it was nothing, really. All in a day's work for a bank security officer of my military experience and my courage. . .."

Winterkill laughed at how the big lug gladly took all the credit.

The bank manager leaned in, shook Winterkill's hand, and said, "Thank you, Mr. Holiday. I would like to say that we would offer you free checking for a year if you want to open an account here. I will even throw in a new umbrella too. Can I help you now? What business did you want to conduct this afternoon?"

"Ah . . . ah, yes, a checking account. I was going to ask about a checking account. However, time is kind of short now, and I am a little shook up, so I will consider it. I want to go lie down and rest from the, ah, ah, shock. Thanks. I have to go. If you need me for anything else, just give me a shout there, Detective Dalton. Here is my card."

Detective Dalton nodded and took the business card and mumbled, "Winterkill Enterprises, huh? Interesting. Video gamer, dude, huh?"

Winterkill smiled and waved, and out the door he went. Naivety was not part of his soul. Courage was, and certainly, a huge dose of confidence was, in fact, the confidence bubbled over and bordered on cockiness. However, Winterkill was not naïve. Within seconds his eyes scanned the scene in front of him, taking mental snapshots of everything, and true to form, Winterkill did not miss anything along the busy city street. Just as Winterkill did when his skills assessed the scene in front of the bank and his keen gaming skills allowed him to identify the situation as well as the criminals, Winterkill made the rounds of the city streets, buildings, vehicles, and side streets. The area around the bank was crawling with law enforcement; a crime scene team was already there, scouring and pouring over the remaining vehicles.

'Okay,' Winterkill thought, 'you blew it on the pickup truck, so stay on the ball now.'

Despite the presence of law enforcement, Winterkill knew the criminals were here somewhere. Watching and waiting. He listened deep and hard to the threats spoken by the mastermind of the robbery, and that was the voice of intent and determination as well as the voice of a career criminal. That is how all the criminals spoke in video games and in the gaming world! Winterkill knew they were there, hiding somewhere and right now, their intention was to find out who he was, where he lived, and to make sure he paid a dear price for helping to ruin their plans and abort the bank robbery.

"Bring it on, jackasses. Find out where I live, so I can find out who you dudes are too. We have the technology. Besides, I am Winterkill and I never lose a game. Ever."

The cockiness and self-assurance made Mr. Mark Holiday into Winterkill, the best competitive video gamer in the world, and it was going to bring him through this situation, his new role and the mission that the quiet stranger assigned him to perform. Furthermore, he took the stranger's warning seriously and after meeting these crooks, he knew that it was "game on."

He vowed that no harm would come to anyone on his watch. No way.

Winterkill squinted at the bright sunlight and made a mental note, always to bring his sunglasses. He thought how Winterkill would look cooler if he wore sunglasses during his missions. He needed all the "cool" that he could muster up.

With a wide smile plastered across his face, Winterkill grabbed his phone. He picked the ear buds off his chest and popped them in his ears. After dialing up his favorite tune, Winterkill put his hands in the pockets of his jeans and listened to the music while cockily strutting down the street to his home. His body swayed to the beat, along with a brash hop and a bounce to his steps.

Between songs, Winterkill spoke aloud, "Maybe, along with the sunglasses I should get some metal tips for my sneakers so that I can walk around all cool like the quiet stranger does. I can make those cool clicking noises on the sidewalk too." He stopped walking and thought about it for a second or two. With a shake of his head, he laughed and said, "No, no, bad idea. No one is as cool as the stranger is. Last thing that I want is to get on the stranger's bad side. I better just stay being, Winterkill."

He began walking again and turned in the direction of his apartment house.

Winterkill snapped his fingers to the beat of the song playing in his ears and swayed his body even more.

Above the music, he announced to the world, "I love this song. It is one of my faves. Yes indeed, the stranger is so damn cool, but I am kind of thinking that Winterkill is pretty damn cool too."

Early in the evening, a few hours after Winterkill and the "hero" security officer thwarted the bank robbery; Winterkill sat in his chair in his command post and scanned his world. He laughed at the local news buzzing in front of his eyes and the beautiful news reporter falling all over the handsome, muscular security officer as she interviewed the hero who saved lives as well as the bank. No one mentioned Mr. Mark Holiday and his skillful swinging of an umbrella, and certainly, no one mentioned Winterkill. That was fine, and Winterkill knew that his best strategy was that he had to fade to black. The video game of the robbery that had played endlessly the past few days was now silent, and the monitor screen for the game was blank and black now too. Even if Mark tried to load a game on the console, it would not play. Mark now knew the strategy, and when the game returned to playing, he knew it would be a prelude to the next round of the mission. For now, it too had faded to black. An ominous and silent black.

Under the pretense of working with a video game development team from one of his subsidiaries, Winterkill made a rare on-line live appearance, and he asked many questions on one of his own chat forums. He asked questions about self-defense tactics, common tools in self-defense, security gizmos and gadgets, and advanced technology. Within an hour or thereabouts, Winterkill tapped some of the best minds in the world. The network of gamers available to Winterkill was astounding, and the collection of the various genius minds overflowed with diversity. A retired Scotland Yard investigator in the United Kingdom had Winterkill all set up in self-defense. A teenager who was an electronic and computer wizard, and who used the gaming handle of "Skateblade" (and a teenager with what Winterkill suspected was a terrible habit of part-time hacking of various websites) living in British Columbia, Canada, provided electronic security and software advice. Even though Mark Holiday was a genius too, he gladly tapped into his network of fellow geniuses. The gaming world teemed with them. All of his schoolteachers told Mark that he was a genius after he aced everything from stacking blocks in kindergarten to his breezing through trigonometry. By the time that Mark Holiday was twenty-three years of age, he had two degrees, one in general sciences and one in mathematics, all earned ahead of time in advanced progressions, but school was not his bag. His university wanted Mark to stay on, earn higher degrees and teach there someday, but he had other things on his mind. When Mark reached the age of twenty-five, he had this apartment in the upscale apartment building, as well as his businesses and his empire. His parents lived a few miles away from the outskirts of the city, with his mother being a successful accountant with her own practice, and his father was a sales and marketing executive in a large corporation. While his parents never fully understood what it was that Mark did, they could not argue with his success. His parents always thought with his intelligence that Mark could pick his career and that there was no limit to what he could achieve, but Mark took a different route. What his parents did not realize was that their son was indeed world famous in his own manner.

Now, in the chat forum, it was bedlam with the famous Winterkill making a rare appearance and chatting with everyone. Other contacts jumped in and out and offered advice and expert commentary, and by the time that Winterkill signed off from the chat group, he had all he required to defend the perimeter of his apartment building and to identify the criminals that Winterkill knew would be prowling around waiting for an opportunity to even the score.

Another hour or so later, after perusing the huge shopping cart of the internet world, Winterkill had all he needed heading his way via overnight delivery. Proximity sensors that could transmit electronic beams of sound and could detect, even a bird landing on his balcony, would be guards of the perimeter, the hallways and all the exterior of his apartment and the building too. Laser beam type signal detectors would broadcast beams throughout his apartment, and even if someone broke the perimeter and gained access to the apartment, the beams would be the final line of defense. High-tech mini cameras, equipped with motion detectors as well as night vision, would constantly scan the same areas and all of these electronic sensors and eyes in the sky would communicate all the captured information, images and data to new software that could broadcast alarms and information to his command center console and to his cellphone too. Winterkill knew the building management would help to install the new equipment. He was their prize tenant and Mark Holiday paid a handsome rental fee to live here and he tipped the building maintenance team very well too. Truly, it was in the best interest of Winterkill Enterprises, the building management, and the other tenants, too. These days, you can never have enough security.

In addition, speeding Winterkill's way via the internet delivery fleet was an assortment of the best handcuffs available to law enforcement, and many, many packets of high-tech plastic ties, not the kind for bundling wires, but the kind to bundle humans. Courtesy of solid advice from his retired Scotland Yard Inspector, Winterkill also ordered trigger locks to fit the triggers of various weapons of all types. The inspector told him many of the tricks that the unarmed English "Bobbies" used to hold and detain criminals until the heavy artillery arrived. He purchased a backpack to hold all of this gear in as he made his way in the "gaming fields," in order to push the pause button on the "bad guys" and win the game. All geeky gamer dudes, toted backpacks and Mark Holiday already owned a wide assortment of them, but this one was larger and was a special backpack. More tactical than geeky. The final piece of his crime-fighting equipment took a long time to find, but when he found it on an exclusive website, Winterkill did not hesitate to pay an exorbitant price for this specific item. The item was a man's umbrella, all dressed out in the color of flat black and equipped with a heavy and extra-sturdy oak wood handle.

A sturdy oak handle that would deliver one mean-ass blow if the umbrella just so happened to swing in the air and by some remote chance, it happened to strike a blow across a person's head.

Or just by chance . . . a person's neck.

Mark Holiday's cellphone beeped and dinged with a text message.

Hailee: *Hi! Whatcha doin' today?*

Mark Holiday stared long and hard at the screen of the cellphone while pondering the answer to Hailee's text message.

While thinking aloud, Mark said, "Okay, let's see, my dear Hailee. It is a little difficult to explain. Let me try to ask . . . by chance, do you recall that very cool, but mysterious dude dressed all in black at the restaurant the other night? Do you remember, you know, the dude sitting next to me that all the women swooned over? Well, it seems as if he is a superhero, or an alien, or some kind of dude from another world. Hell, I don't really want to know who he is. However, he gave me special powers, and a mission to help him defeat evil dudes and he gave me the power to control the world as if it was a video game. I do not have full-control, I can only stop the world from moving and evolving for ten minutes by hitting a make-believe pause button and the world stops for about ten minutes. I only can hit the pause button . . . the rest is up to me to figure out. Therefore, to answer your question very factually, today, Winterkill stopped a bank robbery. Yeah, that is right . . . the robbery you will see on the local news. I know that the news is reporting that it was some hero security officer, but really, it was Winterkill, who stopped the robbery. Me."

Mark rolled his eyes and laughed at the thought. Yet, he could not lie or fudge the truth to Hailee, the young woman whom he had instantly fallen in love with, so he picked up his cellphone and texted back to her:

Mark: *Oh, just being Winterkill. U know the drill.*

Hailee: *Yes, I get it. Running your gaming empire, raking in the dough and winning all the games.*

Mark paused for a few seconds over the keyboard of the cellphone and he smiled. This time he did not have to lie because the game was not over yet.

Mark: *Yes, sort of. Kind of. As far as the winning goes, have not won the game yet, just the opening rounds. Game is a long one . . . it goes on for a long time.*

Hailee: *Cool. Well, I know u will win because Winterkill never loses. Ever.*

Mark nodded his head and realized that he was still smiling. He always smiles around Hailee. Either in electronic chat, text, or in person. Hailee has been studying Winterkill. She knows the tagline. Before Mark could answer, the phone beeped again with another text.

Hailee: *Are we still good for meeting up on Saturday after my shift ends? My mom is cool with watching Ingrid, so we have plenty of time! I get off at eight P.M.*

Mark: *Oh yeah! I will be at the restaurant around 7. If the weather is nice, I will chill with a drink on the patio and then we can book after ur shift ends. U working the patio?*

Hailee: *I am now! Gotta go. A customer just came in. Text u later.*

Mark: *K. Have a good day. Later.*

Hailee worked in a small retail convenience store during the day and waited tables at Silverado's Restaurant at night and in between hours on the weekends. She worked very hard, and if things pan out the way that Mark Holiday felt in his heart, then someday, Hailee will not have to work so hard. Right now, though, there was a mission that required his attention. A mission to save Hailee and many other people from some type of danger, and Winterkill would be ready.

By the end of the week, the command center of Winterkill Enterprises took on a new look. The virtual defenses that Winterkill used in his games also now transpired to Winterkill's reality world. With some very generous tips, a team of happy building maintenance men, along with Mark, installed all the new technology. Mark fiddled with the software and with his genius-level skills; Mark had the database and software smoothly humming along within a half-day of effort. It was very sophisticated and all this had been quite expensive, but worth it. The cameras watching the exteriors that his retired Scotland Yard contact recommended were (other than his umbrella!) Mark's favorite tool. Until Mark installed it and fiddled with it for a few days, he did not realize that it could determine a person's height and estimated weight and he could snap a face shot, upload it to his database and the system would allow export for potential facial recognition and identity of the individual. If the kingpin of the robberies showed up outside, and Winterkill managed some type of snapshot that included facial details, he knew that Skateblade could tap into somewhere and find out who he was. Winterkill would not ask any questions and Skateblade would not ask any either.

After all, Winterkill was simply developing a new video game. . ..

Friday morning arrived, and the hot and steamy

weather arrived along with it. Clear, but hot and steamy, and the loudmouthed weatherman on channel six said there was a chance of thunderstorms for the next few days and evenings.

Perfect umbrella weather.

Winterkill had, as of late, changed up his sleeping versus waking hours and while he skipped one or two competitions; he was back in full-force on Thursday evening, easily winning an on-line game. Now, from either a lack of sleep or a lack of any action from the reality world and the "bad guys" within it, Winterkill found his intake of coffee had proportionally increased as the action ground to a halt. He sat in his gaming chair, headphones on, watching his network and various screens, and until now, everything was very quiet. Too quiet. Winterkill programmed his software, utilizing the cameras that were scanning the exterior of the building, to alert him to any person fitting the rough height and weight description of the kingpin. As a result, the system would lock on track and alert Winterkill to a detection of such a person, and the cameras would immediately snap as many pictures as possible of the detected person. Winterkill grew tired of how many persons fit that height and weight description. He never realized how many large people roamed the city street outside of his apartment building!

As noontime on Friday now approached, he found, as his eyelids grew heavy, a large element of complacency crept into his activity and attention. His networks mostly ran themselves and the money poured into his coffers without much attention from Mark Holiday or Winterkill. That was part of the beauty of his empire.

Winterkill might have been nodding off when the scanning software peering into the city street sounded an alert. Nodding off to the point where he might have curled up in his chair and dismissed the alarm. Instead, he opened one eye and looked over to the monitor displaying the image that triggered the alarm. He was ready to dismiss the alarm, click on the "acknowledge" command, and go back to a glorious nap creeping in on him, when the camera automatically zoomed in on the subject.

He was now wide awake . . . and then some. It only took him microseconds to decide that it was the kingpin of the gang. A gang that the local news and law enforcement recently labeled, "The Brazen Daylight Heist Gang." Even though Winterkill never saw his face, he just knew it was the leader of the gang; by the way he stood, the way that he moved his head, his size, his frame. He jumped onto the keyboard of the computer controlling the camera, and he quickly typed the commands to override the automatic features of the controls of the camera. Using a joystick controller, he panned, tilted and zoomed into the man, while the software captured the images. He was standing across the street, next to a tree, watching the apartment house from there, while hiding behind some dark sunglasses. Winterkill smiled as he adjusted the zoom setting on the camera to move in closer and the lens focused on the man's neck. A neck where there remained, fading, but still visible red welts that formed across the muscles of his neck. Similar to red welts that might have formed . . . if the man had encountered a blow from a sturdy object.

Such as the wooden handle of an old umbrella.

All criminals eventually make a fatal mistake, an error, no matter how smart they are, or how skilled they are at deception and criminal activities. All criminals think that they will never slip up and that the "good guys," will never capture them. This man was no exception. For a few seconds, he lifted his sunglasses to wipe some sweat away from his face and eyes. The camera and technology snapped merrily away, and within seconds, it captured facial shots. Mistake number two out of four. The first mistake was trying to rob the bank, the second was showing up here to plan his revenge on him and the third was allowing the heat of the day to get to him. Mistake number four will be when the kingpin does whatever stupid thing that he has planned next. Winterkill just won this round and, as the kingpin, began to walk up the city street and head in the opposite direction of the apartment house, Winterkill knew that he had the information that he needed to enact his eventual revenge. It was game on; the kingpin's thirst for vengeance just lured him into a technology trap.

Within a few more keystrokes and a few clicks of the mouse, the image of the kingpin's face was on the software. The software, adjusted the light, optimized the features and his face was now clear as a bell.

Next up was to dial in the one person that Winterkill was sure could identify this character. It might be a few hours behind as far as time zones, but he knew that the chances were very good for Skateblade to be active on the social media messenger site. A quick check on the site found a green light next to Skateblade's profile picture and Winterkill typed out the message.

Winterkill: *Say, hey, Skateblade. How U doin? Favor. If I sent you a Jpeg of a man's face, could you find out his identity?*

Immediately, the message bubble popped up with the response.

Skateblade: *Hey, Winterkill! Just chillin' here. Ah, for you, I might be able to do that. For the new game, huh?*

He followed the text with a winky-face emoji.

Winterkill: *Yeah. The new game. Cool. Thanks. Where do I send it?*

Skateblade: *My website has an email address listed there. It is on my own secure server. Attach the jpeg to an email and send it there. Where is this dude located?*

Winterkill: *Paterson, New Jersey. Jpeg coming ur way. Thnx.*

Skateblade: *K. Gimme an hour.*

No sooner than Winterkill finished sending the email to the gamer known as Skateblade, the video game console and monitor that had strangely remained dark and silent since the bank robbery game ended, jumped back to life. Winterkill studied the new game playing, and he realized that the next mission was at hand. The quiet stranger in the black hat reappeared and just as he had done for the prelude to the bank robbery, the stranger gave away hints as to what was going to happen next. This time, the game gave Winterkill some shivers up and down his spine as he watched the scene unfold in the game. He picked up the game controller and held it in his hands, waiting for the right moment to hit the pause. The scene playing was an open-air patio of an exclusive restaurant and the patio looked very familiar. A gorgeous hostess smiled and greeted guests as they came and went while she posed at the hostess station. A team of bartenders frantically worked behind the bar, taking orders and preparing cocktails while pouring beer mugs and filling wine glasses for the patrons. No seats were empty at the bar and the tables of the patio were full of patrons, too. Patrons all dressed for a night on the town. When the three gun-toting criminals brandishing weapons and shooting warning shots in the air burst into the patio, Winterkill grew even tenser. They all wore ski masks and dressed in black military tactical gear, and they all wore black tactical gloves. Two criminals had handguns drawn, but the leader had a semiautomatic weapon and when the leader of the gang, grabbed for a hostage, a gorgeous young woman, who was working as a server, put her in a headlock, and held the weapon to her head, Winterkill could not take any more and he hit the pause button. His breathing was heavy, his forehead was full of sweat, and his hands were so sweaty that he felt as if his finger would fall off the pause button.

"Hailee," Winterkill whispered aloud, "oh, dear Lord. What have I done? They will tail me to you on Saturday and I have brought you into this game."

He pounded his fist upon the desk. He ran his hands through his hair and his eyes focused and grew wider and wider as he studied the game. No doubt it was now . . . game on.

A message bubble popped up in the game and in uppercase letters, Winterkill watched the message type across the screen:

"ON SATURDAY NIGHT, BE SURE TO BRING YOUR UMBRELLA ON YOUR DATE. WEATHERMAN SAYS THERE IS A VERY GOOD CHANCE OF RAIN. A DOWNPOUR."

The cockiness and confidence that made Winterkill, the best video gamer in the world, returned and it combined with the love that he felt for Hailee to create an unstoppable force. The momentary fear left as another message bubble popped up on his social media site and his email dinged with a message arrival in his in-box.

Skateblade: *Check ya email, dude. BTW, whatever this "game" is, and if I can help, then, I am in.*

Winterkill: *K. Thnx. Yeah, man, ur part of the team.*

Winterkill leaned in and opened the email message. It was plain and succinct.

He read it aloud, "Greg Vander Waal. Age, thirty-seven. Six-feet four inches, two-hundred and thirty pounds. A career criminal. In and out of prison for various crimes, mostly car theft and armed-robbery, since he was a teenager. Home city is Paterson, New Jersey. No recorded address since his last prison stint. Badass guy, known for ruthless assaults during robberies. Whatever the "game" is, be careful. This dude is no joke in the evil department."

Winterkill tapped off a message thanking his friend for the effort and info, and he sat back and studied the video monitor with the face of Greg Vander Waal on it. His original intention was to identify this man, then pass the info along to Detective Dalton. When he did so, he would figure out a cover story of how he discovered his identity. Now, in light of the game playing on the screen in front of him, a game currently in the pause mode, he knew that his initial plan would not work. If the police were going to capture this criminal and his gang, they would have already done so. The quiet stranger in the black hat recruited Winterkill for a reason, and the reason was that the stranger already knew the police would not capture Greg Vander Waal. This evil man was going to kill people in his quest for money and within his crime wave of horror. Someone needed to stop Vander Waal. He was quite sure that the quiet stranger could stop him, but for a reason that might be beyond his understanding, or in fact, any person's understanding, the stranger recruited Winterkill in order to stop the criminal and his evil intentions.

Winterkill picked up his game controller and hit the pause button to allow the game to play. He closed his eyes when the gunshot occurred and the young woman crumbled dead at the feet of the kingpin who then proceeded to shoot and kill many more while the gang raided the cash registers, and they quickly stole wallets, jewelry, and other valuables of the patrons.

The game ominously warned, with flashing letters, that this round was lost and he reached over and shut off the game and the monitor.

In his mind, while he fingered the pause button, he knew that he would not lose the next round, nor would he lose the game.

Winterkill never lost a game. Ever, and there was no way that he was going to lose this one. The stranger was counting upon him, as were Hailee, Ingrid, and countless other innocent people. Winterkill would not let them down and he would do whatever it took in order to win this one.

"I love your little backpack, Mark!" Hailee exclaimed as she stood on her tippy-toes and kissed him gently on his cheek. Now, who knew that an innocent kiss on his cheek could create so many emotions for Mark Holiday? However, it could. Mark felt it ripple from his head to his toes.

"It is so you, to pack a little backpack with stuff to go out on a date with me. You are so cute. Do you have your laptop in there? Still working, huh?"

Once more, Mark Holiday would never tell a lie to the woman that he loved. Mark did not have to search too deeply within his heart to know that he was madly in love with Hailee. Despite their just meeting a week or so ago and barely knowing her—Mark already knew that he was in love. Perhaps the stranger's influences brought them together. Mark realized that the stranger's powers seemed to be at work in every aspect of his life. Hailee appeared even more radiant than she did last Saturday. And, despite being in and out of the kitchen and dashing about in the lingering heat of the day, her scent was glorious. Mark sampled it and thought how it was the scent of fresh rose blooms. Her smile was so perfect and her languishing eyes were not even describable.

"Ah, well, no, actually, I have my gaming tablet in here . . . along with other . . . stuff. I was going to connect to the Wi-Fi and check out some sites while I waited for you."

Hailee nodded, and she fingered the hem of his tee shirt and studied Mark with love in her eyes.

"I missed you. Texting is cool, but I am so looking forward to getting to spend some more time with you and to get to know you better. Same attire, too. You are so adorable! Here you are, wearing your canvas sneakers, and those black, but faded jeans, and the tee shirt with the logo for your company. You are so cute, but I have to ask. What is with the umbrella?" Hailee held out her hand and pointed in the direction of his new umbrella. Mark smiled and placed the umbrella in her petite hands. "Whoa, a heavy umbrella and such a thick handle, too. Wow," Hailee said while she tested the weight with both of her hands and handed the umbrella back to Mark.

"Yes, well, that loudmouthed weather guy on channel six said that there were chances of thunderstorms and I thought we might need to walk somewhere. I don't own a car." Mark studied her eyes, and Hailee's smile grew even wider and the lick in her eyes twinkled and glowed.

"You are so thoughtful as well as cute. C'mon, adorable, Mark Holiday, or is it, Winterkill? I will get you a table and your red wine. I have a few tables to finish serving yet, but the floor manager said that I could book out a little earlier tonight. I want to change, so I brought a fresh set of clothes," Hailee said while she waved Mark over to a table and he gladly followed her. Mark admired the rear view of Hailee Nathanson and he thought how the rear view of her was almost as grand as the front view was!

"Okay, but tonight, please, Hailee, just pour me a lager beer. Whatever you have on tap. I am not really a red wine guy. That was sort of a fluke. In fact, that whole night was special in so many ways. Mostly for meeting you, but, no, right now, believe me, I am Mark Holiday. Although, I cannot say for sure if Winterkill will make an appearance tonight or not. You just never know." Hailee stopped and pointed to a table, and Mark studied the location. Within microseconds, his mind and his eyes reverted to Winterkill's mind and eyes and Winterkill quickly scanned the situation and view. This was perfect. Close to the entrance and a perfect view of the entrance, bar and hostess station. There remained only two other access points, and they were fire exits with only one way out and no handle on the outside of which to enter the patio from the street side. The other doorways led to the kitchen, and to the inside of the restaurant, if a patron needed to visit the restrooms or did not want to remain dining outside on the patio.

Perfect table. Perfect location.

"This is a great table, Hailee. Perfect. Thank you."

"Yes, perfect. Like you are. I will be right back with the beer," Hailee said, and she took two steps, whirled around, and caught Mark's eyes studying her.

"Oh, and I am so glad you are here. I am so looking forward to tonight!"

"Me too, Hailee. Me too."

She smiled, pushed the strands of her hair behind her ear and scooted off. Mark took a deep breath as he watched her dash away. Goodness gracious. Was he head over heels in love, or what? Yes, he was.

Mark also knew that somewhere close by here, Greg Vander Waal and his team of thugs tailed Mark here and right now, they were figuring out how this was a solid target to hit and that Mark could easily be a target in and amongst the mayhem. Here were the high rollers of the city, all out enjoying an extravagant night out on the town, in the city's most exclusive restaurant. Here they all sat on their fat wallets, with fancy cars parked in the valet lots, diamond jewelry on their fingers and around their necks, and cash registers filled with the busy day's earnings. Was it a bank heist? No, but it was an easy target, with multiple and easily accessed escape routes that with a few quick turns led to an interstate highway, and the bonus of little to no emergency alarms, just some patrons dialing emergency numbers with hidden cellphones. However, the ace in the deck was the thirst for revenge by kingpin Vander Waal and his promise to make good to even the score and take out Winterkill. The kingpin knew that Winterkill was here. However, what he did not know was that what he thought was just some lean, lanky, skinny, geeky guy, was actually not as he seemed. Winterkill had a few surprises at his disposal.

In Mark's competitive mind, he earned a point in the game already. Right now, it was Winterkill, one point and the bad guys earned a big, fat zero.

Hailee delivered his beer, and she stole another quick kiss on his cheek and dashed away. She was so happy, such a joyous evening planned, and as most of the patrons here were doing, they were enjoying the evening. It was still warm, still a little humid, but not overly hot. Just a touch of heat remained in the day, and while there were some dark clouds looming as the light of the day faded away, the clouds did not seem quite as ominous as did the threat that Mark Holiday sensed looming on the horizon. Terror loomed, sheer terror and as he took the first sip of his beer and felt a slight breeze pick up and flow in and across the patio, Mark Holiday gave way to Winterkill. The keen eyes took over, and his mind tuned to the game at hand, snapping each movement, scanning the scene and the faces. Assessing the angles and situation. Slowly, Winterkill unzipped his backpack, pulled his tablet out, and while he had little to no intention to use it for any significant reason, it did give Winterkill the opportunity to check on the status of his tools for tonight. Handcuffs, plastic ties, trigger locks. Yes, indeed they were all there, as was his weapon of choice.

As Hailee had noticed, it had a sturdy and thick handle. After all, it looked as if it was simply an umbrella.

When he watched Hailee pick up a drink order from the edge of the bar and turn in the direction of the entrance, Winterkill knew that it was time. Surprisingly, he was very calm, when he realized that the scene played over in the game yesterday, just materialized in front of his eyes. Hailee was now carrying a tray with drinks. The hostess was standing at the podium smiling and waving goodbye to some patrons who were leaving, and the entrance gate to the restaurant's patio slowly swung wide open. Winterkill took the scene in and, just as he would in any video game action, he processed it and made his move.

The only trouble was that this was reality and not a game.

What he was not ready for was the way his heart almost stopped, and the way every single fiber of his body shook when Greg Vander Waal and his two sidekick thugs appeared out of nowhere and forced their evil way into innocent people's lives. Out of nowhere, they appeared, brandishing weapons, with black ski masks over their faces and loudly shouting about a hold up and for, "Everyone to get down and to start to toss their wallets and jewelry out in the aisles! Now, or we blow her head off in front of everyone!"

The kingpin grabbed Hailee and forced poor Hailee into his body as he wrapped his huge arm around her neck. Winterkill realized that the kingpin must have been watching from afar, saw their interaction, and realized that Hailee would flush him out. Right now, this was about revenge as much as it was about stealing money and valuables. The tray of drinks went flying and crashing to the ground, and the thugs reached for their weapons. Hailee's scream went right through Winterkill, and patrons screamed and dove for cover as they saw the gang suddenly appear in front of them and the kingpin takes Hailee as a hostage.

Winterkill recovered, and he knew that he had to move now before they wrapped their fingers into the triggers of the weapons. If they did so, he would not be able to slip the trigger locks into the triggers because if the rules of the game held true to form, he would not be able to move their fingers. Moving now, risked Hailee as well as his own life, but he had to do it. Instantly, he jumped off the chair. He assumed his traditional gaming position, and just as he saw the kingpin turn his gaze in his direction and move his finger toward the trigger of the semiautomatic rifle; he hit the pause button.

"Pause!"

Once again, the world did so.

Winterkill exhaled in some sort of relief. He quickly made a note of the time and punched the ten-minute timer into his watch that he programmed earlier. This time, he knew the rules of the game and he was not wasting any precious time trying to figure anything out. Not when he looked into the look of horror on the frozen face of Hailee and all the other innocent people. Quickly, he moved into action, and first, he reached into his backpack and pulled out his tools. He slipped the trigger locks on the weapons of the two sidekick thugs. Luckily, the pause button worked just in time, because the two of them were reaching into their jackets for their weapons and their fingers were inches away from grabbing the handles. Not surprisingly, Winterkill perfectly nailed the timing of this pause. With the trigger locks securely in place, Winterkill slipped multiple plastic ties around their ankles and pulled the ties snugly so their first steps would result in a big surprise. Then, he closed the handcuffs around their wrists and in the case of the two thugs, who were trailing behind their leader; he was able to handcuff both of them to the metal post of the entrance gate for the patio entrance.

Winterkill, three and the bad guys, zero.

He carefully studied the situation that Greg Vander Waal presented. The kingpin's left arm wrapped around Hailee's neck and he pulled her in very tightly to his body. Hailee's feet barely grazed the ground and Winterkill tried hard not to focus on her horror, but at what he needed to do right now. Greg Vander Waal's right arm held the rifle at his side and the shoulder strap for the weapon hung loose in a loop and his fingers were thankfully not on the trigger. Winterkill snapped the trigger lock in place and double-checked the lock. A glance at his watch told him that he still had five minutes or so of time left. Next, after a careful study of the situation, he slipped multiple plastic ties on Greg's ankles and while doing so, Winterkill found a large knife strapped to his ankle in a sheath. A few plastic ties took care of lashing the knife in place to where he could not pull the knife out of the leather sheath. The next step was to handcuff the kingpin's left arm to a steel hook supporting the entrance gate directly behind him. As a good measure of extra reinforcement, the shoulder strap of the weapon received multiple plastic ties to the entrance gate too.

He stood back and smiled as he said to the frozen and paused world, "Well, now, you evil dudes stopped in such a convenient place. Thank you for your outstanding cooperation. So many things to tie you up with right at my fingertips. When I hit the pause button and release the world, my goodness, you are all in for a surprise. Watch out for the first step. It is going to hurt. Right now, it looks as if this round is over and I have a feeling the game is too. The score, which is flashing on the screen right now, is Winterkill, four and bad guys, zero. Man, oh man, I am going to have a helluva time explaining this one to Detective Dalton." Winterkill ran over to his table, and he packed up the rest of his gear into the backpack, slipped his tablet in there and downed the rest of his beer. After all, it was his beer.

Grabbing his umbrella, Winterkill strategically placed his body in just the right spot to make his swings of the handle count. His first shot would be to the face of the kingpin. He then visualized the timing of one of his best moves from a video game, with a quick spin and two smashes to the faces of the two sidekicks as they woke up to the biggest surprise of their lives and came crashing down to the ground in front of Winterkill. He just had to make sure that Hailee fell into his arms as Greg tumbled down. He looked at his watch and he had less than a minute left. He tested his position and ran the scenario through his mind, one, last, time.

With just a few seconds to spare, Winterkill stood with his trusty umbrella next to his leg, assumed the gaming position and took a deep breath. As he exhaled, with his hand and fingers outstretched in the position, he hit the pause button. This time, he kept his eyes wide open.

"Resume!"

Using all of his best gaming reflexes and impeccable timing, Winterkill grabbed the umbrella. He swung it hard and fast at the kingpin's face, just as he saw the world return to life. The solid feel of the blow and the eyes of Greg Vander Waal rolling back into his head confirmed that it was a perfect blow. Screams from the innocent people filled the air, and blood spurted from the face of the evil kingpin. Winterkill, just as he practiced, spun on his heels and delivered two more blows to each of the sidekicks as they took their first steps and virtually fell into the handle of the umbrella. Winterkill dropped the umbrella and dove to grab Hailee just as the kingpin pushed her away as he tried to reach for his face from the pain of the blow and the sheer surprise at what happened. Winterkill caught Hailee just before she crashed to the ground, and he wrapped her up in his lanky frame and surprisingly strong arms.

Winterkill's mission was complete.

"You're okay, Hailee. It's over, baby. You are safe. Everyone is safe," Mark whispered as he held her tightly and gently picked her up. The screams of the patrons ended as everyone realized that the thugs were now defenseless, and they were thrashing around in front of them in vain, while they tried to grab at what were now useless weapons.

"Are you hurt, Hailee?" Mark asked while he gently pushed that glorious dangle of hair behind her ear.

"No, no, other than my heart nearly jumping out of my chest and the fact that I am in shock, I am fine. But how the hell did you do that? I mean . . . one second that big guy grabbed me and I was screaming and in the next second, you have them all tied up and bleeding . . . and, I am safely wrapped in your arms."

"Well, baby, you will find out that I move fast. Really, really, fast. I play video games, you know. My reflexes are amazing. Besides, these bad guys move slowly. Very slowly. Hold on a second." Mark turned and addressed the stunned crowd of patrons and then pointed at the equally stunned hostess, "Ah, can you call 9-1-1 for us? Tell them that we have a bunch of bad guys here."

The open-mouthed hostess nodded, picked up the telephone, and dialed the phone. Mark turned, and he gazed at the captured thugs all thrashing around, while realizing that they were helpless and captured. He peered in, looked at the kingpin, and pointed at his face, as the head thug sneered at him and tried to wipe his face of the blood pouring from his nose.

"Geez, well, hello there, Mr. Bad Guy. Also known as Greg Vander Waal. Yeah, I know who you are and unfortunately, for you, and fortunately for the rest of us, I am not exactly who you thought I was. Man, oh, man, you are gonna need a new nose there. Luckily, you will have plenty of time to heal while sitting in prison."

Greg pulled and pulled, as he tried in vain, to pull free of his ties and handcuffs.

While Winterkill gently kicked the useless weapons away from all of them, the kingpin growled at Winterkill. "Just who the hell are you? You son-of-a-bitch. I swear . . . I will get you someday and I will get, Miss Pretty, here too. You can bet on it."

While the police sirens wailed in the distance and the stunned, but grateful patrons and management of the restaurant gathered around to congratulate and thank

Mark . . . he transformed into Winterkill once more.

He leaned in and, almost in a whisper, said, "Guess what? For a guy sitting on your ass all tied up and for a guy with no nose, you sure are confident. Please, you can call me, Winterkill, and as I told you before, bring it on. Heed my warning again and this time, pay better attention because I swing a mean-ass umbrella. I never lose a game. Ever."

Mark slowly walked away, and in and amongst many slaps on his back and heartfelt words of thanks and congratulations, he stopped, grabbed Hailee and held her tightly in his arms.

She lovingly looked up at her man and said, "I think there is something else going on here, and the fast reflex thing is bullshit, but this is usually where the woman kisses the hero."

"Works for me. I think I have seen that scene in a game or two, so, yes, bring it on."

The kiss was long and glorious and the cheers and claps of the many spectators made the kiss seem all that much sweeter.

Detective Dalton sat next to Mr. Mark Holiday and Hailee, while Mark enjoyed a few beers on the house from an appreciative management of Silverado's Restaurant. Hailee sipped a glass of red wine and swooned over her hero.

"You know, Mark, I am kind of sensing a pattern here. You seem to have a knack for being in the right place at the right time type of thing. A cliché for sure, but true." Detective Dalton made the comments; he scratched at his head with his pen, while in the background, a team of police officers and paramedics worked on the crime and medical scene. Due to the power of a certain sturdy-handled umbrella, there were a few bad guys with bleeding noses and faces. After the paramedics applied first aid and medical care, the officers read their rights and arrested the team of thugs.

"So, let's give this interrogation another little bit of a go around. After recognizing them as the same criminals from the bank, you somehow did an end around, because, I know, you tend to move very fast, and you came up from behind these guys, snuck up on them and whooped the living stuffing out of them with your, cough, cough, ah, umbrella."

Mark nodded, while Hailee smiled and while taking another sip of the beer, Mark answered, "That is about right, Detective Dalton. Say, do you want a beer? I have some pull with the management here."

Detective Dalton scratched some notes on his pad and said, "I would love an ice-cold beer. In fact, after this investigation, I might need a few shots of fine whiskey, but I am on duty. Let's try to stick to the subject here. This is an official investigation."

Mark smiled again, and Hailee suppressed a laugh at Detective Dalton's frustration.

"Okay, and while they were all stunned and bleeding, you managed to secure the weapons with trigger locks and tie them up with plastic ties and some handy sets of handcuffs. You just so happened to have these plastic, law-enforcement ties and handcuffs, along with a smattering of trigger locks in your backpack, because I know . . . you are doing research for a video game and needed them. This, by the way, is technically illegal for you to use these cuffs and ties, but it is private property and the management suddenly claims that you are part of the security team. Oh and, yes, I know by reviewing my notes, the reason that you have this umbrella with a handle made of oak that could knock a hole in a brick wall, is because. . .."

Detective Dalton stopped his statement short, lifted his

eyebrows, and looked at Mark for him to finish the sentence.

"Well, Detective Dalton, yes, indeed, that loudmouthed weather dude on channel six is always wrong. Besides, the bank owes me a new umbrella, but I know it will be a cheap piece of junk, so in the meantime, I bought a better one. Did you see that bad comb over on the bank manager? C'mon, the guy is cheaper than cheap can be. Did you ever get one of those free toasters from the bank for opening an account? All they do is burn stuff."

Detective Dalton suppressed a laugh and shook his head, closed his notepad, and put his pen inside his suit jacket. "You know, something, Mark, I think you are one, extremely brave and intelligent young man. A hero, and while I am not sensing your complete honesty over this situation, or in the bank situation, I accept the fact that a very bad group of guys is now in our custody, with a ton of witnesses to make an ironclad case. However, I cannot understand all of this . . . but I might be convinced to look the other way. I mean, after all, this is *not too* strange! Let's see now, there were about a hundred witnesses who say they cannot even tell me what exactly happened here and they cannot account for lost moments. . .."

Mark interrupted and waved his hand in the air in an effort to dismiss the testimony, "Oh, c'mon, it is cut and dry. Just another Saturday night at Silverado's Restaurant. Lots of booze flowing in those witnesses, hazy thoughts, fueled by booze and good times, ya know, blurred reality. Besides, bad guys are overrated."

"They might be, Mark, but unfortunately, there are a lot of them. They are relentless and unforgiving too and they just keep coming."

"I guess so and we will be ready for them."

"Good. Stay ready. I assure you that there are tons of them. My pension is counting on it. Remember, some criminals are in it for money, or a warped sense of fame, but some are in it for pain and for revenge. Criminals who harbor pain and revenge in their hearts are the most dangerous of them all because in my experience, they eventually always act upon those emotions."

Mark nodded and said, "Thank you for your words of wisdom and of experience. I will take them in and never forget them."

"Good. Please, do so."

Mark smiled and said, "Say, Detective Dalton, I love ya and all, and ya a really cool dude, but my woman and I want to scoot out for our date now. We planned tonight all week. Until now, it has been a little crazy. I guess that is kind of sugarcoating it. It has been wild. Even my games are calmer than tonight has been. Anyway, how about you go off duty and I get you a beer on the house? The Scottish Red Ale is awesome. Be careful, twelve percent alcohol on that stuff. Then, Hailee and I, well, we can be on our way and enjoy our date. You have my card and we can talk if you need me for anything else."

Detective Dalton smiled, and he stood up, extended his hand and while the two men shook hands, Detective Dalton said, "Thank you, Mark. Sure, sure, I am off duty. A free fancy beer in a fancy joint that I cannot afford on a lowly detective's salary sounds good. Enjoy your special night. You deserve it and you have quite a gorgeous gal there. I understand . . . I was young once, too. As of the last few days, I think I have aged, but yes, I have your card."

"Sure, sure, and yes, Hailee is beyond amazing. She is beyond awesome and I am a lucky dude."

Hailee remained silent. She finished her wine, her face filled with a red blush of love combined with embarrassment and she stood and lovingly took Mark's hand.

"We will get you the ale, Detective Dalton. Please stay in touch."

Detective Dalton nodded, and then he reached out and

gently grabbed Mark's arm.

Mark and Hailee stopped and Detective Dalton said in a serious voice, "I meant what I said, you are a hero, but Mark, or should I say, Winterkill, please, you need to be careful out there. I know you are a special guy, with special skills, but there are many bad guys out there. The world is full of evil and it is not a video game. It is a dangerous place. I cannot and will not support any type of vigilantism."

Mark nodded and said, "I understand and I will be careful."

Mark stopped both in his words and in his steps, and Mark stared at the detective and pensively reflected for a few seconds before speaking.

"I have to say, Detective Dalton, that you are a very cool guy and you are on top of your game. I can tell. Can you stop and imagine for just a moment if this world had the ability to stop and pause whenever it wanted? I mean, when a politician is about to tell a lie, or say something stupid that he or she knows will be some dumb-ass, bullshit, promise that they can never keep and instead, they hit a button. A pause button as I can do in a video game. They stop, think, and tell the truth instead of a lie or more spreading of bullshit. Or, when a person is about to say something mean, deceitful, or demeaning in a fit of rage or in a moment of despair and instead, they hit the pause button, think about it, and change their mind. Instead, they say something heartfelt and sincere. They say some words full of praise, and some words full of honor and both of those people are suddenly in a wonderful place. A step or two nearer to Heaven because of praise as opposed to criticism. Think about a crook, a real badass, and he hits the pause instead of the trigger of the gun held within his hand. Better yet, two lovers are about to hold each other and share their first kiss ever, and they hit the pause button to make sure everything is perfect and nothing is lost. It is perfect. Can you imagine how wonderful this world could be if we could just stop and think before we react? If only, for a pause, this world would be so much better of a place."

Detective Dalton smiled, nodded, and then stumbled on his own words.

His thoughts were lost within Mark's profound words and he only managed to mumble, "Yes, if only for a pause. I agree. Ready, aim, fire, instead of ready, fire, aim. I get it and agree with you. This world would be such a better place. It is a wonderful thought and wish."

Mark smiled, and he wrapped his arm around Hailee, pulled her into his body tightly, and gently kissed her on the cheek.

"An awful lot of things have changed for Mark Holiday in a very short amount of time. Winterkill, well, he needs to respect Mark Holiday. I assure everyone that he does, and he will. Now, Winterkill has many people to love, to protect, and even more reasons to be careful for, and the cool part, is that I am not alone. There is an entire network of very talented people at my fingertips, and in particular, one very powerful and unique friend comes to mind. Regardless, I will be careful. Thank you for the good advice and the reminder, Detective Dalton, but rest assured, Winterkill, never loses a game. Ever. If only for a pause."

The summer passes along so quickly. Of all the seasons, it can often feel as if it was a blur in time. For Mark Holiday and Hailee Nathanson, this was a summer filled with falling in love. A summer full of sharing their hearts, getting to know and to understand each other, a time of sharing their bodies and sharing the hope and joy of new love. It was a glorious and magical time in their lives, and little Ingrid fell into it all and felt it all. Mark and Ingrid bonded immediately. Their laughs and joy at finding each other seemed to be so natural, so loving, and they quickly became inseparable.

As if it was all by the design of a much higher authority and meant to be.

It was now late in August and the dog days of the middle of the month slowly gave way to warm days, instead of stifling heat and humidity, and August faded into cooler evenings filled with gentler breezes and awe-inspiring sunsets.

Late in the afternoon on a Sunday, in the local city park around the corner from Mark's apartment, Mark Holiday pushed Ingrid while the little girl sat strapped in a swing. The little girl's laughter filled the air and the park with exuberance and joy. Hailee sat on a nearby bench and she smiled widely at the scene playing out in front of her eyes. The man of her dreams, loving her little girl as if she was his own flesh and blood. Perhaps flesh and blood matters very little, especially when compared to the spirits within our hearts and souls. It was readily apparent that Mark and Ingrid bonded in spirit and in their souls.

"YAAYYYYYY!" Ingrid cried out in glee as Mark pushed her just a little higher, being ever mindful of exactly how high the little girl was flying. As Mark smiled and laughed, and carefully watched the little girl soar to new heights and her laughter filled Mark's heart, his ears perked up. Just above Ingrid's laughter and broadcasting of joy; Mark heard a familiar noise. It was the unique sound of the metal tips of boots striking hard upon a city sidewalk, and the rhythmic noise sparked a shiver up and down Mark's spine. In search of the source of the noise, his eyes glanced over in the direction of a copse of trees lining the edge of the park. The trees did not catch Mark's eyes. No, it was not the trees that captured his glance, but instead, it was the sudden appearance of an immense man dressed all in black and wearing a wide-brimmed black hat that captured his attention. The immense man was now standing on the grass near the edge of the tree line. Mark smiled and nodded as he found and confirmed the source of the familiar sound, and he clearly studied the details of the man. The quiet stranger in the black hat tipped his hat and smiled in return. Hailee spotted her lover's eyes glancing over in the direction of the trees, and she turned her gaze to what had caught Mark's attention. At first, she seemed stunned at the appearance of the stranger. Her worries eased when she saw Mark's reaction.

"I will be right back, Ingrid. Mommy will take over pushing you for a few minutes," Mark advised the little girl and with a nod, Mark indicated to Hailee to switch places with him, while he took some time to meet with the stranger dressed in black.

Ingrid protested a little with a moan and groan while the swing slowed down as Mark and Hailee switched places. Hailee jumped off the bench and she stood next to the swing with one eye on Ingrid and the other one on Mark.

Hailee gently touched Mark's arm, and she asked, "Mark, is everything okay? Isn't that the handsome stranger who sat next to you in the restaurant on the night that we met?"

"It is, baby. It is."

"I don't understand. Mark, please, I thought you only met at random that night. . .."

"We did, but we exchanged some small talk and, well, he gave me something for safekeeping. Perhaps, he wants me to return it now. I am not sure, but please . . . do not be upset. Everything is fine. I love you and Ingrid with all of my heart and soul, and everything is fine. In fact, it is better than fine. It is amazing, just like you are."

Hailee searched his eyes for more clues and a further explanation, but his warm and loving smile and calm demeanor caused trust to replace her worry.

Mark sensed her caution and to ease the apprehension, Mark quickly explained, "He is a good guy. A very good guy. A friend. I assure you that everything is fine. It is a little complicated, and I will explain more, but right for now, please watch Ingrid and I will be right back. Okay?"

Hailee quickly nodded and smiled, and the trust and love that she felt in her heart chased away any lingering doubts and worries.

"Okay, Mark, will be right back! Mommy will push you! Are you ready?" Hailee took over on the swing duty and Mark slowly walked over to the quiet stranger in the black hat.

As he approached, he marveled at the immense size of the man and while he grew closer, he caught the amazing sparkle of the fading sunlight in the stranger's dark eyes. Eyes full of marvelous adventure, not eyes that were dark and ominous, but eyes full of caring and eyes full of warmth. Mark thought in his mind how he would not want to be on the wrong side of those eyes if they turned deep and ominous. Mark extended his hand to shake the stranger's hand. The stranger reached out and grasped Mark Holiday's hand, and they warmly shook hands. Mark Holiday was tall and lanky, but he was not a small man. His long fingers helped make his legendary abilities at effortlessly working video game controllers even more famous, but as large as Mark's hands and how long his fingers were, his hand eclipsed within the grasp of the stranger's enormous hand.

"I wondered how long until we would meet again, dark stranger. It's nice to see you and I hope that Winterkill fulfilled the mission and did not disappoint you in any way."

The stranger did not answer, but he nodded and tipped his hat in acknowledgment of Winterkill's efforts.

Surmising that this would be a decidedly one-way conversation, Mark picked up the conversation with his thoughts, "I am very grateful to all that you have done for me and for us," Mark turned and nodded toward Hailee and Ingrid and he explained some more, "I know that this was all part of the plan. They are both my life now. All of my heart and all of my soul, and I will protect them at all costs, even with my own life and so much more. I know that part of the plan was for Hailee and Mark to meet and fall in love, and for that gorgeous and amazing little girl to capture my heart, too. I have found my soulmate, and one day, she will be Mrs. Mark Holiday and Ingrid will be our daughter. Ingrid's biological father is out of the picture. Ha1 I know that you are aware of all of this! I have never loved like this before, so thank you, quiet stranger. From the deepest depths of my heart, I need to say thank you. I am not dumb and I understand all that this means."

Once more, the stranger only nodded and smiled.

Mark found it difficult to suppress a laugh, and he waved his hands in the air while saying, "No doubt, you are the quiet stranger in the black hat. Yet, your lack of words is not a factor when your actions pack one helluva punch. I will not be a dope and try to figure out who you are, or where you came from, or other crazy thoughts such as that, because I understand and know that this is a strange and mysterious world and there are many things that are very real and defy explanations. Why try? Because most of humankind has to be dopes and quantify everything, and try to put the unknown of this world into neat little boxes to explain it and understand it. I do not dwell, but I accept. Above all, I want you to know that I will always do the best that I can for you and for those two wonderful women that I love so dearly. I also admit that despite all the flaws, the evil, and the meanness that I love this weary world and I recognize that things can be, and will be, very different, if only for a pause."

The stranger's eyes burned with understanding and Mark continued, "Quiet stranger, if I might ask of you, why me? Why? I get the reflexes and the skills and such, but why me? I am just some geeky, video game dude. Nothing special. So why me?"

Finally, the stranger spoke and his deep, melodious voice filled the entire world, "Because, Mark, you are a man of special skills but even more so, you possess a wholesome heart. You have a brilliant mind, full of understanding. You are a man of courage and fearlessness and a man of honor. At times, my ability to intercede in this world is quite limited, so I recruit special allies to assist me along the way. Winterkill is one of my allies and not only do you possess the intelligence and skills and courage to perform our missions, but you also have a network of very special friends, who will assist us in the missions. Please, do not thank me, for it is this world that should thank you."

Mark stood motionless and silent, while feeling and watching the stranger's eyes, while the stranger studied Mark's eyes and his face for a reaction. Wisely, Mark chose to remain silent. The stranger seldom spoke; therefore, Mark knew that he was best to stay quiet and allow the words of the stranger to flow when and if they did finally arrive.

"There will be future missions. Unfortunately, evil seldom rests. However, I assure you that I will be right there with you, watching and waiting in the shadows."

Mark turned and pointed at Ingrid and Hailee and concern filled his words and his voice conveyed the concern, "I will protect them at all costs and can never allow them to be endangered."

The stranger acknowledged the concern by saying, "I can assure you that both goodness and kindness always will prevail over evil. Goodness, will never fail."

The tension eased and Mark relaxed and put his hands in the pockets of his jeans, and his posture reflected his relaxation.

"Okay, cool, then I am in and Winterkill is in, too. All in, and you can count upon us. I guess that I will watch the video screen for some games and clues as to the next mission."

The stranger only nodded, and Mark sensed that the words now stopped flowing.

"Say, gotta ask you and this might be pushing my luck, but you know, you have the cool black hat, the handsome face, the all-black thingy going on with the vest and shirt and pants and the boots with metal tips and cool clicking noises. Whoa, you are mega-cool and well, Winterkill, he is kind of a dweeb. C'mon, geez, my weapon of choice is an umbrella. I mean, it is one mean-ass umbrella, but ah, ya know, it is a little dorky. Can I have something, ya know, a little cooler?" Mark stopped speaking, and he studied the stranger for a reaction, but the immense stranger simply stood silently in front of Mark. "I was thinking of a laser beam gun or maybe a freeze gun or something, super cool such as that."

The stranger shook his head, and Mark smiled at the reaction.

"Okay, I get it. I have all that I need. Right?"

Now, the stranger nodded in agreement. He reached out, and gently placed his powerful arms on Mark's shoulders and slowly turned him to face Ingrid and Hailee.

The stranger removed one arm and with his hand, he waved and then pointed in the direction of Mark's two loves. Mark stood there watching them laugh and play and he understood what it was that the stranger was trying to convey to Mark. It was then that Mark thought for a brief second that he should give way to Winterkill and that he should pause this scene in front of him. Instead, Mark chose to take it all in and to relish it forever in his heart. To hold it near and dear and capture the scene and the love. Mark nodded and despite his best efforts, he could not hold back the tears and he gently wiped them away from his cheeks as they ran down his face.

Mark marveled at how the quiet stranger in the black hat's dark eyes sparkled with what Mark could only imagine or believe were rays of joy and hope that seemed to broadcast straight to his heart from Heaven.

"Yes, indeed, I have all that I need. I have love, and when the games are all won and the bad guys are all defeated, love is all that remains and all that really counts in this weary world."

The stranger nodded. He tipped his hat, smiled, and quickly turned and walked briskly away.

Mark stood there. He watched, and listened as the metal tips of the stranger's boots made that amazing and wonderful clicking noise, as they struck hard upon the sidewalk. He stood there watching and listening until the stranger faded away from his view and he could no longer hear the noise of his boots walking along the sidewalk. Slowly, the stranger disappeared into the world once more.

Mark wished for a way to hold this moment in his heart forever, and his only thought was, 'If only for a pause.'

THE END

Epilogue

Mr. Lionel Shearing sat behind a huge desk in the luxurious office for the Senior Pastor of the Golden Cathedral of Praise. The office was located deep within the bowels of the sprawling complex. Needless to say, the luxurious office suite was not for the use of the general parishioners.

The office suite was beyond exceptional. The best of everything as far as furniture, flooring and finishes go. Deep pile carpets with the occasional high-end Turkish throw rugs here and there. Intricate oak wooden finishes fitted and crafted by the finest carpenters lined the walls, the baseboards and the trim work. You will find no "home improvement" quality fixtures or finishes here. Only the best of everything. Elegant light fixtures hung from the ceiling and decorative lights on the walls glowed in soft blue, red and yellow glows. On the walls were paintings and photographs of modern art and landscape scenes and just in case . . . a random visitor ventured in here. There were a few token art pieces displaying Bible scenes and stories. After all, this was a ministry dedicated to the glory of God.

Or so it seemed to be.

Yet, ever since the dramatic collapse, confession and breakdown of Pastor Rutherford Bartholomew Waxworth in the pulpit of the cathedral, right in the beginning of a major service, television and radio contracts ended, and attendance at services had nosedived. The money, which used to roll in, was drying up now. The publicity was all-negative and it seemed as if the empire was crumbling. An empire that Mr. Lionel Shearing conceived, built and created, and sucked the money out of, as well as sucked the lives out of some dedicated parishioners. You would think that the well-played news report of the elderly widow who lost her home, her life savings and everything that she had when she decided to give everything to follow the Prosperity Gospel that Pastor Rutherford Bartholomew Waxworth preached and promised would have discouraged Lionel from continuing his mission of greed and deception. On the other hand, at least it would have opened his eyes, as well as many others, to the evil going on here. However, Mr. Lionel Shearing was a conniving and cunning man and the mastermind of the Golden Cathedral of Praise was able to spin the story and perform enough damage control to resurrect part of the empire from the gathering storms of dust. After all, it was easy to make Pastor Rutherford Bartholomew Waxworth the evil scapegoat. The mastermind was at work, speaking on the telephone and desperately working with a key contact to find the replacement for Pastor Waxworth. The perfect candidate seemed to have crossed his desk and now Lionel narrowed the field and zoomed in for the kill.

"Look, I like how the guy looks. His voice is perfect, he is handsome as a movie star and his hair is perfect. Best of all, he has huge, white teeth too. All these buffoons need huge, white teeth and wives with huge chests, perfect asses, and big hair. Send me a picture of this dope's wife. Huh?"

Lionel listened hard to the other person on the telephone, and the answers that he heard did not make him too happy. He elevated his voice level as his blood pressure increased.

"Well, tell him to find some gorgeous chick on the side and dump his wife then if she is a flat-chested dog. This could mean a fortune for this idiot. Everything is on the line now! Everything! What?" Lionel paused to listen once again, and he sighed before he answered. "He does not need to be a pastor any longer. He needs to be an actor. This is an acting job, not a religious job. You need to get your head out of your ass and understand that this is it. The end of the road if we do not find the perfect jackass for this job. You like your paycheck, right? Convince his sorry ass, then! Huh?"

Lionel tapped the telephone receiver, and he jiggled the handset wire. He placed the receiver to his ear, listened, and then said, "Are you there? Suddenly, I can't hear shit. The line just went all full of static and noise." Lionel spun on the pivot of the chair to look out the windows of the office as if he expected to see a herd of thunderclouds bearing down on the building. The sky was bright blue and clear. "I dunno. Maybe something went wrong with the connection. If you can hear me, call me back or better yet, do your damn job and sign his handsome ass up!"

Lionel Shearing slammed the phone down in the cradle of the telephone and shook his head while speaking aloud to the walls of the fancy office, "Friggin' weird how the line went crazy. As if a storm was brewing."

The words we speak often prove to be prophetic.

The office door suddenly swung open, and it opened with such force that the door bounced upon the wall of the office, and it flew off its hinges and burst into splinters because the door opened with such ferocity. The exploding door and the loud burst of violence and noises shocked Lionel and he looked up from his chair in horror. He was aghast with fear as he saw an immense man standing in the doorway to the office. His heart thumped in his chest, and he gasped for air. This was the largest human being that he had ever seen.

"WHAT! Who the hell do you think that you are? You just cannot blow my door off and come stomping in here! Get the hell out of here, or I will have my security officers throw your big ass out of here. This is private property and these are private offices."

The ominous visitor simply stood in the doorway and Lionel studied him as his spine shivered in fear and sweat poured from every pore of his body. The man standing in the doorway stood there with dark piercing eyes that seemed so dark they were as if they were holes in his head. His focus was solely and intently upon Lionel Shearing. The man was dressed all in black; his black vest covered a perfectly pressed, black, buttoned-up shirt, black pants and shiny black boots upon his feet that reflected the lights in the office on the tips of them. Upon his head, he wore a wide-brimmed black hat.

He was the quiet stranger in the black hat.

The stranger took a few steps toward the desk; the metal tips of his black boots did not make the usual noise while the stranger glided on the deep-pile carpet of the plush office. The deep stare continued and Lionel recalled the bizarre testimony of Pastor Waxworth and Mr. Claude Buxton, of an ominous visit from an immense man dressed all in black that threw Claude aside as if he was a rag doll and tore the door right off their limousine. A dark, strange visitor, whose words and visit caused Claude to flee in terror and Pastor Waxworth to repent of his life of chicanery and return to a legitimate ministry. Lionel and others thought the strange testimony, and the imagined stranger in black were simply the result of a drunken vision during an intense drinking spree and wild binge. Now, Lionel knew better, because he was sober and this immense and menacing stranger standing a few feet away from him was not a vision. He was real. Very large, very frightening and very real.

Lionel cowered in fear as he reached for his telephone.

"I told you to get the hell out of here. I am calling security!" Lionel shouted as he picked up the receiver, only to find the line was dead with no dial tone. Now, his fear grew even more, since the immense stranger still did not say a single word, but he only stood and stared at Lionel.

Lionel pulled out his cellphone and to his sheer horror; the cellphone . . . was dead. He frantically pushed at all the buttons, but the phone would not turn on or respond.

"Get out! Leave me alone! Do you know who I am?" Lionel screamed in desperation.

Suddenly, those words and the resulting question invoked a response from the quiet stranger, as he slowly nodded his head to indicate that he did know who Lionel was. The stranger followed the head nod with some words. Words spoken in a deep and melodious voice that seemed as if they shook the walls of the office.

"I know exactly who you are, Mr. Lionel Shearing. I know everything about you and, I can, not only look into your mind, but I can see the final fate of your soul. A soul that I am about to consume and deliver to a new owner. The trouble for you right now, is that, in your wildest dreams, you could never even imagine where it is that I come from and exactly who it is that I am. I can assure you that, unfortunately, you are about to find out."

"For an angel went down at a certain season into the pool and troubled the water: whosoever then first after the troubling of the water stepped in was made whole of whatsoever disease he had."

The Gospel of John 5:4

King James Bible

ABOUT THE AUTHOR

If you ask Paul John Hausleben, he will tell you that he is not an author, he is just a storyteller. His mission is to continue to write and tell stories to warm your heart, make you laugh, and sometimes make you cry, just a little. Most of all, he deals in memories, and helps you to remember the good times of your own life, and the special people who touched you along the way. Paul was born and raised in Paterson, and then nearby Haledon, New Jersey, and began writing at an early age. He revisited a writing career later in his life, and he now is the author of a number of novels, compilations, short stories and audio and video works. Most of his work touches upon nostalgic remembrances of simpler times, and tells the stories of heartfelt, humorous, and special human relationships. Other than writing, among many careers both paid and unpaid, he is a former semi-professional hockey goaltender, a music fan and music reviewer, an avid sports fan, photographer and amateur radio operator. He now resides in Somewhere, U.S.A., but his heart always remains along Belmont Avenue in good old Paterson, and Haledon, New Jersey.

Other Work by Mr. Paul John Hausleben

The Time Bomb in The Cupboard and Other Adventures of Harry and Paul

The Night Always Comes, Another story from the Adventures of Harry and Paul

Reunion, A sequel to the Night Always Comes and Another story from the Adventures of Harry and Paul

The Autumn Collection

The Christmas Tree and Other Christmas Stories. Tales for a Christmas Evening

Crows on a High Wire

The Miracle Tree, Another story from the Adventures of Harry and Paul

The Summer Collection

Tales of the Quiet Stranger in the Black Hat

The Return of the Quiet Stranger in the Black Hat

Geyer Street Gardens
Beneath the Mask of a Hockey Goaltender
Another story from the Adventures of Harry and Paul

And a few others too!

You may write to the author at ctte27@gmail.com

Published by God Bless the Keg Publishing
Somewhere, U.S.A.

You may write to the publisher at
Godblessthekegpublishing@gmail.com

"Life's simple pleasures are so often the best ones!"

www.ingramcontent.com/pod-product-compliance
Lightning Source LLC
LaVergne TN
LVHW091039080826
845145LV00002B/555
9780998630052